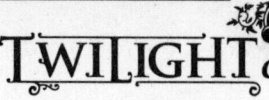

ENGINES of the APOCALYPSE

The soul-stripped were not moving because they could not move. Each of them was quite, quite dead, rivulets of blood congealed beneath their mouths, ears and nostrils. Where their eyes had been were simply empty sockets still slowly oozing gore. It was as if someone had taken hold of their heads and squeezed until they popped.

Kali raised her fingertips to her own nostrils, and they came away red and wet. The dwarves had established no defences here because no defences were needed. The spider machines had been built to maintain the hub once it was running because the dwarves knew the overwhelming magnetic forces at play would prove deadly to any living thing, including themselves. While Redigor's puppets were no longer strictly alive, their bodies were still flesh and blood, subject to the same physical vulnerabilities as anyone.

Kali wondered if Bastian Redigor had felt the agonising pain that must have accompanied the soul-stripped's deaths. And she wondered, more resilient than most or not, how long it would be before she started to feel her own.

WWW.ABADDONBOOKS.COM

An Abaddon Books™ Publication
www.abaddonbooks.com
abaddon@rebellion.co.uk

First published in 2010 by Abaddon Books™, Rebellion Intellectual Property Limited, Riverside House, Osney Mead, Oxford, OX2 0ES, UK.

10 9 8 7 6 5 4 3 2 1

Editor: David Moore
Cover: Greg Staples
Design: Simon Parr & Luke Preece
Marketing and PR: Charley Grafton-Chuck
Creative Director and CEO: Jason Kingsley
Chief Technical Officer: Chris Kingsley
Twilight of Kerberos™ created by
Matthew Sprange and Jonathan Oliver

Copyright © 2010 Rebellion. All rights reserved.

Twilight of Kerberos™, Abaddon Books and Abaddon Books logo are trademarks owned or used exclusively by Rebellion Intellectual Property Limited. The trademarks have been registered or protection sought in all member states of the European Union and other countries around the world. All right reserved.

ISBN: 978-1-906735-37-1

Printed in Denmark by Norhaven A/S

No part of this publication may be reproduced, stored in a retrieval system, or transmitted in any form or by any means, electronic, mechanical, photocopying, recording or otherwise, without the prior permission of the publishers.

This is a work of fiction. All the characters and events portrayed in this book are fictional, and any resemblance to real people or incidents is purely coincidental.

TWILIGHT of KERBEROS

ENGINES of the APOCALYPSE

MIKE WILD

Abaddon Books

WWW.ABADDONBOOKS.COM

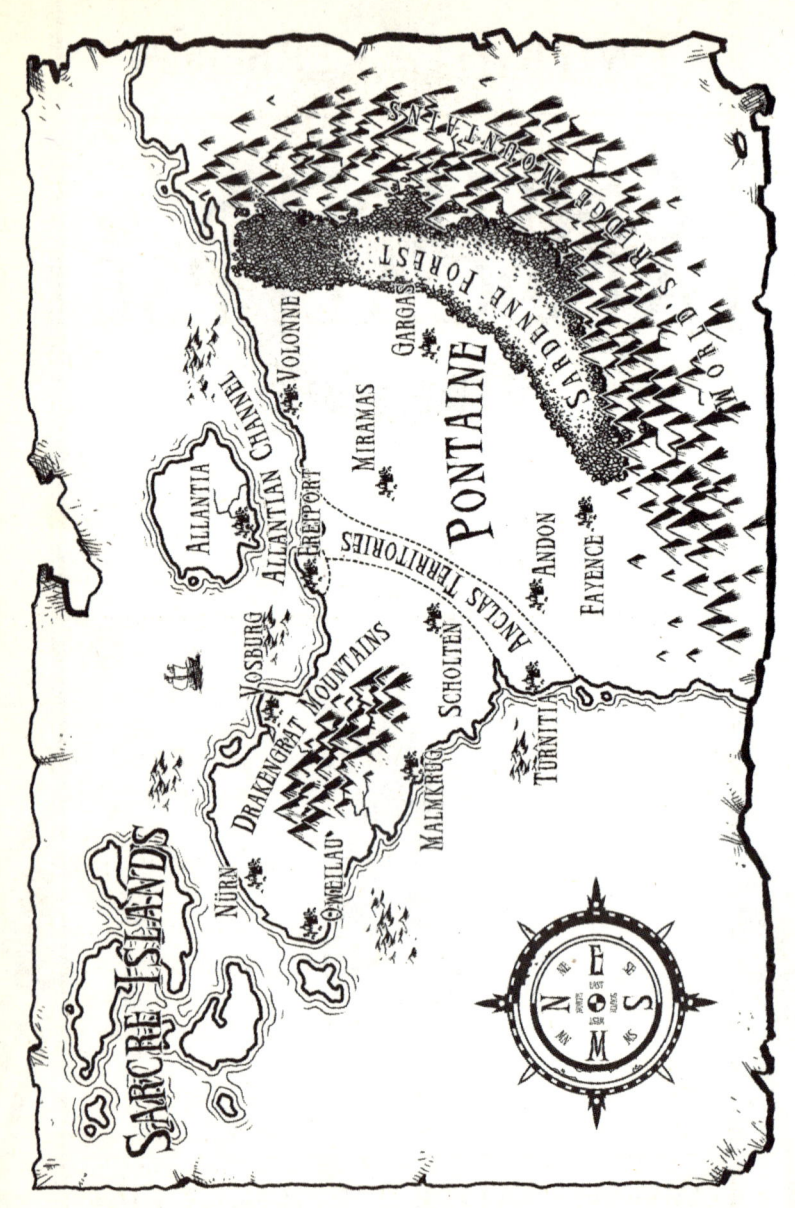

Chapter One

The end of the world began with a scream. A very high-pitched, girly scream.

Not Kali, then. She wasn't a girly scream kind of girl.

No, the scream in question came from her guide, one Maladorus Slack, hired only hours before in the *Spider's Eyes* when he'd claimed to know the location of a lost passage leading directly to the fourth level of Quinking's Depths. It was an audacious claim and it wasn't every day Kali trusted the word of some ratty little chancer in a seedy tavern, but there had been something in the way he made it – with wariness as well as greed in his eyes – that had made her take a gamble and hand over fifty full silver for the privilege of having him share what he knew.

As it turned out, it was money well spent, Slack guiding her at twilight into a cave in the hills above Solnos and, deep within, tearing creepers off an ancient cryptoblock he swore, once unlocked, would enable her to bypass the Depths' upper levels and find treasure of such value that she might, as he put it, come over all tremblous in the underknicks. Kali had been forced to have words with him about this, pointing out that it was *her* business what went on in her underknicks and also, while she had him pinned against the wall, that she wasn't your common or garden tomb raider doing what she did for the money. Unless her taxes were due, of course.

Later, she would feel a bit bad that Slack had spent some of his final moments being throttled, especially when she recalled the hungry roar that followed the poor sod's scream. Not that what happened to him was her fault. Nor Slack's. In fact, there was no way either of them could have guessed what was going to happen after she picked up the Claws.

Okay, okay, okay, she'd been at this game long enough so perhaps she *should* have known better. Perhaps, given the way things had been going until then, she should have sensed the whole thing was going to go tits up.

"This cryptoblock..." Slack had queried as she worked on the numerous etched blocks that formed the seal. The conditions in the cave were cramped, and he was balanced awkwardly between the skeletal remains of earlier treasure seekers who had found their way to the threshold, trying to ignore the fact that all their bones were utterly and inexplicably shattered. "It is some kind of puzzle, yes?"

"Not some kind of puzzle," she replied. "A very specific kind."

"You have seen such puzzles before?"

"Once or twice. Cryptoblock seals are typical of an ancient race called the dwarves."

"The Old Race?" Slack said. "Tall with pointy ears and bows?"

Kali sighed, but took time to set the man straight because he had at least heard of the Old Races, which was more than could be said of most people on the peninsula, especially out here in the sticks. "No, the other lot. Short-arsed with attitude and axes."

"But surely both are stories for the children, yes? These Old Races did not exist?"

"Oh, you'd be surprised..."

Slack sniffed. It was the kind of rattling snort where you could hear the contents of his nostrils slap wetly against his brain and

Kali grimaced in distaste. But the man seemed to accept the truth of what she was saying.

"The dwarves. They were supposed to have been masters of deadly traps, were they not?"

"Not supposed."

"Then this door is a trap?"

Kali glanced at the skeletons on the floor of the cave. "Either that or these guys had a very bad case of the jitters."

Slack glanced fearfully around the cave, looking for hidden devices.

"You won't see a thing," Kali advised. "They were master engineers, too."

"You *do* know what you are doing?"

"Wish I did," Kali said. She ran a finger down the join between two blocks, concentrating hard, tongue protruding between teeth. "Trouble is, no two cryptoblocks are the same... springs, balances, counterbalances... you just have to feel your way around." She gasped as something suddenly sprang inside the cryptoblock and slammed together where she delved. "Farker!" She cursed, whipping out her fingers and sucking their tips. Then she almost casually grabbed Slack's sleeve and pulled him aside as a solid stone fist the size of an outhouse punched down from the cave roof onto the spot where he'd stood, reducing what remained of the skeletons to dust. With a grinding of hidden gears, the fist retracted, and Kali returned to her work, smiling slightly as Slack had, himself, come over all something in the underknicks, a small stain forming on the front of his pants.

"Sorry about that," she said, wrinkling her nose. "Might be a while."

She'd worked diligently on the puzzle well into the night, Slack staring warily about him all the time, flinching or whimpering each time there was a click, clunk or clack from the door. At last, though, there was a sound that was different to the others – somehow *final* – and, as he watched, Kali stood back with a sigh of satisfaction, brushing the dust off her hands.

Slack regarded her and the cryptoblock with some puzzlement, because, at first, nothing happened. Then, with a soft rumbling and puffs of ancient dust, the blocks making up the door began to punch in and out. Some then slid behind those next to them, which in turn slid in front of others next to themselves. Yet more ground up or down, obscuring or obscured by their neighbours, or simply retracted backwards into darkness, never to be seen again. The movements became faster and more complex, the cryptoblock shrinking all the time, until at last all that remained was a single block, floating in the air, which Kali grabbed and casually tossed aside. Slack found himself staring at the discarded stone.

"I do not understand," he said. "It is gone. How can it be gone?"

Kali frowned. Questions, always questions. "Translocation mechanics," she said, adding in response to his puzzled stare, "It's a dimension thing." It might well have been, for all she knew; the truth was, despite having cracked a few of these bastards, she really hadn't a clue where they went.

Luckily, Slack hadn't been interested in analysing her statement too deeply. His attention had been side-tracked by the passage that lay beyond the cryptoblock, and the ore that glittered in its walls. It was only triviam, all but worthless, but its shine held the promise of greater things, and as Slack wiped sweat from his lips with his arm, she frowned. The man might have saved her the trouble of negotiating the first three levels of the Depths, but there was a growing air about him suggesting that, while he'd been happy to guide her to the cryptoblock, he'd never really expected her to *open it*, and now that she had was having second thoughts about who deserved the treasure beyond. Her suspicions were confirmed as Slack raced ahead of her into the opening.

Kali cursed and threw herself forward, grabbing his tunic from behind – just in time, as it turned out. Slack was already skidding helplessly down a sharp incline and, now a dead weight on the end of her arm, wrenched Kali onto her stomach and pulled her down after him. The stone floor of the passage was rough beneath her, tearing her dark silk bodysuit, and grazing her exposed torso with sharp scree. She ignored the pain, concentrating instead on jamming her legs against the sides of the narrow incline in an effort to slow their progress. The walls tore at her ankles, stripping them of skin, but she ignored this, too, groaning as she stretched out her other hand to get a firmer grip on Slack. He suddenly yelped and lurched, and Kali willed all her weight onto the floor of the incline, praying for enough traction. She was yanked forward and her arms were almost pulled from their sockets, but the two of them came, at last, to a tentative stop – again, not a moment too soon. Kali sighed. Below her, Slack dangled over a seemingly bottomless abyss, too terrified to struggle or even object to the rain of stones that bounced off him, clattering down into the dark.

Kali twisted herself into a stable position and heaved him up. "Looks like I need to keep an eye on you in more ways than one," she growled.

"I was only... making sure it was safe," Slack said, breathlessly.

"Of course you were." Kali winced and rubbed her bare stomach, ignoring Slack's hungry stare. "But there are rules to this game," she added. "Rule one is watch *every* step."

A flash of resentment crossed Slack's face as he dusted himself down, but he turned to stare into the dark, swallowing deeply. It was not in reaction to the end he had almost met, however, but a stare of undisguised greed.

Kali joined him at the edge of the abyss, wondering fleetingly whether it might have been less bothersome if she'd just let him fall, but considering what it was they faced, it was obvious Slack could make no move without her.

As always, her research had given her some idea of what to expect when coming here, but the expectation never quite did the reality justice. The two of them were staring into a vast cavern that must have extended beneath the whole of one of the hills above Solnos, an underground expanse hung with immense stalactites and dimly lit by a strange, golden glow in front of them. The glow was the only illumination and emanated from the top of an isolated pillar of rock, maybe six feet across, which thrust thinly and dizzyingly up from the abyss. It appeared unreachable from their position. Kali bit her lip and studied her goal. She could not yet make out the source of the glow, but was sure she knew what it was. The light was pulsing, dreamlike. The glow of something magical.

Kali had no doubt that she'd found what she'd come for. All she had to do was reach it.

"There?" Slack observed incredulously. "But there is no way across!"

"Rule two," Kali said, pulling a small object from a pocket in her bodysuit. "Plan ahead."

Slack stared at a small, ornate piece of stone – some kind of key – that Kali held in her hand, then watched her move along a narrow ledge to a carved niche. She brushed lichen away from an indentation in the stone, inserted the key and, with a grunt, turned it solidly to the right, the left, and then twice more to the right. Something grated behind the niche as, below in the darkness, something rumbled. Slack watched in amazement as another rock pillar rose judderingly from the abyss, shedding thick cobwebs, dust and the detritus of ages as it came. The top of the pillar stopped level with the ledge on which they stood, some hundred feet out into the void.

Kali withdrew the key from the niche and smiled. Slack, meanwhile, stared at the pillar and then Kali, regarding her quizzically.

"I do not understand," he said. "That is still too far away to reach."

Kali nodded. The fact was, it was too far away for a running jump, even for her. But even had she been able, she wouldn't have tried. Revealing her abilities to a man who would, for the price of a shot of boff, tell all and sundry about it was not a wise move in a backwoods such as this. It could easily reach the ear of some overzealous Final Faith missionary, and she had no wish to be dragged to a gibbet and burned as a witch. Besides, jumping would take the fun out of it all.

"Rule three," Kali said. "Be patient."

She smiled again as, from under the lip of the ledge where they stood, a scintillating plane of blue energy snaked out towards the newly risen pillar, zigzagging around the stalactites in its path to form a translucent bridge wide enough to take them both. Slack squinted, frowned, and Kali realised he hadn't a clue what he was looking at. It was easy to forget that while she'd come to live

Engines of the Apocalypse

with such wonders on an almost day-to-day basis, the average peninsulan hadn't much experience of magic.

"It isn't witchcraft," she explained. "The bridge is made of something called threads."

"Threads?"

"An elven thing but the dwarves weren't averse to their use when needs suited. They –" Kali paused and contemplated. How exactly *did* you explain the threads of magic to a man such as Slack? "They allow you to use the world around you... to do things with invisible tools."

Slack looked enlightened. "So, I could use these tools to dig a new dump-pit?"

Kali pulled a face. "Uh, yeah, I suppose," she conceded, thinking that she was the only one digging a hole around here. "Let's move on, shall we?"

A wary Slack dibbed a toe onto the bridge, clearly not trusting its solidity, while Kali strode casually by him into the void, slapping the stalactites she passed and humming a happy tune. She reached the pillar and waited for Slack to catch up before inserting the key into a second indentation carved in its centre. This time she turned it left three times, right and then left again. There was another grating sound, and another rumbling from below.

"Six pillars," Kali explained as another rose ahead of them, "six combinations. If all are entered correctly, they form a bridge all the way to where we want to go..."

Slack sniffed. "This is really quite easy, then."

"Easy?" Kali chided as she waited for the bridge to form before skipping onto it. "You think I got this key from some adventurer's junk sale? Oh, no. This key is a complex construct of separate components, each of which was hidden in a site rigged to the rafters with every kind of trap you could imagine. These past few weeks I've been shot at, scalded, suffocated, stifled, stung, squeezed, squished and squashed, so maybe, Mister Slack, you should rethink your 'easy.'"

"And you say you're *not* doing this for the money?"

"Nope," Kali said. "Holiday."

"*Holiday?*"

"Holiday."

The fact was, she was still reeling from recent revelations about 'the darkness' coming to Twilight – so much so she'd had to get away, from friends, the *Flagons*, all of it. Not that there were actually that many friends around right now. Slowhand was off avenging the death of his sister, and she'd barely seen hide or hair of Moon or Aldrededor since she'd rescued the *Tharnak* from the Crucible – the old man, whose shop was being rebuilt after the k'nid attacks, and the pirate were spending all their time tinkering with the ship in Domdruggle's Expanse. Dolorosa had dismissed it as boys and their toys but there was a serious side to their tinkering, readying the ship for when – and for *what* – it might be needed. Not that she missed any of them – her holiday had been chosen specifically to keep her busy. She had, in fact, lost count of the times she'd barely avoided it becoming a funeral. In short, she'd had one hells of a time, and the acquisition of what lay ahead was the last challenge she had to face. Because what she had so far not told Slack was that forming the bridges was only half of it.

"One wrong move," she said, "and the entire mechanism resets itself. Bridges gone, pillars back where they came, carrying us with them into the depths."

Slack peered down and glimpsed something huge, white and serpentine slither through the darkness. "But there is something down there! Something horrible!"

Kali looked over her shoulder, smiled. "Of course. There's always something horrible."

With the more restrained Slack in tow, Kali negotiated more bridges, coming eventually to the last one – the one to the resting place of the artefact.

This time she wielded the key but hesitated as she held it before the lock, drawing a worried glance from her companion.

"There is a problem?" Slack asked.

"No, no, no problem," Kali responded.

Well, not much of one. It was only that at this point she might most likely get them both killed. The fact was that while her studies of the dwarven key had revealed a pattern to her, she'd been sure of all the combinations except this last. The combinations represented a really quite simple series of nods to the inclinations of the dwarves' multifarious minor gods – lightning equalling from above, or up; sunrise, east, so right; sea, which at this point on the peninsula was to the west and therefore left. The problem with the last combination was that it contained a glyph for the god of wind and, frankly, that one had left her stymied. Wind, after all, could come from any direction, so how in the hells was she meant to know which was correct? In the end, she'd whittled the possibilities down to two answers – up, because the wind in this valley was predominantly northern, and down, or south, because... well, because.

Hesitantly, she inserted the key in the final niche, turned most of the combination and stopped before the final twist.

North now, or south? If she guessed wrong, the last thing she'd see would be Slack wetting himself again, and she could think of better images with which to depart the world. She stared at the odorous little man and, in doing so, made up her mind. It had to be, didn't it?

Kali turned the key south, locked it in place and, after a few seconds, the bridge appeared.

She sighed heavily; she'd gambled correctly. On a dwarven joke. A crude but effective joke, much like the dwarves themselves, and she could imagine them roaring with laughter when they had thought of it.

Hey, Hammerhead, how about this? There's more than one kind of wind!

Kali was not about to tell Slack that she'd just gambled both of their lives on the strength of a fart gag, so instead she sauntered nonchalantly across the bridge, finally setting foot on the reassuring solidity of the central pillar. And right in front of her was what she had come for.

The Deathclaws.

Legend had it they had been forged by the renegade blacksmith Dumar, who had pledged his allegiance to an elven rather than dwarven court. Commissioned by that court's Lord, the mysterious metal from which they were made was said to have washed up as jetsam near Oweilau millennia before. That the metal *could* wash up – that it could float – was just one of its unusual qualities and had led many to speculate its origin lay with those said to live deep under the sea. True or not, the metal was unlike any worked before. It was pliable yet all but indestructible. When fashioned into the claws, they were sharp enough to slice through anything, natural or man-made, most importantly the unbreachable brodin armour in which the dwarves of that time garbed their warriors. It was even said that, wielded with skill, they could bypass the armour completely and slice away a dwarf's soul.

Unsurprisingly, the Lord who wielded the Deathclaws became unstoppable on the battlefield, and thousands of dwarven warriors had fallen before him, until, one night, the claws had simply vanished from the Lord's chambers.

The fact that, thereafter, Dumar returned to live among his own people in such circumstances that ten lifetimes' smithing could never have paid for may or may not have had something to do with the disappearance. But, by whatever means the dwarves acquired the claws, they had thereafter sealed them here, on the lowest level of Quinking's Depths, so that they might never be wielded again. They were, in short, a priceless treasure, a one of a kind artefact that Kali had had on her 'to find' list for as long as she could remember.

She sighed and lifted them from the podium on which they rested, then slipped them onto her hands. As light as silk, each of the metal handpieces was attached to five curved rune-etched blades by intricately crafted hinges and studs that allowed for perfect freedom of movement. It was hard to believe that something so delicately and lovingly constructed could have been intended for such deadly use. It wasn't simply the workmanship that belied their purpose, however. The legend also said that the elven Lord had imbued the runes with additional sorcery that ensured the blood of the fallen never tainted their beauty, and it was this that gave them their golden glow. Kali couldn't resist wielding them for a short time – slashing at the air like a cat, grinning as they cut the air with a hiss – and then she moved to return them to the podium.

"What are you doing?" Slack asked, aghast.

"Putting them back," Kali said.

"Are you *insane*?"

"Nope. I made a promise to a friend a long time ago that certain things should stay where they are, for the good of Twilight."

Behind her back, Slack hopped up and down, gesturing at the key, the bridges. "Then why all *this*?"

"Because I could."

"Because you could?"

Kali nodded. "It's about the thrill of the chase."

For a moment, Slack stared at her open-mouthed, then moved with hitherto unsuspected speed, putting a knife to Kali's throat. It was as dull as a twig compared with the treasure she had found but could still cause a nasty gouge. More uncomfortable by far was the fact that Slack was pressing himself tightly up against her rear, rubbing her exposed midriff slowly and panting in her ear. Kali sighed, but only with bored resignation.

"I will be taking the claws, Miss Hooper," Slack said.

"You sure about that?" Kali responded.

"What? Of course I am sure!"

"Only it's just that if I drop them to the ground you'll have to pick them up, and while you're doing that I'll kick your nuts so hard people'll be calling you 'four eyes.'"

There was a pause.

"I told you, Slack, plan ahead..."

"Then pass the claws to me slowly, between your legs."

Kali drew in a sharp breath in mock sympathy. "Or 'no nuts.'"

"Over your shoulder, then!"

"'Twilight's silliest hatpins'?"

Slack tightened his grip. "You are toying with me, woman."

"Actually, I'd prefer to get this over with. Have you any idea how much you *stink*?"

"*Give me the claws.*"

"Won't."

"Will."

"Won't."

Slack sighed in exasperation and Kali smiled. All you ever had to do was wait for the sigh that said your opponent was off guard.

She elbowed Slack in the ribs and flung him around in front of her, kicking his legs out from under him as he came. It should have pinned him to the ground with the Claws at his throat, and that was exactly where they would have been had the entire cavern not begun to quake violently, almost spilling the pair of them into the depths. As it was, Kali stumbled to her knees, the Deathclaws skittering from her grip, and Slack took advantage of the moment to grab them and run. Kali growled and made after him, then suddenly stopped dead in her tracks.

What the hells?

That some kind of quake was occurring was beyond doubt, the cavern shaking and thick falls of rock dust pouring from the roof. The rumbling was almost deafening. The quake, though, was not what had caused Kali to stop in surprise. Something seemed to be interfering with the thread bridges throughout the cavern. As Kali watched, they faded and flickered. The magic seemed to be destabilising for some reason and, if it disappeared completely, she and Slack were going to be trapped down here.

Slack himself had a more immediate problem, however. Oblivious in his flight, the rat was already running across the fifth bridge and, from her vantage point, Kali could see it was the most unstable of them all.

"Slack, come back!" Kali shouted, but the only response she got was a backward flip of a finger. "Fine, you moron, run, then! Just get off the farking bridge!"

She'd meant the warning to galvanise him but it actually had the opposite effect. Slack paused in his tracks, turning to face her. That he was listening was good, but it was also the worst thing he could have done.

Kali stabbed a finger downwards, trying to make the man aware of his situation, and comprehension slowly dawned as Slack looked down. His mood turned from triumphant glee to undisguised panic as he saw the bridge flickering in and out of existence. The sudden realisation that, at any moment, there might be nothing between himself and an abyss filled with *something horrible* spurred the thief into running for his life but, unfortunately, time had run out for Slack.

"*Aaaaaaaaaaiiiiiiiiiiiieeeeeeeeeee!*"

"Bollocks," was Kali's honest response. But she couldn't help raising her eyebrows when she saw the Deathclaws remained where Slack had been, still held in his bloody, severed hands, amputated by the flickering bridge the moment he'd fallen through. For the bridge, like the others, had not yet gone for good. She had time – though not, necessarily, any to waste.

Kali ran. As the six bridges continued to blink on and off, she knew that crossing each successfully was going to be a matter of a timing, using the pillars that connected them as staging posts.

The first bridge was, at that moment, in an either/or state of flux, and she ran on the spot until she felt it safe enough to traverse, then put on a sudden burst to reach its other end. She did the same with the second, and then the third. The fourth presented a problem, almost as unpredictably erratic as the one on which Slack had met his doom. The effects of the quake on the cavern were worsening. What the dwarves had intended to be a protective sanctum for as long as the hill above existed was now starting to come down about her ears. While she ran on the spot waiting for safe passage a rain of dust and stones left her coated in a grey shroud, and she had to dive out of the path of several large chunks of debris.

Then, when the bridge finally seemed stable enough for passage and Kali began to race across, all of the pillars began to move up and down.

Kali felt her stomach lurch as the pillar ahead rose and the one behind sank, taking the bridge with them so that she suddenly faced an uphill flight.

Oh, you have got to be kidding.

Kali pumped her legs until she neared the rising pillar ahead, and, with a bellow, threw herself onto it, rolling into a ready position for the next, crouched to leap.

There were only two bridges left now, but she was painfully aware that the next was the one that had so abruptly ended

Slack's time on Twilight. It was once more flickering every half second or so but, interestingly, the claws had still not fallen through, which suggested it was stable enough to take her. The problem lay in timing it right, because if she moved at the wrong moment the pillar ahead would have risen too far and she'd once again face a steep incline to reach the end.

Kali ducked as the cavern shook violently and further falls of rock poured from the roof all about her, and then scowled at the bridge ahead. It looked as right as it was ever going to be.

Kali moved, faster than even she thought possible, but once again the quake scuppered her plans. As she began to race for the final pillar a massive boulder detached itself from the cavern roof and plummeted straight down. The boulder seemed to hit the pillar in slow motion, splitting asunder before bouncing off into the abyss, and in its wake the pillar started to crack and break apart. What was worse, it severed the link with the last two bridges. Kali staggered and yelped in protest as the threads there began to sputter and die, and now it was her mind rather than her body that raced. She took in all of the possibilities presented by the changing circumstances and moved again, heading not for the pillar but for the Deathclaws. It had never been her intention to remove them from the cavern but now they were coming with her whether she liked it or not. In fact, they might even save her life.

Kali didn't even slow to pick the ancient weapons up, executing a rolling somersault as she ran, one hand slipping into each of the claws and shaking to lose Slack's disembodied grip. His appendages spun down into the abyss, arcing trails of blood, until something white snatched them out of the air to join the rest of him, but Kali was already gone.

Her sole interest now was in reaching the collapsing pillar before the bridge died or it broke apart completely. The pillar was more or less level as she reached it, though far from intact, and as Kali landed on its buckling and crumbling surface it finally relinquished its hold on the bridge ahead, which blinked out of existence before her eyes.

She didn't need to turn around to know that the bridge behind her was also gone, but neither did she let the fact that she was seemingly now trapped on a disintegrating finger of rock hinder her pace. Kali ran full pelt across its surface and then, even as she felt the pillar tipping and tumbling away beneath her feet, she let out a loud "gaaaaaah!" and launched herself into the air.

Arms and legs flailing to stretch as much distance out of the leap as possible, she seemed to hurtle though the air for ever. But then she thudded into the stalactite ahead of her, the claws embedding themselves effortlessly into the spine of rock.

Kali simply hung there for a second.

"Oh, yes," she breathed to herself.

From the stalactite to the ledge and the exit was now only a minor jump, and Kali made it with ease. She would have taken a moment to pay her respects to Slack but the cave was rapidly filling with rubble. But as Kali moved into it she did cast a backward glance into the cavern that had almost claimed her life. The last of the bridges were flickering out now, leaving the ages old resting place in darkness but even as the roof caved in, she sensed that it hadn't been the quake that had caused the bridges to go away. No, something else had killed the magic.

Maybe when she reached the surface she'd find out what the hells was going on.

CHAPTER TWO

Hells was the right word. As in all of them breaking loose. Kali dragged herself spluttering and squinting up into the dawn light, disorientated and wrong-footed. Not only because the landscape she remembered from before her descent was now obscured by a dust cloud so thick she could *bite* it; she also immediately found herself dodging rivers of scree flowing rapidly down the hillside. As the treacherous stones threatened to sweep her off her feet, Kali hopped left and right.

There was no escaping it. The whole range rumbled as if the world itself were coming to an end. The boulders she dodged smashed into others below, cleaving apart with cracks like thunder, the guttural, groaning, thrashing sounds of uprooted trees and vegetation and the strange, hollow clattering of falling rock everywhere. There was another sound, too, not particularly loud in comparison, but one to which demanded Kali's attention. It was the agitated snorting and roaring of Horse, whom she had left tethered nearby – safely, she'd thought at the time.

Kali scanned the hillside, trying to locate the bamfcat in the chaos. As she did she caught sight of a dark, spherical object, the size of a fussball, darting here and there through the dust-filled air. As she saw it, it stopped dead, hovering right in front of her eyes. Kali recoiled instinctively, thinking *what the hells?* But by the time she'd recovered enough to try to work out what the sphere was it had already gone, darting away into the fog as quickly as it had come.

Weaving to dodge the tumbling descent of yet more stones, Kali began to work her way across the hillside once more, at last spotting Horse rearing against his tether, horns and armour plating deployed to deflect falling rubble. She moved to him quickly, slapped his side solidly and whispered calming words in his ears, and, though his nostrils still flared and he bucked slightly beneath her, the bamfcat no longer fought her. One thing was for sure, though – she had to get him out of there. Kali quickly untied his tether and led him away from the quake. At least that was her intent. The problem was, there didn't seem to be any *away* to get to. What Kali had thought to be a phenomenon specific to the hills was actually affecting an area much wider.

Exactly how much became clear as soon as she and Horse topped the next ridge.

When she had ridden up into the hills with Slack the previous evening, she had left below her a town lying peacefully in the savannah and forest lands east of Andon. Solnos was positioned beyond a sun-bleached but solid wooden bridge, the river meandering gently around its northern outskirts, and at the other end of town a grassy escarpment rose to the south before sloping away in the direction of Fayence. The town itself was a little smaller than Kalten, without defensive walls because none had ever been needed, and its buildings were one or two-storey affairs, constructed of blindingly white plastered bricks over a wooden framework. The buildings were centred around two squares, each strung with bunting and paper lanterns, one lined with shops selling everything from food to farming implements to bolts of silk, the other home to the town's well and church, a twin-turreted and bell-towered affair that was rurally typical of the Final Faith. The Faith's 'missionary' presence in such an otherwise idyllic spot had been the only thing that had stopped Kali musing on the possibility of opening a second *Here There Be Flagons* in the town, but it had been something she'd remained willing to consider should the Faith ever be kicked out on their arses, as they thoroughly deserved.

Now, it was likely she never could. Solnos was turning rapidly to ruin.

Where only the previous afternoon children had been laughing and playing in the streets, their parents sampling the exotic fare of the town's communal dining plaza, all had degenerated into chaos.

The white buildings were now criss-crossed with a growing number of cracks, each widening by the second as the buildings were shaken to their foundations. Many of the inhabitants of the town were racing in and out of the buildings, desperately gathering valuables or loved ones, or rushing in panic about the streets, trying to understand what was happening to them. The destruction wasn't limited to the buildings, either – even those who had safely evacuated their homes could not escape the effects of the quake, as they found themselves fleeing dark, jagged rents in the streets themselves, bunting and lanterns falling and fluttering about them like dying birds.

It was utter calamity and confusion. The people of Solnos hadn't the slightest clue what was hitting them. But Kali did. From her vantage point on the hillside, she could see it, even if she couldn't quite yet take it in.

"Okay," she said with a levity she didn't feel, "that's a new one."

To the west of the town, in the midst of its farmlands, massive machines were drilling out of the valley floor. There were three of them in all, emerging one after the other, the first already risen to the height of the ridge on which Kali stood, filling the sky and dwarfing her with its mass. The machines resembled, of all things, giant fir cones. The comparison was hardly apt, however, because these were not the products of some unbelievably huge, nightmare tree, but things of metal which spouted steam as they rose. Things which crackled with electrical energy. Things which Kali had no doubt had been *manufactured*, which only served to make them all the more staggering.

She could only stand stunned beside Horse as the second and third machines rose to join the first, churning slowly out of the ground with a deafening crunching of substrata and roots, carrying with them great scoops of soil, shrub, and even whole trees, sloughing from their sides in lethal downpours. Rising ever higher, they inevitably became visible to the town beyond the ridge, and Kali's gaze flicked to the people of Solnos, who as one had momentarily forgotten their immediate concerns to stop and point, or scream.

As one, the massive machines had begun to turn slowly on their vertical as well as horizontal axis so their pointed peaks would eventually face towards the ground. As they did this they emitted a siren sound that reminded Kali of the last, desperate calls of some dying leviathan, or of some impossibly loud and haunting foghorn, blaring endlessly into the night. The sound drowned out everything, even the clatter of the crumbling hills.

What in the pits of Kerberos were these things? The style of their construction and the runes Kali could make out carved into their eaves were dwarven, and the devastation they'd caused upon emerging suggested they had lain underground for millennia. Their history and reasons for construction were only two of the questions that intrigued her, though. What had brought them to the surface? Who or what controlled them? And why?

No, Kali mentally kicked herself. *Honestly, sometimes...* The question she should be asking was, what could she do to help the people below?

Kali turned her attention back to the west of town, to the farmlands. There, a number of Solnossians, little more than dots from her vantage point, were scurrying across the fields, their tools abandoned. Kali had no doubt that when these most unexpected of crops had emerged from the ground, the farmers had been as staggered and transfixed as their neighbours in town and now that they had collected themselves to flee, reaching safety appeared to be almost impossible.

The fields were nothing less than a disaster zone, subsiding not only into the three gaping pits that the machines had created but into rents in the ground like those that had split the streets of Solnos. Even as she watched, Kali saw two of the fleeing figures sucked into oblivion, clawing desperately for purchase as they went, and she knew that things were only going to get worse. Beneath all of them was the subterranean expanse that she had only just escaped, and if Quinking's Depths collapsed further, Solnos might as well say goodbye to anything or anyone this side of the ridge.

Kali mounted Horse and spurred him down the hillside towards the fleeing figures. She frowned, the fleeing men and women were some distance apart, and to aid them all she and Horse would have to perform some pretty fancy manoeuvring.

With a "hyahh!" she drove the bamfcat toward the nearest group, shouting at them to raise their arms as she leaned sideways to scoop the first of them up. The man arced up onto Horse's back, landing with a thud in the saddle, and Kali repeated the rescue with a second farmer and a third. She could carry no more behind her for the time being and reined Horse away from the landslips and to the safety of a patch of stable ground.

Kali had no choice but to ignore their pleas about rescuing husbands, wives or brothers and wasted no time, turning Horse again and scanning the fields for those in the most immediate danger.

One group of five or six – in the chaos it was difficult to tell – were struggling, their escape route cut off by a fresh fissure. Attempting to backtrack, they were once more caught in the middle of the subsidence.

Another "hyaah!" sent Horse hammering towards them and, almost as if he had read her mind, the bamfcat deployed more of his natural armaments. The extra horns which had just sprang from Horse's body were, for once, meant neither as defensive or offensive appendages but provided hand and footholds for the group of farmers it would otherwise have been impossible to carry. Quite what the farmers made of the great armoured beast as it pounded towards them she'd never know, but as they staggered back before his fearsome sight, Kali had to indicate as best she could what they should do. Thankfully, in their desperation, the men and women seemed quick learners, and as Horse galloped into their midst, they leapt for and clung to the armoured protrusions.

"Hang on!" Kali shouted and, wondering vaguely if there was some kind of obscure world record for the number of farmers dangling from a bamfcat, she quickly reined Horse around once more, riding him into a jump across the fissure that had earlier stymied the farmers' flight.

The bamfcat roared triumphantly as they arced over the collapse, and, as they thudded down on the other side Kali, too, let out a whoop. But it wasn't over yet.

"My girl!" One of the women pleaded as Kali dropped them off with the others. "Please, she was frightened, she ran, I couldn't reach her..."

"Where?" Kali said, already turning Horse.

"She ran *beneath* one of those things. Lord of All, please, you have to help her!"

Kali stared back into the chaos, seeing no sign of the girl but spotting instead another group of stranded victims, whose escape route was blocked by fallen trees. They were attempting to hack through the barrier of vegetation but their going was slow and all the while, behind them, the ground broken by the machines was growing ever larger.

Kali swallowed. She had no choice but to ride to help these people, and all she could do was hope she'd spot the youngster on route – the problem being, if she did, what the hells was she going to do then?

A second later, the dilemma became stark reality, a scream managing to make itself heard over the strange wailing of the machines. Kali stared hard and spotted a small figure struggling on the edge of the pit in the shadow of the first of them, and cursed. There was no way she could reach both the girl and the others in time, and for a moment she reined Horse's nose left and right, left and right, tortured by the decision to save the lives of a whole group or of one, however young. Thankfully, it was a decision she didn't have to make, the sound of further heavy hoofbeats signalling the arrival of a second horse by her side.

"You take the girl!" Its flame-haired rider shouted from her solid white mount. "I'll fetch Treave and the others!"

There was no time to think about who the woman was or where she had appeared from. Once more Kali booted Horse's flanks and steered him towards the girl. But if her chances of success had been precarious so far, they had just gotten a lot worse.

Kali found herself weaving Horse through the masses of soil that poured from the machine hanging above the girl in a deadly rain, at one point even having to turn him abruptly as a tree crashed back to the ground directly in their path. It was a close run thing with far too many near misses and, the further in she rode, the thicker the falls became, leaving Kali with no choice but to ignore the painful hammering of falling detritus on Horse's hide and on her own, far less protected flesh. At last, though, she reached the girl and scooped the dishevelled, but miraculously unhurt, child up behind her, turning Horse for the return trip.

But again, she cursed. What seemed like a whole field by itself was falling in a solid curtain that would be impossible to pass without being crushed. Nevertheless, Kali spurred Horse on, leaning forward as she did to whisper in his ear, "If ever there was a time for you to do your thing, my friend, it's right now."

Horse was of the same mind, galloping straight ahead. One moment the bamfcat, Kali and the girl were heading into the roaring soilfall and the next they were heading away from it, on the other side.

Kali kept Horse at a gallop until they had reached the waiting farmers, slowed him to a trot, and stopped beside the anxious mother to swing her daughter down into her arms. She dismissed the woman's thanks, but not ungraciously, being more concerned with the fate of the one who had come to aid her in the rescue attempt. She stared back into the disaster area, a hopeless mass of uncontrollable landslides now, and bit her lip. Long, long seconds went by but then, bursting through a cloud of debris, a white, if somewhat soil-stained, horse appeared at full gallop. The farmers she had rescued clung to her saddle in much the same way Kali's had clung to Horse's horns, and a moment later they were with their own.

Kali watched the woman dismount, nodding modestly as the farmers thanked her for what she had done, but seemingly more interested in tending to the welfare of the animal she had ridden. Kali dismounted Horse and walked to the white horse, casually palming between its gravestone teeth one of the bacon lardons she kept for sentimental reasons, and then, without a word, the two women stood side by side to stare up at the strange, rotating machines which had come to dominate the whole sky.

All three of them now fully inverted – or perhaps the right way up, who was to tell? – their rotation appeared to be speeding up. The sound of their sirens faded to be replaced by a strange and very deep thrumming that seemed to be produced by the rotating eaves. The faster the machine turned, the more intrusive and painful the thrumming became, and all in the fields were forced to press their hands to their ears to block it out. The painful effects seemed to last no more than a minute, however, although both bamfcat and horse snorted in protest a little longer. As the animals calmed, Kali guessed the thrumming had passed beneath the range of anything's hearing, leaving the machines to rotate in apparent silence.

Kali glanced at the woman beside her. She still stared up at the machines with narrowed eyes and a steely set to her jaw, as if these things were an affront to her. There was also the same determination on her face that she felt herself – to find out just what these bastards were and what they would do next.

"Hells of a morning," Kali said.

"Not exactly what I expected when I got out of bed," the woman said.

"Kali Hooper."

"Gabriella DeZantez."

Kali studied her more closely. With her bone structure and fiery red hair she looked like a younger version of the Anointed Lord, Katherine Makennon. Kali didn't usually notice such things but it was also clear to her that the hair had been cut by her own hand rather than the prissy fingers of the primpers and preeners who'd begun to appear in the cities. She could tell immediately that Gabriella was different, like herself having little time for people's expectations or normal conventions. Her attitude was reflected in her clothing, too, the woman dressed for practicality rather than fashion, in a dusty surplice and working trews. Unfortunately it was the surplice of the Order of the Swords of Dawn, the Final Faith's warrior elite, bearing the faded crossed circle of the church. Kali had no idea what had caused Gabriella to end up as she was in a backwater such as this but she knew instinctively that she liked her. Which made it all that more of a shock when, with no preamble at all, the woman's next words were, "As the Enlightened One of the town of Solnos, I am placing you under arrest."

"What?" Kali protested. "Why?"

Gabriella DeZantez turned to face her directly for the first time, and Kali started slightly. Gabriella's eyes were unlike any she had ever seen, one a clear sapphire blue, the other a striking almond flecked with gold.

"I should have thought that was obvious," she said.

Kali surveyed the devastation. "You mean this? I had nothing to do with this."

"There is evidence to the contrary."

"Evidence? What evidence? Now wait one farking minute!"

But before she could argue her case further Gabriella DeZantez quickly unsheathed her twin blades, whirled them full circle and slammed their hilts into her temples.

Kali dropped to the ground like a stone.

"Treave, Maltus, bring her," the Enlightened One said as she strode by two of the farmers in the direction of what was left of the town. "As the Overseer has decreed, this 'Kali Hooper' must answer for her crimes."

CHAPTER THREE

For the last hour the archer's aim had been unwavering, the tip of the arrow pointing precisely where it had pointed when his wait had begun. It had not moved a hair's breadth in any direction. In the hands of any normal bowman, the strain of holding it so would have long ago become too intense. The bow would have begun to shake and skew, the shaft unstable and tremulous between two crooked fingers of the right. The nock of the arrow would, by now, have begun to buck spastically on the bowstring, and the strain would have transformed the tendons of the arms into agonising webs of red hot wire. Under such circumstances the bow would have to have been relaxed, lowered, and the trembling, cramped limbs exercised and massaged. The intended target of the bow might, as a result, have been lost.

In the hands of *this* archer, there was no such concern. The bow remained steadfast and its aim true. Everything was perfectly still, the only sounds in the flue where he hid the subtle creaking of wood and his soft, measured breathing. His concentration was sublime. Where others' gaze would have long ago started to wander, their vision to blur and lose focus, his blue eyes remained focused and alert, waiting for the moment – *the one, fleeting moment* – that he knew would eventually come.

Man and weapon were the best there were.

It was why the bow was called Suresight.

And why the archer went by the name of Slowhand.

The moment arrived. A small flicker of shadows betrayed motion some twenty yards outside the flue, framed in the one inch square formed by four bars of the iron grille through which his arrow was aimed. Despite the imminent arrival of his target, Slowhand's breathing remained calm. All that changed was that he smiled.

Smiled because this was not the first time in the last few days he'd waited for the perfect shot, and depending on how things went it might not be the last. For the last thing Slowhand intended was to kill the man whose shadow approached – that would be far too easy. He did not want Querilous Fitch to die *quite yet*.

Oh, Querilous Fitch. Slowhand so much wanted the psychic manipulator to suffer. He wanted him to suffer in the same way the corpse-like bastard had made Jenna suffer, stripping from his sister everything that had made her who and what she was. It might have been Slowhand himself who had given the order to fire upon her airship, and consequently end her life in a flaming crash, but in truth it had been Fitch who'd ended it long before. Independence, spirit, freedom of will: Fitch had taken them all until Jenna was nothing more than a puppet of the Final Filth. Slowhand did not have the abilities that Fitch possessed, of course – to literally stick his filthy little fingers in unspeakable pies – but he had his own, and so far they were working just fine.

During the past days, wherever in Scholten or beyond Fitch had been, he had been also – unseen, undetected, undetained. And on each occasion he had sent Fitch a message to let him *know* he was there, an arrow despatched from whichever hiding place he had used which could almost, but *not quite*, have dropped him dead where he stood. By these means he had gradually robbed Fitch of the very same things the bastard had taken from Jenna, reducing him to his current state – a furtive, quivering hostage to mortality, unable to do anything or go anywhere without the presence of the living shield of bodyguards he had so desperately employed.

There the bodyguards were now, Fitch huddled in their midst. The passage along which he walked was one that rose from the cells and torture chambers beneath Scholten Cathedral to the central level of the Final Faith's sprawling underground complex. It was a route Fitch followed daily at roughly the same time, depending on how thoroughly he had attended to his 'guests.' The fact that he had not varied his routine was probably reflective of the fact that he considered himself safe in the bowels of the secret stronghold, but the time had come to prove him wrong.

Slowhand waited until Fitch was outlined in the dead centre of the one inch square and let his arrow fly. It cut perfectly through the grille, flew through the narrow gap between supply crates that blocked the flue from view and then embedded itself solidly into the wall next to Fitch's face. The psychic manipulator and his guards fell into immediate, blind panic; Fitch, clearly torn between gathering them more closely about him or sending them in search of the origin of the arrow, settled for half and half. Some guards pounded towards the flue, while others bundled Fitch away, swords raised defensively as they attempted to get their charge out of sight.

As the first batch of guards kicked open the flue and examined its interior, Slowhand was already gone, having slipped out and replaced the grille the moment he'd released the arrow. Now he circled the crates, keeping out of sight but, as the opportunities presented themselves, unleashing more arrows in Fitch's wake, until a line of them dotted the wall of the passage along which he fled.

Turning with a look of horror each time one hit, Fitch made the decision that might make these his final moments after all. He ordered his protectors to guard his flank.

No problem, as far as Slowhand was concerned – he simply clambered up onto a stack of crates, leapt for a support beam and passed over the guards' heads.

Fitch, he thought, *you really should have invested full gold and bought in decent mercenaries from Allantia. The kind with brains, because you only get what you pay for.*

It was just him and the psychic manipulator now. As Fitch fled into the warehouse and distribution area, Slowhand followed, passing the Faith workers there unopposed, creating confusion as they hurried through. Once or twice Fitch looked to his rear, trying to defend himself by unleashing fireballs, but, born of haste and panic, they ricocheted wildly off the walls.

Querilous Fitch reached the other side of the central area and entered one of the railway tunnels that fanned off it, dodging between the couplings of stationary wagons. The expansive network of tunnels that spread far across the peninsula – beneath both Vos *and* Pontaine – were thought to be the remains of dwarven mines which the Faith had extended into a transport network, and the cable-driven, funicular trains which rode their rails simply developments of the ore-collectors once used. It was what the Faith did – purloined technology and then adapted it for their own insidious purposes – but it gave Querilous Fitch no advantage here.

Just the opposite, in fact. In his panic, Fitch had clearly neglected to take into account what lay some distance into the tunnels – and Slowhand knew what lay there because he'd had to bypass one to enter the Cathedral.

Since last Slowhand had been here with Hooper, security had been upped dramatically on the surface, and without offing every guard between himself and Fitch he would have had the pits' own job of reaching him undetected. But, as was so often the way, when security was increased on one front, it was often left vulnerable on another. Instead of heading for Scholten Slowhand had made his way to a tiny and purposefully underwhelming Faith mission some leagues east. The Church of Divine Intervention was more than it seemed, the fact that it had never been open for worship a clue that it had another purpose more fitting to its title. The mission was but a hollow shell concealing an access shaft to one of the Faith tunnels that led from Scholten to Volonne.

The mission also had only one guard, and he was swiftly despatched with an iron-tipped arrow to the helmet that concussed rather than killed. After that it had been easy to gain entry to the shaft and drop onto the first train heading back west. The train had been carrying naphtha for the cathedral gibbets, and he had used some of the oil mixed with grime to apply facial camouflage before he reached the complex.

But before the complex, of course, had been the shields.

Fitch had forgotten about the shields.

Slowhand smiled. The tunnel along which the psychic manipulator now fled was not the one through which he had rode the train – appeared, in fact, to be long unused – but that didn't matter, for its defences would be the same. He allowed Fitch his rein, letting him increase the distance between them, exhaust himself as he fled into the darkness. Slowhand followed at his own pace, knowing he had all the time in the world.

Fitch now gasping and staggering had negotiated most of a broad bend in the tunnel, and the blue glow that he could see illuminating the walls seemed to him to be some kind of salvation, a heavenly exit, perhaps, which would end this dark pursuit. It was nothing of the kind, of course, and as Slowhand appeared along the tunnel behind him, the stark reality of what he faced hit home.

The magical force barrier that sealed all of the tunnels against intruders into the sub-levels of Scholten Cathedral closed off the tunnel, its surface rippling gently. The only things capable of passage through its lethal charge were the trains, their front carriages embedded with crystals that momentarily nullified its destructive effects. Given time, Fitch might have been able to use his own sorcerous powers to break the barrier down, but time was something he no longer had. The psychic manipulator weaved left and right, as if trying to find some alternative escape route, but unless the first train in who-knew-how-long came through the shield in the next few seconds, there was no way out.

Fitch turned to stand against Slowhand, his brow darkening and hands dancing in an attempt to weave threads. Slowhand gave him no chance, rapidly loosing two arrows that nicked the tops of Fitch's hands and drew blood, breaking his concentration. Fitch tried again and Slowhand loosed more arrows, deepening the same wounds. The archer's message was clear: he was in absolute control. Any of his arrows could be solidly embedded in Fitch's forehead in an instant, if he so wished.

That, though, would be far too quick.

Slowhand didn't want it to be quick.

The archer sighed and closed on the man responsible for Jenna's death, Suresight now slung casually by his side. As he came, Fitch fell to his knees, tearing away parts of his robe to wrap around his bloodied hands. He stared up at his nemesis, trying and failing to disguise the fearful bobbing of his adam's apple, and was wise enough not to raise his hands again. He studied Slowhand intently, working out his identity through the smears of camouflage the archer still wore.

"The brother," he said, with disdain. "So it *was* you all this time."

"The brother," Slowhand confirmed. "But isn't that a redundant term?"

Fitch smiled coldly. "From what I've heard, she died at your order, not mine."

Slowhand paused. For Fitch to know that meant there had to have been a survivor of the *Makennon* and he'd thought all hands had gone down in the battle with the airship above the Crucible. Not that a survivor was necessarily a bad thing. News of the Faith's comprehensive defeat might very well serve to deter them from taking to the skies again anytime soon. In any case, it didn't alter the facts – Jenna would not have even been aboard the *Makennon* when it crashed in flames, were it not for Querilous Fitch meddling with her very being.

Speaking of which, the bastard was trying it with him, right now.

Slowhand recognised the slight dip of the head and pulsing of the temples that signified Fitch was trying to *influence* his actions as they spoke, but he wasn't going to be turning his bow on himself today, thank you very much. He tutted and raised Suresight, aiming an arrow directly at the manipulator's head.

"Don't try it, stick-insect. If I feel the slightest scratching in my mind..."

Fitch capitulated but, Slowhand got the impression, not wholly because of the warning he had just received. The man seemed confused, troubled somehow, as if he had been trying to gather the mental reserves to pull off his insidious little trick but had, for some reason, failed.

"Maybe you should try to *talk* me round, instead," Slowhand suggested. "Though I can't really guarantee that will work."

Fitch glared up at him, but there was an element of desperation in his gaze.

"There's something..." he began, then shook his head, unable to grasp what. His mind was, in any case, on other matters. "So what happens now, *brother*? Do you plan to execute me in cold blood?"

"Actually it's running a little hot at the moment. But yes, that's the plan."

Fitch began to laugh, softly at first, but then with a volume Slowhand knew was designed to unnerve him. It was exactly the type of tactic he'd have expected – mind games of a more prosaic nature than Fitch usually played, but mind-games nonetheless. And he knew what they were about. Fitch didn't believe that Slowhand had it in him. He saw him as one of the good guys who, when it came to it, wouldn't actually *murder* someone in revenge.

Fitch didn't know Slowhand at all. Didn't know what had made him not really care.

Slowhand drew the bow tauter still, pressing Fitch's head down with the tip of his arrow. The creaking of the weapon was the only sound in the silent tunnel.

"Say goodbye, Querilous Fitch."

The psychic manipulator began to tremble beneath him, waiting for the arrow that, in all likelihood, he would never feel. And in the eternity that he seemed to wait he became aware that Slowhand could play mind games, too.

"What are you waiting for?" He hissed. "*Do it!*"

"Get up," Slowhand said.

"What?"

"On your feet, you bastard. Move away from the shield."

Fitch sneered. "What is this, some kind of trick?"

"No trick. Do it."

Dazed and pained, Fitch regarded him with confusion. But Slowhand's attention was fixed above him. Because what had stayed his delivery of the fatal arrow hadn't been sadism on his part. As he'd been about to loose his killing shot something had drawn his gaze. Something beyond the energy barrier.

A horde of people – hundreds of them – were approaching. And each and every one of them appeared to the archer to be dead.

He plucked Fitch up and span him around. "You wanna tell me who *they* are?"

Fitch gasped, actually staggered back. The apparently dead things, meanwhile, walked into the barrier in a single mass, recoiling from its charge in waves, but otherwise unharmed.

"I think they want to come in," Slowhand said. "Fitch, are these things your doing?"

"No," Fitch said quietly.

From his expression, though, he clearly recognised what he was seeing, and his face was as white as those beyond the barrier. Even when he'd been facing death Slowhand wasn't sure he had looked so afraid.

"So," Fitch continued, "the First Enemy moves at last."

"The First Enemy?"

"We have to get out of here," Fitch declared, pushing past him. "Now."

"Whoa, whoa, whoa, tiger," Slowhand persisted, grabbing him by the arm. "Whatever these things are, we're safe behind the barrier, right?"

"It was designed to be impenetrable."

"Then why are you so afraid?"

It was Fitch's turn to rail on Slowhand. "*Because the barrier is shutting down.*"

"What?" Slowhand said, and saw that what Fitch said was true.

The Final Faith's shield was flickering on and off, as if something was interfering with the magic that made it whole. He stared at the figures pushing against it.

Engines of the Apocalypse

"Are they doing this?" He asked. "The First Enemy?"

Despite his evident fear, Fitch began to chuckle. "*They* are not the First Enemy, archer. They are only his representatives here."

"Fitch, what in the pits of Kerberos is go –"

Slowhand didn't finish his question. The barrier had vanished completely. His nose wrinkled as it was flooded with the stale air of the long unused tunnel, but it was nothing compared to the stench of those who approached them now.

Slowhand could see that his first impression of their health hadn't been entirely accurate, but neither had it been wide of the mark. Grey of flesh and white of eye, with chests that barely rose with breath, they were alive, but not in any usual sense of the term. They seemed suspended, somehow, between life and death, and had an odour about them that reminded him of an outbreak of the tic. An odour that came when bodies ceased to function properly, when things were fundamentally wrong inside. The odd thing was, none of the people seemed wounded or showed any obvious illness. It seemed to Slowhand to be more of a spiritual thing.

That was it, he thought. The clothing these people – men, women, and even a few children – wore was blackened or torn but still recognisable, and it betrayed them as being from the woodcutting villages that bordered the Sardenne. He knew these people, had spent time with their kind, and they were hard-working, rugged individuals. But now, from their empty eyes, to their emotionless expressions and the way they moved as one, they may as well have been the walking corpses he had first taken them for.

They began to move towards himself and Fitch. Each shambling figure brandished an axe, cleaver or scythe.

"What the hells?" Slowhand breathed.

The archer raised Suresight and unleashed an arrow which thudded into the chest of a man at their front. He faltered slightly but continued walking. He hadn't made a sound. Slowhand swallowed and unleashed another into a different target, with the same effect. As the group continued to advance towards them, he backed Fitch along the tunnel and loosed Suresight again and again, into hearts, necks, right between the eyes. The shambling group just kept coming.

"That will do little good, archer," Fitch said. "As you've seen for yourself, these things are no longer normal flesh and blood."

"What *happened* to them?"

"They have become puppets. As such, even an arrow into the brain will barely slow them."

"Whose puppets? No, forget it. You wanna tell me what *can* stop them?"

"I can," Fitch said after a second.

Slowhand shot him a look. The psychic manipulator was displaying his bandaged hands, clearly seeking permission to use his powers without penalty.

"Magic is the only thing that can stop them," Fitch insisted.

"Do it." Slowhand said.

Fitch raised his arms towards the group, his temples pulsing. But moments passed and there was no sign of lightning bolts or fireballs or any offensive magic at all. Not a fizzle.

"Fitch," Slowhand said, "this is no time for projectile dysfunction."

"I – I don't understand," Fitch said.

"What's to understand?" Slowhand countered. "This, Fitch, is the day the magic died."

The stick insect gave him a horrified glance. "What do we do?"

Slowhand glanced towards the approaching figures. The walking pace which they had so far adopted was turning into more of a trot.

"Run maybe?"

"For once, archer, we are in agreement."

The two of them began to pound back along the tunnel, but at the same time the pace of their pursuers increased even more, until it was almost a charge. The eerie thing was that, other than for the sound of their footfalls, they proceeded in absolute silence. There was no need for them to utter a battle cry to chill the blood because the *thud, thud, thud* of their relentless and accelerating progress was chilling enough. Within seconds, Slowhand and Fitch were near to being overwhelmed, and the archer pushed the manipulator to the side of the tunnel, deciding the only thing to do was to make a last stand.

He wasn't sure whether to be relieved or offended by the fact that, other than an instinctive swing of weapons from those on the group's edge, their supposed attackers passed them by. It made him sure of something else though. These things weren't interested in the two of them, they were merely in the way. The horde's purpose was to reach the cathedral.

"We have to warn them," Slowhand said, and pushed Fitch on.

Paralleling the horde's advance now, he could see the light of the warehouse sublevel and, silhouetted before it, the wagons Fitch had dodged between on his way in. There were now also a number of workers who, guided by some Eminence, were delicately loading boxes onto them, oblivious to the deadly wave heading towards their way.

Slowhand had no love for anyone of the Faith but they *were* people. "Get out of there!" He shouted. "Get out of there now!"

The workers looked toward the sound of his cry, and tools were instantly dropped. They stared in incomprehension, something for which Slowhand could hardly blame them, but that reaction and their position – right in the path of the horde – cost them their lives. The horde met them and they were reduced to a pile of twitching, dismembered body parts by axe and cleaver and scythe.

The carnage did not last long but it gave Slowhand and Fitch enough time to overtake the horde and burst from the tunnel, the archer shouting warnings. But the distribution centre had already been alerted by the workers' screams, and the cathedral's cloister bells were sounding a security breach.

Guards were pouring from the sublevel's barracks to take up position before the tunnel. Slowhand bundled Fitch behind their lines, amazed that he had started the day intending to kill the man and was now getting him to safety.

"Arrest this man," Fitch ordered, intercepting two of the guards. "He tried to kill me."

The guards stared at Fitch questioningly.

"The First Enemy moves. For all we know he is in league with him."

The guards faces paled at the mention of the name, but they nodded and seized Slowhand by the arms. The archer glared – that was what you got for being the good guy.

"Fitch, don't be a fool," he pleaded. "I don't know what's going on here but let me help."

"Take him," Fitch ordered, and headed for safety.

"Dammit, Fitch! Can't you see this is about more than just saving your skin!"

Slowhand's protests fell on deaf ears as the horde continued to pour from the mouth of the tunnel. The guard commander hesitated for a moment before barking orders to his men. Crossbows were loosed and fifty or more quarrels slammed into the front ranks of the horde, the archers reloading instantly to despatch a second volley. By their sheer weight of numbers the quarrels slowed the horde more than Slowhand's arrows had, but they were as ultimately ineffective at stopping them and, despite a third volley, the horde gained ground into the sublevel itself.

Ordering his crossbow men to continue firing at will, the guard commander turned to a number of robed figures who had hastily shuffled into position at the rear of the line, and with a downward sweep of his arm instructed them to deploy their defences.

Nothing happened, for the figures were shadowmages, and the magic here, too, was gone. A wave of desperation crossed the guard commander's face and, despite his evident fear, he changed tactics, breaking forward from the line and unsheathing his sword, ordering his men to follow and do the same.

It was a mistake and a massacre. Only Slowhand and Fitch had so far witnessed how the horde behaved in close combat, and it hadn't just been the utter lack of mercy with which they had mutilated the tunnel workers, it had been the way they had done so with no regard to mutilation to *themselves*. They didn't care, didn't feel anything, and the only way to stop them was utter dismemberment.

The cathedral guards didn't get the chance. As they ploughed on, swords raised, into the front of the horde, the grey-fleshed intruders responded in kind, their makeshift weapons all the more deadly because of the suicidal way in which they were wielded. The guard commander and first wave of his men were bloodily felled without claiming a single foe, and even those who miraculously survived the sweeping attacks died horribly moments later, torn apart. More guards joined the fray and the horde began to slaughter these, too, fighting in eerie, absolute silence. The only noise was the wet sound of butchery, and the desperate cries and screams of the dying.

"Stop!" A voice commanded suddenly.

Slowhand glanced towards its source and saw that reinforcements had arrived, summoned from the upper levels by the tolling of the cloister bells. The Anointed Lord herself – Katherine Makennon – stood at their fore.

The archer drew a sharp intake of breath. He hadn't forgotten how striking Katherine Makennon could be, but as the Anointed Lord strode towards the tunnel, shoulder to shoulder with her men, his thoughts were not on the way her shining armour accentuated rather than hid her statuesque form, nor on the feral mane of long red hair that swept behind her like a fiery comet's tail. All he could think was that, for once, she might be biting off more than she could chew.

"Makennon, don't," he implored her as she passed. His words were barely heard above the clanking of her armour. "I don't know what these things are but I'm not sure they can be stopped."

The Anointed Lord halted briefly, her face a mix of recognition and curiosity at the archer's presence, swiftly replaced with cast-iron determination. "I will stop them. This is *my* cathedral."

Slowhand struggled against the guards as Makennon strode on, but their grip was firm. All he could do was watch as the Anointed Lord marched at the horde, her battleaxe swinging down before her with an audible *swoosh*. Scholten might well have been her cathedral but for the moment at least she was no longer its Anointed Lord, reincarnated instead as the battle-hardened Vossian general she had once been.

Makennon directed her men to the peripheries of the horde and then, roaring, waded into the heart of them, battleaxe carving a path as the invaders' weapons sparked and clanged on her armour. While it looked as though she was wielding the heavy weapon with as much carelessness as the enemy were wielding theirs, it was in fact with great precision. Its twin blades bypassed, by hairsbreadths, her own people fighting beside her, cleaving only into the things that flailed about them. The horde might have been unaffected by damage from lesser weapons but the sheer mass of Makennon's axe, to say nothing of the expertise with which it was used, was something they could not withstand. Within seconds she had reduced their numbers by twenty or more. As damaging as Makennon's incursion was, though, the numbers involved were great, and as more guards fell beside her it was clear she faced a war of attrition with an inevitable conclusion. This did not deter Makennon from continuing her impassioned defence of her domain, however, and while she shouted for what few men remained to pull back to a safer position, she herself continued to wade forward until she had carved a sea of body parts that reached almost to the tunnel entrance. There, fatigue at last started to get the better of her, and she was forced to stand her ground. Breathing heavily and slightly bowed, her blood-slicked hands nevertheless levelled her axe before her, ready to swing it in a circle and cut down any or all of the horde who closed in about her.

But the horde did not close in. Instead, as one, they collapsed to the ground.

Slowhand's surprise was as great as the Anointed Lord's, but their interpretations of the unexpected development differed. Obviously concluding her efforts had somehow won the day, Makennon's heavy breaths turned into shuddering gasps of relief, and slowly she raised her gaze to him, displaying flaring and victorious eyes. The archer was considerably more wary. Puppets, Fitch had called these things, and if that was the case their strings had just been cut. But he seriously doubted that, with such an advantage, this First Enemy – whoever he was – would have cut them in defeat.

Something was wrong.

Every one of the horde that remained intact began, slowly, to laugh. They didn't stir from where they had collapsed, and their faces showed no more emotion than they had before, but from each of their upturned, gaping, black mouths came the sound of laughter. It was a cold and calculating laugh that echoed throughout the now otherwise still battlefield, and it seemed to come from very far away.

Makennon turned in a circle, her eyes on the collapsed forms, her axe ready to be wielded once more. And as she turned, she faced the tunnel.

She stared into the darkness. Something darker still seemed to grow there.

And then that darkness exploded in her face.

Chapter Four

Kali stirred, blinked in confusion. After the clout she'd taken from DeZantez she guessed it was normal to see stars, but the Enlightened One's clout had clearly been an Almighty Clout because she was seeing balloons, bunting and flags as well. There was also a worgle right in front of her nose, staring at her in what seemed to be a very accusing way. Worgles had no eyes but it *still stared*, conjuring up flashes of Horse's darting tongue and a pang of guilt she'd never realised she'd felt.

Kali shook her head to free it of weirdness, then groaned. She was surrounded by the stuff of festivals and fun, but the way DeZantez had turned on her she wasn't feeling much like either. Wincing at the pain in her bruised temples she gently picked herself up off the floor to see she'd been confined in a small storeroom with a tiny window and solid wooden door. She tried to open the door but, naturally, it wouldn't budge, no doubt barred on the outside as there was no lock within. She pulled a crate under the window and climbed up. The window was too small for even her lithe frame to squeeze through but at least the view enabled her to glean where she was and how long she'd been out.

By the look of the sun, it was just after midday, and she was in Solnos – what was left of Solnos anyway. The storeroom had clearly been sturdy enough to survive the quake – which explained why it was serving as a makeshift jail – but outside was devastation. She was looking out onto the town plaza, which was now deserted, many of the tables and chairs upturned, plates shattered, the remains of meals scattered across the mosaic floor. There was smoke everywhere, a pall of it pouring from a jagged rent that split the plaza in two. Beside the rent was the body of a small dog.

Kali craned her neck so that she could see beyond the plaza. The destruction that the machines and the quake had wrought had flattened almost half the town, spreading as far as the second square, where, though the well and church had survived, the adjoining graveyard had disgorged its dead, many of the coffins lying broken in the sun, others half sunk in the river along its edge.

A few people were gathered around the well, cleaning and caring for the wounded as best they could. More simply cradled those who were beyond care, slowly rocking them back and forth. The only sounds were those of distant coughing and gentle weeping.

Kali sighed. If there was one small mercy, it was that it all seemed to be over. The quake had ceased completely. The strange machines, still dominated the horizon, and as she narrowed her eyes to discern the spinning objects against the brightness of the sun, she thought she could make out pulsing waves radiating from them, as if the inaudible sound they made was almost physical.

What the hells are *these things?* she found herself wondering once more. She had to find out. But that wasn't going to be easy in her current circumstances.

Kali considered her options. Horse had to be somewhere nearby, likely constrained like herself, and for a moment she considered whistling for him. Little would hold the bamfcat for long and, at full gallop, his armour would make short work of even these walls. She quickly rejected the idea, however, knowing that if she used the steed to instigate a jailbreak it would only confirm her guilt in the minds of her captors, however the hells they had concluded she was responsible in the first place. No, she had no desire to have her face on bounty posters all across Pontaine. It was better to get things cleared up.

Speaking of which, figures were moving towards her from the church right now: DeZantez and some fat, shaven-headed, jowly guy in fancy Final Faith robes. With him were a pair of meatheads, Faith again, who appeared to be his bodyguards. What a Faith dignitary was doing in Solnos she had no idea, but while she was never pleased to see one of Makennon's lackeys, if he was coming to sort this mess out, fine.

Kali heard the sound of a bolt being drawn back and the door opened, light momentarily flooding the room. Then fatso filled the gap, plunging it into shadow.

"I'm sorry about what's happened," Kali began. "but –"

"My name is Randus McCain," the fat man said, speaking over her. "It is my honour to be the Overseer for this region."

Kali's eyes narrowed – she didn't like to be interrupted. What she liked less, however, was the detail she could now see on her visitor's fancy robe. The usual crossed circle of the Final Faith was present but at its centre the pattern had been interwoven with the symbol of a wide open eye. Kali felt a tug of concern. She knew the Faith hierarchy fairly well but the eye and this 'Overseer' role were new ones to her.

"Nice eye, Randus," she said. "What's that about, then?"

"Bring her," the Overseer ordered the two bruisers. He moved back into the sun and the two men grabbed Kali roughly by the arms.

"Hey, now, wait," Kali protested, struggling in their grip. Her instinct was to nut one and knee the other but the sound of sharp metals being unsheathed halted her action before it began.

Gabriella DeZantez stood in the doorway, head slightly bowed but gaze fixed on her, twin blades ready for use in her hands.

Kali paused, she could see how perfectly posed for combat the woman was, how honed her muscles were, and, quick as she knew herself to be, realised that to challenge her would be folly. What affected her more than anything, though, was again the appearance of her cat-like eyes. They had an arresting presence about them – a *genuine* presence, that was, not the kind affected by fatso – that made her feel that, if she could appeal to anyone here, it would be her.

"What's happening?" She asked her, swallowing slightly.

DeZantez didn't answer, merely continued to stare, jaw muscle twitching. Randus McCain loomed behind her.

"You are charged with the manipulation of forbidden artefacts," he said. "You are to answer for your crimes."

Forbidden artefacts? Kali thought. McCain could only be referring to the machines. So the Faith were taking it upon themselves to police Old Race finds now? They really were arrogant bastards.

"Look, I keep trying to tell you –" she tried once more, but the Overseer merely nodded to his guards and she found herself being dragged from the storeroom.

Gabriella DeZantez stood aside as she passed but Kali sensed her immediately swing back into position behind her. Herded as she now was there was little chance of escape. Just one of DeZantez's blades could sever her spine before she managed a step.

It wasn't just the presence of the woman she sensed, though. There was more than a whiff of resentment coming from her, too. Resentment directed not at her but McCain. That was interesting and something she might be able to use when she found out what was going on. For the time being Kali allowed herself to be marched towards the church, noticing two things. The first was the fact that DeZantez faltered slightly as they came within view of the graveyard, as if someone close to her had suffered the upheavals there. The second was that Horse was chained beyond the well, guarded by more goons who had presumably escorted McCain into town. The bamfcat registered her predicament as she drew closer and began to snort and pull against his chains.

Kali knew he could snap them in an instant but stared into his flaring green eyes and shook her head. Horse calmed.

Prisoner and escorts reached the church and paused. McCain turned to DeZantez.

"Wait outside," the Overseer ordered. "Ensure we are not interrupted."

DeZantez protested. "I am the Enlightened One of Solnos. My place is inside the church, where I should witness these proceedings."

"I have given you an Overseer command, Sister of the Swords of Dawn. Need I remind you that yours is a temporary position and that our office holds jurisdiction over your own."

DeZantez's face darkened, her hands tightening on the hilts of her blades. "Need I remind *you* that your office did not, until recently, even exist. This town has been my responsibility for months and I have lost many of my people today."

Kali noticed McCain's goons go for their own weapons but the Overseer shook his head. "Very well. But you are to take no part in these proceedings, do you understand?"

DeZantez glared but nodded briskly. Kali could hardly blame her for her attitude. If she'd just had her authority stamped on like that, she'd be pitsed off too. The irony was, DeZantez could have whittled both goons down to a knucklebone in a second but, as a Sword of Dawn, the Faith's chains of command were sacred to her, whoever rattled them.

The interior of the church was pleasantly cool as Kali was ushered in. The wooden door was shut firmly behind her, DeZantez taking up position before it, and Kali looked around. Where she had expected some one-to-one questioning from McCain she found herself instead confronted by a number of townsfolk filing into pews as if to act as a jury. And when the Overseer stood in a shaft of light at a podium before which she, in turn, was forced to stand, she knew exactly that a jury was what they were going to be.

Hang on, she thought. Things were getting a little out of hand here. Moving a little too fast for her liking.

This was no questioning.

This was a trial.

"Kali Hooper, you stand accused –"

"What the hells is this?" Kali shouted over him. "I've done nothing to be tried for."

"Nothing?" McCain retorted. He pointed at the jury, raising his voice. "The loss of this community's loved ones at your hands is 'nothing'?"

Kali faltered. She was being charged with these people's deaths? Oh no, this was wrong. Wrong, wrong, wrong. She stared helplessly at the jury and then steadily at McCain.

"You're talking about the appearance of those machines. I had nothing to do with that. What happened was as much of a surprise to me as to you."

"A surprise?" McCain repeated. "A *surprise*? You make it sound like those *machines* were nothing more than some cheap trick gone wrong!"

There was a mumbling in the jury, shaking of heads, and Kali swallowed. Scant few hours had passed since the disaster, and these people's horror and anger were still raw. Even though she knew she shouldn't have to, she sought another choice of words.

"A shock, then."

McCain let her response hang in the air a second. "A shock," he said, nodding to himself. "A shock. What are you girl, an adventurer? One of those tomb raiders who make their living scrabbling for shiny things in the dirt?" He paused and gripped the sides of the podium, rattling it until his jowls shook. "In doing what you do," he thundered, "how many other shocks have you caused by sticking your nose where it doesn't belong?"

The jury stirred angrily, and glared at Kali. She, in turn, glared at McCain. And he had the gall to accuse *her* of cheap tricks, the fat bastard. McCain didn't care about these people's feelings, wasn't interested in meting out justice for them. All he wanted to do was manipulate them, and her. The shaft of light, the shouting, the flair for the dramatic – McCain, wherever in the hells he'd sprung from, seemed to have his own little travelling roadshow, and the trouble with roadshows was that they always ran to a script. Just as well, then, that this hadn't been a 'one-to-one' discussion because she would have been wasting her time. If she was to avoid being rail-roaded into whatever outcome McCain had in mind, she'd need to appeal to the jury directly. And to DeZantez.

"You were *there* this morning," she said to the Enlightened One, and then turned to the jury, "some of you people too. You saw how I tried to help. Ask yourselves – would I have done that if I had caused the quake in the first place? Why would I have *wanted* to cause the quake? To hurt you? Again, why? It makes no sense."

Faces remained impassive.

"These... machines," Kali continued, "I want to know why they've destroyed your town as much as you do, but to find that out the first question you should be asking isn't who's responsible, but what in the hells *are* they?"

"Exactly that, tomb raider," McCain said from behind her. "Instruments from the very Pits of Kerberos. From the hells themselves. Instruments which *you* made rise from where you plotted beneath the ground."

Kali whirled to face the Overseer. Though his office might, as DeZantez had suggested, be new to the Faith, McCain himself clearly wasn't. His jowls and girth evidence of a number of comfortable years in its hierarchy. As such, he'd know very well that he was talking bollocks, that his so-called 'instruments from the pits' were Old Race technology, whatever their purpose might be. This wasn't something he'd necessarily care to share with the people of Solnos. After all, the Lord of All Himself might struggle to create such wonders and He couldn't be seen to be inferior in their eyes. But that didn't explain why McCain was pursuing her with such zeal. He might still think her guilty, yes, but why not deal with her quietly rather than persist with this whole charade?

There was only one reason she could think of. McCain enjoyed it. The fat bastard had been tempted to stir from behind his dinner table by the chance to play god.

"How did you know?" She asked McCain. She and Slack, had, after all, headed to the cave when no one was around and had told no one their destination. "How did you know I was underground?"

McCain smiled. "Because, Kali Hooper, the Eyes of the Lord are everywhere."

"Of course they are." But what she'd meant as a flippant response took a darker tone when McCain addressed the jury.

"Would you like to see, my children?" He asked. "Would you like to see what this woman has done?"

In response there was a murmuring. Kali, meanwhile, looked about in confusion.

McCain thrust both hands towards Kerberos. "Then let me show you what the Eyes of the Lord beheld!"

Oh, for fark's sake, Kali thought, *enough!*

But then she froze. Because, between herself and the jury, an image had flickered into view and before their eyes they saw Slack leading her towards the cave and out of sight.

The view segued to show the machines burrowing from the ground, starting the quake, and then fleeing and terrified townsfolk, trying desperately to escape the effects of the catastrophic machines. Again the image segued, and this time showed Kali alone, emerging from the cave, moving across the crumbling hillside towards Horse, and then mounting him and riding away. There was a collective gasp from the jury as she did, both at what the recording implied and because Horse, with his armour fully deployed as it had been, was something of a disturbing sight.

The images began to loop, showing themselves again and again, and with every loop the jury shifted more uneasily in their pews. McCain certainly knew how to charge an audience, allowing the images to play a couple more times before raising his hands to stop them.

"With your own eyes, people of Solnos, you have witnessed how this *careless adventurer* and her pits-born beast activated the machines that destroyed your town. With your own eyes you have seen her guilt!"

"Hey, fatso!" Kali shouted. "Horse is no pits-born beast, he's a bamfcat, okay! And your little performance here proves nothing! The destruction of your town began while I was underground, yes, but that doesn't mean I started it!"

"Really?" Randus McCain said slowly, and once more an image appeared.

This time the image zoomed into Kali's face in a sudden close-up, dusty and bloodied after her ascent from the cavern, and recoiling, wide-eyed, in shock. "Do you see the blood?" McCain went on. "Proof she murdered your own kinsman lest he interfere with her plans! Do you see the startled look upon her face? Proof she believed she could deliver this act of evil upon us without realising that the Eyes of the Lord see all!" He paused again. "Ask yourself, people of Solnos, why would the Lord of All reveal such things to you unless he wished this evil act to be punished!"

"But that isn't what happened!" Kali shouted.

She was about to launch into an attack on McCain that would reveal him to be the charlatan he was but then realised she was taking the things she had seen in her stride. It had been immediately obvious to her that the images McCain had presented to the jury had come from the dark sphere she had fleetingly encountered on the hillside, but how was she to explain that to the people who, thanks to McCain's manipulation, held her fate in their hands? Explaining the presence of such technology to them was like explaining magic to Slack. Here, in this once idyllic town, they simply had no knowledge of it, and the Old Races were stories for children.

Kali looked around. True enough, it was reflected in their faces. Even the face of Gabriella DeZantez. The woman was clearly intelligent, but she was also a dedicated Sword of Dawn, and the Faith carefully chose what they exposed the Swords to. Without something tangible to contradict it, why shouldn't she accept what she had just seen?

Only Kali knew otherwise. She stared up into the shadows of the church, following the flickering light that created the imagery, and saw it. The sphere. It had to contain one of the memory crystals she had encountered in the Crucible of the Dragon God, the same kind of crystal that had recorded Jenna's messages to Slowhand, and was perhaps held aloft by some miniature version of the rotors that had driven the Faith's ill-fated airships. Makennon's mob might have lost their battle for the skies in the Drakengrats but they had adapted both technologies for another far more insidious purpose. The Eyes of the Lord were no messengers of the Lord of All, they were surveillance devices.

Overseers.

Gods, no wonder McCain was enjoying himself. The Filth had a new toy for its voyeurs to play with.

Despite how difficult it might be to explain, Kali knew she had to tell the people of Solnos what was going on. It wasn't just for her or their sakes, but for those of everyone where these things might already have been deployed.

"This isn't divine proof!" She shouted to them. "This is a *recording* of only part of what occurred. The Lord of All didn't see what happened underground because 'He' couldn't follow us there!" Kali paused, looking up. "There is a device," she went on, "a device constructed with the aid of Old Race science – a science developed long ago by the elves and the dwarves." She stared at the blank faces before her and then turned on the Overseer. "Why don't you tell them, McCain? Tell them about memory crystals and airships and your sphere, and how those machines out there in the sky aren't from the hells but from civilisations far older and more advanced than our own? Why don't you tell them that it was *they* who left the shiny things in the dirt? Or are you afraid? Afraid that if these people learn the truth, know how you use their tools, that you'll no longer be able to bend them to your beliefs?"

McCain gave Kali time to take a breath and then turned to stare at the jury as if he had no idea what she was talking about. Only she caught the knowing flare of his eyes as his gaze passed hers. "'Memory crystals'? 'Airships'? 'Sphere'?" he said with a chuckle that became a laugh. "These terms are unknown to me. The only truth I know is that which is shown to me by the Eyes of the Lord."

The Overseer raised his hands once more and the images returned, playing over and over again.

Keep going, Kali thought, seeing Gabriella DeZantez edging forward from the door, peering up into the shadows.

Unfortunately, just as the Enlightened One was about to become more enlightened, McCain sensed her movement and the sphere, controlled by some unknown mechanism, zipped out of sight.

"It was a trick!" Kali shouted to the jury, but received only unsympathetic glances. She turned to DeZantez. If she was going to bring her onto her side, now was the time. "You have to believe me," she said. "It was there. The images showed only part of the truth, not the whole truth, and certainly not *divine* truth. It's circumstantial. Give me time and I'll show you the sphere. Give me time and I'll prove to you what happened."

DeZantez hesitated. Her gaze alternated between Kali and McCain.

"May I remind you," McCain interrupted, "that the Enlightened One plays no part other than that of an observer in these proceedings. Her opinion carries no weight."

"Hey!" Kali shouted at McCain. "You want an opinion that carries weight, you bastard, I'll show you one!"

She leapt the podium, intending to land a fist in his smug, fat face, but found her neck scissored between DeZantez's twin blades before she could swing. Barely able to speak because of the blades pressing on her throat, barely able to move her head, she strained to look into DeZantez's eyes.

"*Please*," Kali implored.

"Not until I *know*."

So, that's it, Kali thought. With four words DeZantez had declared her independence, but shattered her hopes that she would act on the injustice that was happening here. The fact of the matter was there was no evidence of injustice, and until there was, the Sword of Dawn was bound by her oath to the Faith.

"Ladies and gentlemen of the jury," McCain said. "What is your verdict?"

Kali swallowed, waiting for the word that she knew was going to come.

"Guilty."

"Guilty."

"Guilty."

One after the other, the jury members stood and delivered the same verdict, and Kali was powerless to do anything about it.

DeZantez remained stony-faced during the delivery, even when McCain delivered his sentence.

"The Eyes of the Lord have witnessed your crime. The sentence is death."

"No," Kali said quietly.

McCain nodded to DeZantez. "Prepare the gibbet."

Kali struggled against the grip of the guards that now surrounded her. She had been fully aware that the gibbet was the Final Faith's preferred method of punishment – had been fleetingly aware of it hanging outside as she had been led into the church – but had refused to acknowledge its presence until now. Things all of a sudden became very unreal and she felt a dreamlike coldness ripple through her body. As she watched DeZantez exit the church and found herself being hauled after her into the sunlight, Kali realised that her holiday had finally come to an end here, far out in the backwoods, among strangers who intended to burn her. She felt suddenly, desperately lonely and yearned for Slowhand, Merrit Moon, anyone who could say *no, don't do this, this is wrong*. But all of her friends were far, far away, thinking other thoughts, and all they would know of her death would be that she never returned home. She was alone and, worse, about to die for a crime she would never dream of committing.

Well, hells, she wasn't going without a fight.

Kali drove her elbows into the stomachs of the goons holding her and slammed her fists into their faces as they doubled over. The pair staggered backwards and she dropped to a crouch, swinging herself around her hands and kicking out, knocking their legs from under them. The guards fell on their backs in a clatter of armour and, as they struggled to pick themselves up, Kali punched both in the face, knocking them cold. She sprang upright, twisting to face Randus McCain. The Overseer swallowed and backed up against the church wall before her less than happy gaze.

Then, Gabriella DeZantez casually walked in front of her, between them.

The Enlightened One had both blades unsheathed and assumed a low, defensive stance. One blade was thrust forward, wavering slightly as if tempting Kali to make a move, the other held back and unwavering, ready to follow through. DeZantez was, in short, prepared for a swift and deadly double strike.

DeZantez spoke one word, but it was enough.

"Don't."

Kali slumped, her battle tension reluctantly leaving her body, and the guards once more took her. DeZantez sheathed her blades and returned to the duty McCain had given her. Kali stared at the Overseer as he watched DeZantez manipulate the chains that lowered the gibbet from its hanging position on the side of the church, then open the front of the cage. The look of abject terror he had exhibited moments before had been replaced by a twisted smile, and he wiped a small amount of drool from his mouth as he turned to his guards.

"Strip her," he said.

Strip me? Kali thought.

"Get your farking hands off!" She shouted as the bodyguards began to tear at her bodysuit. Thankfully, she saw DeZantez move forward, at last seeming willing to intervene. Instead of halting their actions, however, she regarded Kali steadily.

"It's better this way," she said. "Trust me, when the naphtha comes, you will not wish it to first burn your clothes."

Naphtha. Perversely, the word made Kali feel even colder than she had before, and she stared at the pipes that ran from the side of the church into the top of the gibbet cage, at the spark ready to ready ignite the substance as it poured onto the victim within. Well, nightmare as this was, she sure as hells wasn't going to entertain McCain more than he already would be.

"He isn't concerned about how easily I die," she said, with disgust. "Let me remain as I am."

DeZantez hesitated, then nodded to the bodyguards. They bundled her into the gibbet, slamming and locking the cage behind her.

"It's your choice," DeZantez said, turning away.

Kali stared after her and, as she did, became aware of McCain laughing.

"What did you expect?" He said. "That the Enlightened One would balk at the horror of what is about to happen to you, force me to release you from my custody?" He shook his head. "The gibbet is an *everyday* occurrence, girl, don't you understand? Your enlightened friend here has burned countless sinners in her career. Have you not, Miss DeZantez?"

DeZantez stared at Kali, still emotionless, and nodded.

"This might seem like the ultimate horror to you," McCain continued. "But it is her *job*."

Kali grabbed the bars of the gibbet. They were rough beneath her grip, coated with a substance that once had been the flesh of 'sinners' but was now only a permanently caked layer, as hard as coral.

"McCain," she said. "You do this and I promise you *I* will regret it."

McCain smiled. "I like a sense of humour. But I equally dislike modesty. Raise the gibbet, Sister DeZantez."

Gabriella DeZantez paused for a second but then turned a wheel on the wall of the church.

Kali felt the cage floor shift beneath her and sway and creak as it was lifted well off the ground. The climb brought her within the full glare of the sun and she blinked and prickled in the brightness and heat. It was nothing, though, compared with what was to come, and she stared down at McCain, DeZantez and the goons, swallowing dryly as they were joined by the jury, filing slowly out of the church to witness what was to come. Any hope she might have had for a last minute reprieve or hint of compassion was instantly dashed as she saw their upturned faces; vengeful and convinced of her guilt. Suddenly she appreciated the awful reality of the situation she was in. To her this was a waking nightmare, but such was the iron rule of the Faith here in the sticks that to these people, as McCain had said, it was just an everyday occurrence. A *normal* way to die.

"The taps, Miss DeZantez," McCain ordered.

"No..." Kali said softly to herself, clenching her fists around the rough bars.

She began to struggle as she watched DeZantez turn the taps on the wall of the church and they vented steam. Drops of moisture fell to the ground. The pipes above her hissed, shook and gurgled as the naphtha entered them and began to build up pressure inside. It would take seconds for the lethal substance to travel their length and Kali was suddenly overwhelmed by how close to death she was. She had never been afraid of dying – had faced it many times – but to have it occur like this was somehow tainted and wrong, and filled her with despair and fury.

She renewed her struggle against the bars, rocking the cage violently on its chains. The pipes groaned under the strain of the protest she unleashed and, for a moment, Kali thought that was the way out. If she could only dislodge the pipes, she would escape this after all. But then she saw that the pipes were flexing with her, joined at various points along their length by some rubbery substance that could presumably withstand the heat of the naphtha.

"Really, Miss Hooper," McCain said, "do you not think that all who have died before you have not tried the same..."

Kali looked up at the pipes and then quickly down again, for the gurgling was louder now and *closer*. Before she jammed her eyes shut in a futile attempt to block out the pain she glanced over at Horse, her loyal mount bucking in agitation beneath the restraining hands of a dozen of the townspeople, and wondered what would happen to him now. Then she felt the first tiny hot spits of naphtha searing the back of her neck.

Something cracked like thunder, and there was the sound of wrending metal. No further naphtha came and Kali opened her eyes.

She saw that the pipes had been torn apart at their mid section and were dancing about in mid air, vomiting their lethal content to the ground. Below, McCain and his goons were stepping back awkwardly, trying to avoid the oil, while DeZantez threw herself at the taps to stop any further release before lowering the gibbet to the ground.

The flow stopped. Kali's gaze turned to McCain, whose face was red with fury. The subject of his fury seemed to be behind her, out of sight, and so she had no idea to whom McCain addressed his next words.

"What," the Overseer rumbled angrily, "is the meaning of this?"

A figure strode into view and Kali frowned. She wasn't sure who she had expected miraculously to have appeared – Slowhand, perhaps, Aldrededor, Dolorosa or Moon – but the man she saw was a complete stranger to her. Tall, muscular, and garbed like a huntsman in leather britches and squallcoat sewn from irregularly cut pieces of hide, his stubbled face with its piercing brown eyes regarded McCain with some degree of contempt.

"The meaning of this," he replied in a voice clearly used to having the last word, "is that your execution is over."

As he spoke, he wound back into a coil a whip made of nine lengths of chain, clearly the weapon which had ruptured the pipes, and moved around to the front of the cage and released its door. He offered Kali a hand down and she took it silently, still assessing what the hells was going on here.

"On whose authority?" McCain demanded.

"The highest authority. That of the Anointed Lord."

I wonder what the Lord of All would make of that? Kali thought.

It was clear what McCain's opinion was. The Overseer narrowed his eyes and beckoned his bodyguards to the fore, where they placed hands on their weapons.

"Forgive me," he said, "but you hardly have the appearance of an agent of the Anointed Lord, and I know, or know of, most of them. What is your name?"

"My name is Jakub Freel."

"Freel?" McCain repeated, dismissively. "I have never heard of you."

McCain may not have heard of him but Kali had, and she stood back slightly in some shock. She stared at her rescuer, her own eyes narrowed. Jakub Freel. This was the man whom Jenna, Slowhand's sister, had married. Other than that, however, she knew little about him. As to his role here, she was as much in the dark as McCain himself.

"How is it that you carry the authority of the Anointed Lord?" asked the Overseer. "What office do you serve?"

"Let's just to say that the office I occupy was once occupied by another, now deceased."

McCain sneered. "And this other was?"

"Konstantin Munch."

Freel's answer gave the Overseer pause. His sneer disappeared and, somewhere beneath his jowls, Kali saw the man swallow, hard. That was hardly surprising. Munch's remit in the Final Faith had been to tackle those jobs that might prove *embarrassing* in others' hands, the head of a shady group whose powers, as a result, transcended the otherwise rigid structure of the Faith, allowing them to go everywhere and exist nowhere at the same time.

Kali found it interesting to note, however, that while Munch had surrounded himself with lackeys, Freel appeared to be working alone, and she got the impression that this was his preference. Whether that was because he was capable of single-handedly dealing with what the Faith threw at him or not, she didn't yet know, but she did know that it was time to start getting her own handle on things.

"So, you're Stan's replacement," she said casually, and nodded at the cage. "I like the new approach to the job. Getting me out of there was not something he'd have done."

"Oh, he might. In these circumstances."

"Which are?"

"I tracked you here because the Anointed Lord has need of your help. We need to leave for Scholten right away."

Kali was stunned.

"You're kidding, right? You're here because Makennon needs *my* help? *Again*? This is the same Makennon whose arse I saved at Orl but who then sent me a map to a dwarven deathtrap as thanks? The same Makennon whose people nicked the plans for the *Llothriall* from my own tavern? The same Makennon whose skewed religion nearly got me fried alive just now? The same Makennon who... fark it, never mind."

Kali turned and began to stomp towards Horse. "Tell her to go to the hells..."

"I wish I could," Freel said, striding after her.

"Wish you could what?"

"Tell her to go to the hells."

Kali span. "Look, at least Munch was an *obvious* nutter. Do you want to tell me what you're talking about?"

"The hells," Freel said. "We fear they have already taken her."

Chapter Five

There was no way that Kali could resist a hook like that, was there? She agreed there and then to accompany Freel, at least until she knew more about what was going on.

There remained, however, the small matter of Randus McCain, who refused to recognise Freel's authority and thus to release her to him. Kali knew full well that it was little to do with authority and more with the bastard's desire – stripping her whether she liked it or not this time – to get his fat hands on her again, and her immediate inclination was to stuff the Overseer in his own gibbet with a naphtha pipe up his arse. She sensed Freel felt the same – seeing through the pretence of procedure to recognise the tin god pervert for what he was – but while McCain himself would prove no obstacle if Freel chose to remove her by force, his goons about the town might. Not than any of them looked as if they'd stand a chance again him – it was just that, new to the job as he was, he might not wish the paperwork that would result from mopping up a town of his own people.

Freel suggested a compromise.

Kali would be returned to McCain if she failed to deliver the help the Faith was asking of her. To ensure her return, Gabriella DeZantez would accompany them where they needed to go.

"What?" Kali said.

Once again she began to stomp towards Horse.

And once again Gabriella DeZantez stepped in front of her, blades drawn.

Kali whirled on Freel. "*Are you serious?*"

Freel folded his arms. "It appears Sister DeZantez is serious."

"But I already agreed to come!"

"Ah. But not necessarily to help."

"I'm innocent, dammit!"

"That remains to be seen."

Kali's gaze snapped between the two of them, exasperated. What the hells was going on here? One minute this... *enforcer* was asking for help, the next taking her into his farking custody! Then a small wink from Freel mollified her. He had no intention of returning her to the Overseer, just getting her away from him without the need for bloodshed.

"It is better all round, do you not think?" Freel said.

Kali did think. Once again the enforcer had demonstrated an approach to the job that was different from Konstantin Munch's and shown himself to be something of a manipulator in the process. It made a refreshing change from a punch in the face, but she realised she'd have to keep an eye on this Jakub Freel.

"Maybe it is," she agreed.

Kali again moved to Horse, and this time actually reached him. She debated manually unshackling the various chains that had been wrapped about his body and legs but, having had more than enough of this town, snapped her fingers instead. Horse bucked, the chains exploded and links flew like rain.

"Good boygirl," Kali said.

She began to check her saddlebags ready for the journey. As she did she noticed DeZantez emerge from rooms behind the church with a single, if fairly hefty, saddlebag of her own. She slung it over a dusty, chestnut horse, and the clank it made suggested it contained her armour.

Kali frowned. Gabriella was something of an enigma and she couldn't quite work out how serious she was taking her assigned role as her custodian. Whether, indeed, she was aware that Freel himself had not been serious about it. Certainly, she had to keep up appearances for now, but the question was, were they more than appearances? Would she, if it came to it, return her to McCain if she failed to help Freel? Would she, even, cut her down if she tried to flee? Kali decided she might have to have a word with Freel once they'd left town, request that he make his little deception clear to DeZantez, because she appeared to be a soldier who followed orders to the letter.

Or... maybe not.

Kali watched as DeZantez returned to the church and emerged with its collection coffers. The gold inside was destined, like them, for Scholten, and it was a cardinal sin to remove it, but DeZantez had no hesitation in distributing it instead to the people of the town. She clearly thought it better used for the repairs Solnos would need.

Kali was about to move forward, tell her that was a kind gesture, but hesitated as DeZantez moved to the edge of the ruined graveyard and stood, staring in. Kali didn't know why, but she sensed that had the graveyard still been intact the Enlightened One might have been a little more reluctant to leave. With its destruction, she had found an excuse for a decision that she had struggled with for a while; that it was time to leave Solnos, and whatever memories it held, behind.

After a while DeZantez turned and mounted her horse. Kali and Freel mounted up too. The three of them rode to the edge of town and then up onto the ridge where, for Kali, this whole affair had begun. They stared at the rotating machines. A rumble of thunder in the sky behind made them seem all the more ominous.

"I was going to find out what these bastards are," Kali said to Freel. "Before you came."

"Actually, Miss Hooper, you were going to die, screaming horribly."

"You know what I mean."

"I know what you mean. And believe me when I say you are still going to get the chance."

Kali snapped him a look, but before she could question him further, Freel spurred his horse on, and she and DeZantez had to gallop their mounts to catch up.

The enforcer kept them to a strenuous pace for most of the journey to Scholten, slowing to rest the horses – the bamfcat needing none – only infrequently. Kali could, of course, have had Horse make a few 'shortcuts' but there seemed little point in reaching Scholten before Freel. Still, she would have liked to see DeZantez's face if Horse jumped right in front of her eyes. What would she do about returning her to McCain then, eh?

It was during one cooling off period – she and Jakub Freel riding side by side in silence, DeZantez lagging a little way behind, lost in thought – that she decided to tackle what had so far been unsaid.

"I know who you are."

Freel simply nodded. "And I, you. In fact, I understand you were something of a thorn in my predecessor's side."

"More like an arrow in his head," Kali said. "But, strictly speaking, I wasn't the one responsible."

"No?"

"No," Kali repeated. "It was my lover. Slowhand. Killiam Slowhand."

The mention of the archer, and her relationship to him, was careful and deliberate. She let both facts hang in the air. She hadn't known how much Freel knew of her and Slowhand's involvement with Jenna's death in the Drakengrats, but got a notion now – a flicker in Freel's eyes that went beyond recognising his wife's brother's name. It was obvious he knew full well that Slowhand had given the order that had killed Jenna.

"Killiam Slowhand," Freel repeated. "A joke of a name. Not even his own."

"He has his reasons."

"That, then, is his role in your relationship? He is your assassin?"

"Assassin? No, of course not. He's a soldier and..." Kali hesitated and decided that she may as well take the bamfcat by the horns. "Freel, you have to understand, what happened... it was Jenna or us."

Freel pursed his lips, nodded slowly, but said nothing. Kali did not press him.

"Was it worth it?" He asked eventually.

"What? Was what worth it?"

"What you fought so hard to save? The reason so many died that day? The ship?"

The question threw Kali and she frowned. The fact was, other than generalities, she had no idea what role the *Tharnak* had yet to play. "Honestly? I don't know."

"Are you saying that it remains to be seen?"

"I guess I am, yes."

Freel turned to her for the first time. "Then, Miss Hooper, if you are trying to discover what my opinions of your lover are, my answer is they, too, remain to be seen."

With that, the conversation ended and Freel spurred his horse on. They didn't slow again until they had reached their destination.

Scholten Cathedral. The last time two times Kali had trodden its supposedly hallowed halls she had been with Slowhand, and on both occasions she and the archer were intruders, either running for their lives or sneaking about in the dark. In either case they had been able to pay little attention to the details of their surroundings, other than to the whereabouts of Faith patrols. She wished she could say it made a nice change to be able to take a good look around but the opposite was true. Everything about the place – the grandiose architecture, the ceremony and particularly the smug faces of the cathedral's Enlightened Ones, tending to their flock in exchange for donations – made Kali sick to the stomach. She wondered why she hadn't, in fact, jumped away with Horse on the way here, as had crossed her mind.

The One Faith, The Only Faith, The Final Faith, she thought. *Gods!*

They were a blight selling the false dream of ascension to their followers, and she wished she could tell every one of those followers what she had witnessed done in the church's name, just what it was that went on behind the gold-thread tapestries and hand-carved wooden doors – show them the real face of the Final Faith.

She, of course, bore scars both old and new to remind her of exactly what that was. The old scars on her ankles, wrists and neck had been acquired deep beneath these very halls, where Konstantin Munch had submitted her to the comforts of his 'nail chair' and the tender ministrations of Querilous Fitch. Though the scars had faded, her disdain for the Faith would never go away. The new scars were the red blotches that she now bore on her shoulders and neck: evidence, if any were needed, of these bastards' propensity to burn first and not ask questions later, to immolate any who spoke out against their cause, as they had done in the thousands over the years.

It gave Kali no small pleasure, then, as, with the sound of the Eternal Choir fading in their ears, Freel led her and DeZantez down into the sublevels', where it seemed the Faith had undergone some suffering themselves. The transition from the ornate cathedral to its gritty underbelly was always dramatic, but the signs of recent battle in the distribution and rail centre made it more so. Bodies had clearly been removed from within it, but cleaved or broken pieces of armour and torn surplice cloth were scattered here and there, some pieces of which still contained the odd chunk of severed flesh. And there was blood. A great deal of blood that had to have come from a great many people.

Something had hit the Faith and hit them hard.

The question was what?

"Come with me," Freel said, wasting no time.

He led the two women to some kind of bunker that, judging by the crates of belongings waiting outside the door to be removed, had recently changed hands. Kali recognised some of the belongings, particularly a small trolley containing a number of needlereeds and vials of viscous liquids and a duplicate of her own gutting knife. This must have been Konstantin Munch's hidey-hole when he wasn't torturing poor unfortunates in the holding chambers below. But as they passed through the door, no further evidence of the dwarf-blooded psychopath could be seen. Freel had put his own stamp on the office.

Kali's eyebrows rose. The bunker could have been an Old Race site, so much of their technology had been installed. Except that where most of the devices she encountered in such sites had been decayed and broken down, rotten after countless years of neglect, this stuff looked as if it had come straight out of the box. Amberglow light-panels illuminated an array of exotic machines of unknown purpose, security cages were sealed with runic arches and, most disturbingly, a raised platform in the centre offered views from a dozen Eyes of the Lord spheres, projecting goings-on in different parts of the Faith's empire. These images were being monitored by a handful of grey-robed men.

Gabriella DeZantez seemed discomforted in the presence of so much technology, as if it had no place in her vision of the church. Freel immediately dropped a few notches in Kali's estimation, too.

"Seems like there's a difference between my manipulating forbidden artefacts and your doing the same," Kali observed, nodding at the spheres.

"Oh, those things," Freel responded, "those weren't my idea." He signed a chit handed to him by one of his men. "The rest, though... well, the Faith has to move with the times. Even if, ironically, those times are the ancient past."

"Still meddling with things you don't understand," Kali said.

Freel paid her little attention, his face darkening as another man entered and read out the latest confirmed casualties – supply workers Bogle, Krang, Rutter and Flank, and an Eminence named Kesar.

The latter name seemed to shake Gabriella DeZantez.

"Rodrigo Kesar is dead?" She said.

The guard looked regretful. "The Eminence was supervising a... volatile incense shipment when the assault began, Sister. Was the Eminence a friend of yours?"

"No," Gabriella DeZantez said quietly to herself, and shook her head.

Kali looked at her, puzzled. The man had obviously been important in some way, but she had already said not as a friend. It seemed almost as if she had had some door slammed in her face. Maybe she'd ask her about it when she had the chance. For now, though, there were more important questions to be addressed.

"You want to tell me what the hells has been going on here?"

Freel guided her and DeZantez to the viewing area and, as he did, three other men joined them from across the room. "General McIntee of the Order of the Swords of Dawn, Cardinal Kratos," he said by way of introduction. "And this is the developer of the Eyes of the –"

"I know who this bastard is," Kali interrupted. "And I should have known. Hello, Fitch."

The psychic manipulator bowed slightly, his hands steepled. They were bandaged, Kali noticed. "Kali Hooper. What a pleasant surprise."

"What the hells are you doing here?" Kali demanded.

"Helping, Kali, just like you. All hands on deck, and all that."

"What – you run out of heads today?"

Fitch smiled and suddenly noticed the burns on Kali's neck. He tutted sympathetically.

Kali snarled.

"I suggest," Freel said hastily, "that we get down to business."

"No argument here," Kali agreed. "You said Makennon needed my help? That you feared she'd gone to the hells?"

Freel nodded. "The Anointed Lord has been taken."

"Taken? By which I presume you *don't* mean she's currently prancing through the clouds annoying the rest of the poor souls with Kerberos?"

"He means abducted," General McIntee said. "Here from the very heart of the Faith."

Kali pursed her lips, nodded. "Neat trick. So who's got her?"

Freel nodded to Fitch who promptly shut down all of the images being projected from the Eyes of the Lord. He then picked up an inactive Eye of the Lord from a nearby table and readied it for viewing.

With DeZantez, Kali found herself watching the horde's assault on the tunnels. She saw an overview of the grey figures pouring from the tunnel, zooming images of agonised or dying Final Faith soldiers and the flashes of the intruders' makeshift but lethal weapons. She had to disguise her shock as she saw Slowhand struggling in the grip of Faith guards. She had already met with indisputable proof that his mission to kill Fitch had failed, and now she knew why. Just like herself, events had overtaken him. Not for the first time, she reflected that she and the archer had a knack for being in the right place at the wrong time. It was almost as if, as Poul Sonpear had pointed out some months before, their presence in these places was somehow predestined. Now was not the time to worry about that, however, or Slowhand's current fate. If she were to make sense of what was happening before her, she had to give it her full attention.

Katherine Makennon was visible in the fray now, the armoured form of the Anointed Lord striding into the sublevel at the head of her men. Again, Kali caught a glimpse of Slowhand, trying to stop Makennon wading in. Wade in, of course, was what she did, and Kali had to give the woman her due – she could certainly bollock the bad guys. What happened next, however, was so unexpected and shocking that she wasn't at all surprised to see Slowhand and his captors reel from it.

Something hurtled out of the dark, darker than the tunnel from which it came. A thing of indeterminate shape, a storm cloud streak that moved at breakneck speed, whose outlines writhed before the eye. A shifting, octopus-like morass and an insane blur at the same time, as seemingly insubstantial as shadow as it shot straight at Makennon and whipped back towards the tunnel, wrapping about her as it did, absorbing her in its mass and carrying her away. In that instant – and only that instant – it was almost identifiable, as a black carriage drawn by wild-eyed, snorting horses from the pits. A moment later the shape and Katherine Makennon with it were gone.

"Farking hell," Kali said, as the image from the sphere flickered and died.

Gabriella DeZantez was a little more controlled. "What in the name of the Lord was that?"

"Interesting, isn't it?" Freel said. "All I can say is that it – and the preceding events – were repeated at twelve other locations across the peninsula. And in each case the leader of that community was taken by that... thing."

"By previous events, I presume you mean the attack from the soul-stripped?" Kali said.

Fitch looked surprised. "You know of the First Enemy?"

The First Enemy, Kali thought. Only the more senior of the Final Faith called him that, those who *remembered*. DeZantez seemed not to be one of them, and so for her sake –

"Why don't you remind me, Fitch?"

Fitch shrugged. "The result of a conceit of the first Anointed Lord, Jeremiah Nectus Dunn. He mistakenly believed the teachings of the Faith could be taken to the farthest reaches of our empi... of the land."

"The Sardenne Forest you mean."

Fitch nodded. "But Dunn was wrong. The people who live in that forsaken hinterland have greater things to fear than the Lord of All, as our people discovered to their cost."

"My, my, Querilous Fitch, that's almost blasphemous," Kali chided.

Fitch could have been talking about any of the multifarious creatures that called the Sardenne home, and it would have served Dunn's missionaries right if they had encountered them and not come home as a result. But he wasn't talking about them, she knew. It wasn't the bogarts and beasties of the great forest coming out of there that they had to worry about – the assault on Scholten Cathedral was far too coordinated for them. This was without doubt the work of the one ruling intelligence that called the Sardenne home. In an area called Bellagon's Rip.

Most people called him the Pale Lord.

"He was the first serious resistance our Church encountered," Fitch continued. "A sorcerer of power unprecedented, then and now. He found the presence of our people in the forest – in *his* forest – distasteful, and made that distaste abundantly clear. Those who 'survived' the encounter remain with him, I imagine, to this day. In the end the Faith and he made a truce. The Sardenne would be left alone and, unless we attempted to return, so would we."

Kali nodded. It was pleasing to see that some things made Fitch sweat as profusely as his victims. But with good reason. In Pontaine, at least, the Pale Lord had become something of a bogeyman. A necromancer by the name of Bastian Redigor, he had been banished from civilisation long ago and had retreated into exile in the depths of the Sardenne Forest, whereafter occasional sightings of his almost albino features and tall, thin, cloaked figure – who never seemed to age – had earned him the nickname of 'the Pale Lord.' It was what the Pale Lord *did* during these sightings, however, that had earned him his fearful reputation over the years. People near to the forest began to disappear, first in ones and twos and then in ever increasing numbers. If these people were ever seen again it was as a fleeting form glimpsed among the trees, empty and grey and engaged in mysterious business. These people had become slaves of the Pale Lord – he had taken their souls for purposes unknown – and they became known as the 'soul-stripped.' As the years had passed, more and more had been taken – the soul-stripped themselves taking people on their Lord's behalf – so much so that unruly children were sent to bed with a promise that, if they did not behave, the Lord or his growing army of minions would come to 'kiss them' and take them away into the night.

Oh yes, Kali knew that, because she'd been one of those children who'd lain awake night after night, peeking out fearfully from under the sheets. Thankfully, rather than turn her into a gibbering wreck, it had eventually instilled in her a curiosity for the unexplained that had defined the rest of her life.

But why, after all these years, and as the Faith hadn't returned to the Sardenne, was the Pale Lord attacking them?

And how the hells had he been able to do what he did?

"I thought your tunnels were shielded," she said. "Weaved so powerfully nothing, not even the Pale Lord, could get through."

"They are. Or rather, were. The shields collapsed before the assault began. Just vanished. As, incidentally, did the abilities of every mage or shadowmage in the complex."

Kali's eyes narrowed suspiciously. "Vanished how?"

"We don't know. They just –"

"Fizzled out," Kali finished, and sighed. "Just like Quinking's Depths."

"Quinking's Depths?"

"Below Solnos," Kali said absently. "The same thing happened there."

"Then I imagine you're thinking that the reason the shields collapsed is related to the appearance of the machines near Solnos. And you would be right. But only partly so."

"Oh?"

"Those machines are not the only ones of their kind. There are three groups of them."

"*What?*"

Fitch moved to a map of the peninsula, pointing out three locations. "Three groups of three machines rising from beneath the ground at precisely the same time. Their appearance was reported to us by our senders, just before their abilities... left them."

Kali hesitated. "Wait one minute. Are you trying to tell me this phenomena is peninsula-wide? That magic has been cancelled out *everywhere*?"

"Yes. Our theory is that these machines have been activated from some central location by forces of the Pale Lord for just that purpose. It is with this that we need your help."

Kali folded her arms. "I thought that's where I might come in. You want me to find out where this location is and shut these things down right?"

Fitch nodded. "Only then would we have an effective defence against the First Enemy. Only then would we be able to effect a rescue of the Anointed Lord."

"And the others who were taken, of course..."

"Of course."

"Okaaay," Kali said. "And just what do you lot do in the meantime?"

"Try and find out more about what the Pale Lord is planning," Freel said. "To that end I ordered an Eye of the Lord despatched to the Sardenne."

Kali was impressed. She doubted very much that such a course of action would even have occurred to Fitch, who could think of nothing to do with his new toys other than spy on his flock.

Sometimes you just needed to think, as it were, outside the collection box.

"Show me," Kali said.

"I will," Freel reassured her. "But the journey to and from the Sardenne takes time. We expect the Eye's return in the next couple of hours." The enforcer shrugged, half-smiled and spread his arms. "In the meantime, I suggest you make yourself at home."

Chapter Six

Make yourself at home, Freel had said. How exactly did you do that in the bosom of the most intolerant religion the peninsula had ever seen? Kali had contemplated popping upstairs to do a few numbers with the Eternal Choir – maybe something with a bit of a *beat* – or perhaps sneaking into Makennon's quarters to grab herself a nice, hot bath, but she didn't want to give Fitch a chance to play with his balls. She had even thought of getting the hells out of the cathedral for a while to down a flummox or three in the Ramblas, but the information she was waiting on was too important to miss.

She tried to get to see Slowhand, But the archer was under heavy guard – access to no one but Fitch – and instead she found herself wandering the sublevels. She came at last to the naphtha chamber where the soul-stripped, who had been left behind after the Pale Lord's assault were meeting, without objection, their ultimate end. The creatures' fate was indicative of how Redigor had used them as nothing more than cannon fodder to draw

Makennon out, and now their purpose was done, they were discarded.

Kali was surprised to see DeZantez in the chamber, watching the mindless victims with sorrow rather than disgust in her eyes. As one soul-stripped after the other was placed within a naphtha cage, mindlessly compliant, she seemed even to sag before the weight of them, as if each victim took with it a little part of her. Maybe it did, Kali reflected. After all, as a Sister of the Order of the Swords of Dawn, these were the people whom DeZantez had sworn to protect, and they had been taken from her by the Pale Lord in obscene numbers.

Watching them burn, Kali cringed, recalling her own close encounter with the gibbet and trying not to think how agonising her death could so easily have been. She was aided in this by what was perhaps an even greater horror. As the naphtha consumed them, the Pale Lord's soldiers remained perfectly still, making no attempt to escape their gibbets and absolutely no sound other than the crackling and spitting of their own burning flesh. By all that was natural, they should have filled the underground with the sound of their screams but, whitened eyes staring unfeelingly ahead, their mortal forms departed the world uncomplaining, supplicant until the last to their dark master's will.

When it was done, Gabriella DeZantez touched all four points of the crossed-circle on her tunic and then placed her right palm on its centre, her head bowed in prayer. When her gaze rose once more Kali was surprised to see teardrops beading the corners of her eyes.

"Maybe now," DeZantez said, "their souls can somehow reach Kerberos."

Kali regarded her, and nodded non-commitedly. Considering the treatment she had received at this woman's hands, she hadn't expected such a human response from her but, then, she had already sensed that there was more to her than the average Filth drone. She shared their devoutness, yes, but she was clearly not part of the pack. There was an air of independence and a sense of humanity and, more importantly, *justice* about her. For a moment she wished she could share her hopes for the victims.

"You don't believe in ascension to Kerberos." Gabriella observed, seeing her expression.

Kali shrugged, bit her lip. "Let's just say I've seen and heard a few things that make me question the received wisdom, particularly the teachings of the Filth."

DeZantez actually smiled at the slur. "That it is our destiny to ascend – to become something greater than our whole?"

"Yes."

DeZantez pondered for a moment. "We have time. What if I could prove to you that when a deserving soul departs its body it does indeed travel to the place to which we all aspire – to the clouds of Kerberos?"

"And just how would you do that? With some Faith parlour trick? No, I don't think so."

"No trick. And nothing to do with the Faith. Except, of course as a reinforcement *of* our faith. No, this is something that was here before our Church. Something much, much older."

Gabriella snapped instructions to a nearby brother, an initiate by his cowl, to fetch something from her saddlebag, and he departed, returning a little while later with a small cloth-wrapped object. Gabriella unfolded the material almost reverently, revealing what appeared to be a shard of glass or crystal.

"This is a piece of Freedom Mountain," she explained. "It was loosened during a recent... let's say *visitation* and removed from the site by a man named Crowe, as a souvenir of what happened there. Travis... he neglected to take it with him when we parted company."

"I don't see what geology has to do with anything here."

"Take it," DeZantez urged. Kali did, and found the shard unexpectedly light. "Now come with me."

Kali frowned, but did as asked, finding herself led along a number of corridors to a small chamber which had been converted into a makeshift field hospital to treat the few survivors of the recent attack. One of the cots held the badly injured body of a Faith brother for whom nothing more could be done. The dying man stared up at DeZantez with dimming eyes as she stood over him, a rattle of recognition at her Swords of Dawn surplice escaping his dry throat. Gabriella smiled with genuine warmth and sat gently down on the side of the cot, taking the man's hand.

"This is Brother Marcus," she explained, squeezing his hand. "Brother Marcus is a good man, with simple beliefs. Chief among those beliefs has always been that when his time comes he will ascend to Kerberos and there find the greater glory that awaits us all, just as the Final Faith teaches." She leaned forward to Brother Marcus's face and spoke softly. "You understand, don't you, Marcus, that your time is coming soon?"

Brother Marcus nodded almost imperceptibly and swallowed, as did Kali. DeZantez had clearly spent time here while she'd been wandering around.

"I am with you," Gabriella said.

Kali shifted uneasily on her feet, but said nothing as DeZantez continued to comfort Marcus and wait for the man to die. There was, she presumed, some point to this. After a few more minutes, Marcus's hand suddenly tightened in Gabriella's, he bucked once and gave a long sigh. This particular member of the Final Faith had breathed his last.

DeZantez sighed. "What do you see?" She asked Kali.

"A man gone to meet his maker," Kali responded. "But who, or what, that maker is I wouldn't want to say."

"Look again," Gabriella instructed. "Through the shard."

"What?"

"The shard. Freedom Mountain had a direct physical connection to Kerberos, and that has given it some unique properties. Look again," she added. "*Hurry, girl, or it will be too late.*"

Girl? Kali thought. There wasn't that much difference in their ages and, in fact, she was pretty sure she was the elder here. Nevertheless, she shrugged, warily raised the shard before her eyes, and caught her breath. Because what the shard revealed was that Brother Marcus hadn't yet gone anywhere. His soul, his essence – Kali wasn't sure what to call it – separated itself from the physical form like pollen shaken from a flower by a spring breeze. It was made up of sparkling, scintillating beads of light as vibrant as anything Kali had ever seen. As they emerged from his lifeless body, they formed themselves into a recognisable semblance of Brother Marcus - albeit distorted, as if viewed through a carnival mirror - forming and stretching upwards, towards the ceiling of the chamber. And then, with an actual, noticeable glance down at his corporeal remains, *through* the ceiling.

Kali continued to stare upwards, working out where beneath Scholten this particular chamber was located, trying to rationalise what she had just seem. But she couldn't. Because unless Brother Marcus was heading for a final tankard in the *Bloody Merry* - which, considering the Faith's abstinence laws, seemed unlikely - there was only one thing up there. Quite some way up there.

"The clouds of Kerberos." Kali said softly.

"The clouds of Kerberos." Gabriella confirmed.

"I... I don't know what to say."

"Then say nothing. But understand that this is why I have given myself to the Faith. That, despite what you think, some of us truly believe."

Kali stared at her. DeZantez turned as the messenger who had delivered the shard returned, in a hurry and bringing news. "Sister DeZantez, Miss Hooper, Enforcer Freel requests your presence," he said breathlessly. "The Eye of the Lord has returned."

The pair looked at each other and began to make their way to the bunker.

"There's something that I need to ask you," Gabriella said en route. "Something I don't understand."

Kali was grateful to return to more familiar footing. "Shoot."

"That *thing* that took the Anointed Lord. It was borne of sorcery, it had to be. Of magic. But I thought the magic had died."

The same seeming contradiction had occurred to Kali, and while she had no answer, she did have suspicions. The threads might have been cancelled by the machines, but what if this wasn't the threads at work? Something close to them, yes, something similar, but not the threads everyone knew? She recalled Aldrededor telling her that while he had been piloting the *Tharnak* he had seen strange *black threads* lying dormant amongst the others, no longer a part of their tapestry but still there. They'd appeared lifeless, he'd told her, but nevertheless occasionally leeched colour from other threads.

"It has," Kali said to DeZantez. "That's what worries me."

They reached Freel's bunker where he and the others were gathered once more about the central platform, where a new sphere had been positioned for viewing. The returned Eye was blackened and damaged, still smoking slightly, as if it had been caught up in some incredibly vicious firestorm. Kali wondered how it had managed to limp home. But limp home it had and, by the looks on the faces of Freel, Fitch and the others, they had already viewed what it had brought back with it.

"I have a feeling this isn't good news," Kali said.

"It isn't." Freel replied.

He nodded to Fitch and the manipulator activated the sphere. The flickering image showed the rolling plains of east Pontaine for a moment, before the target of the Eye of the Lord's flight came into view.

The sphere approached the perimeter of the Sardenne at a height of about a thousand feet, so that the demarcation between the ancient forest and the plains was clearly visible. It was darker than Kali had expected it to look, however, although she had experience of just *how* dark the Sardenne could be. The reason wasn't immediately obvious, the distance still too great, but from Jakub Freel's expression it was going to come as quite the revelation. She studied the image intently as the small recording blimp drew closer, and gradually began to make out exactly what it was that constituted that greater darkness.

Gabriella DeZantez crossed herself once more, praying under her breath.

Soul-stripped, thousands of them, standing shoulder to shoulder in the border of the forest, absolutely motionless and as grey as the shadows in which they stood. Distinguishable as individuals mainly by the whites of their lifeless, staring eyes, they were crowded together in an almost crushing mass but none reacted to the others, none complained, none jostled. Kali had no idea how far back into the forest these witless creatures lurked but, as she watched, more, presumably recent victims, shambled to join them and take up positions by their sides. As if those already assembled weren't enough.

This was a gathering of the Pale Lord's servants on a massive and hitherto unprecedented scale. The necromancer was, it seemed, building an army.

"Their eyes," Fitch said. "It's said that the First Enemy can, if he wishes, see through them all at once, and that when he does his gaze is powerful enough to see people's thoughts."

"What the hells is going on?" Kali asked.

Freel placed a hand on her shoulder. "There's more."

Kali glanced at Gabriella, who looked as confused as she did, and turned back to the projection. The Eye of the Lord was heading beyond the edge of the forest, now, and the vista it displayed was an unending, rolling landscape of ancient and massive trees, a thick canopy that hid the presence of the multifarious creatures and horrors that lived beneath. As the sphere progressed, Kali mentally traced her own journey through the forest almost a year before, the only way that she could map the progression of the Eye of the Lord over the otherwise unchanging topography. She guessed it was nearing Bellagon's Rip, now, which was generally accepted to be the stomping ground – or hiding place, depending on which way you looked at it – of the Pale Lord. Her guess turned out to be accurate as, after a minor alteration of its flight path, the view of the Eye of the Lord changed slightly and *something* hove into view.

"Oh, my gods," Kali said.

The Eye of the Lord had turned to look over the Sardenne's canopy, Kerberos's azure curve clearly visible above the forest. It was neither the canopy nor the gas giant that drew the eye, though, but the space between the two, where a massive pillar of energy, the width of a small village, punched up from the forest *towards* Kerberos. The pillar pulsed regularly and, each time it did, seemed to rise a little higher.

"What are those things you can see in it?" Gabriella DeZantez asked.

"I wish we knew," Freel responded. "Miss Hooper, have you ever come across anything like this in your travels?"

Kali shook her head. She was gaining a better view of the pillar now as the Eye of the Lord moved closer. The 'clouds' were revealed to be an agitation of the entire insides of the pillar, the shapes thick within it, slapping and battering against each other like leaves in a storm. Kali squinted, peering at them to make out more of their exact form when a thought struck her. She nudged DeZantez, indicated the shard and then raised it to her eye to view the projection.

Kali swallowed before speaking.

"They're souls," she announced.

Freel, Fitch and the others snapped their gazes towards her but, before Kali could elaborate, the projection suddenly juddered and flickered and, with the sphere perhaps thirty feet from the surface of the pillar, blackened and disappeared.

"The Eye of the Lord closed at this point," Fitch pointed out. "And returned to me."

"Did you say *souls*?" DeZantez asked Kali, clearly disturbed by what she had seen.

"But the ascension is meant to be a *personal* calling," Cardinal Kratos said, seemingly of the same mind, though Kali wasn't sure she believed him. "An individual journey. Not this... this –"

Kali offered him the shard. "Watch again and see for yourself. I'm sorry but they're souls. One for each of those soul-stripped."

Freel blew out a breath, looked at Kali. "I have to ask again – have you ever come across anything like this?"

She shook her head. "Believe me, it's only recently that I've got aboard this whole 'soul' thing."

Kratos sighed. "I think the enforcer had hoped to benefit more from your experience."

"Hey," Kali protested, "do I look like a farking encyclopedia?"

"No," Fitch joined in. "What you look like is the owner of a disreputable tavern in the middle of nowhere."

"That's it, I'm off..."

Gabriella DeZantez blocked Kali's way.

"I *thought* we'd gotten past that," Kali snarled.

"Gentlemen, ladies, please," Jakub Freel said. "The pressure of this current situation has obviously affected us all. May I just ask you all for your conclusions on what you've seen?"

"What other conclusion can there be?" General McIntee answered. "You saw the number of those things. The First Enemy is planning a full-scale invasion of the peninsula."

Beside him, Cardinal Kratos accepted and read a scroll handed to him by a messenger. His expression turned grim. "Faith riders report that more of the Pale Lord's forces have launched assaults on most of the settlements within twenty leagues of the Sardenne, and are moving farther afield. We believe we are looking at the total loss of Verity, Rasoon, Prayer's End, and countless communities, including Gargas."

"What about the rest of it?" Kali interrupted. There was something very wrong going on here. "That... phantasm that came for Makennon and the other twelve? This... pillar of souls? Where do they fit in? It doesn't make sense."

Freel sighed. "Are you suggesting an alternative theory?"

"No, but you asked for my help, so give me time and I'll have one."

"How much time?"

Kali faltered. "I think it has something to do with the speed at which the pillar of souls is rising. I think its meant to touch Kerberos. And I think whatever is going to happen will happen then." She paused, calculating. "Three days. Give me three days and I'll shut down your machines *and* find out what you need to know."

Freel was silent for a few moments, considering. "Agreed. But in the meantime, I have no choice but to convene a council of war."

"You do that," Kali said. "But there's one other thing."

"Oh?"

"I want Killiam Slowhand to be in on this too. Fitch has him and I want him released."

Freel's expression was unreadable. But he nodded briskly.

"Under no circumstances!" Querilous Fitch objected. "The man is insane, a killer!"

Kali smiled. "That he is. And a very good one. But he only kills those who deserve it."

"No," Fitch insisted. "I refuse."

Cardinal Kratos and General McIntee regarded the psychic manipulator with distaste. McIntee was the one who voiced their thoughts. "The decision is not yours to make, manipulator. In the absence of the Anointed Lord we are responsible for decisions for the good of the Faith." He turned to Kali. "Very well. I'll have him brought up from the cells."

A few minutes later, Slowhand appeared in the doorway, and immediately tried to lunge for Fitch, but Kali, standing unnoticed beside the door, grabbed his arm and pulled him back. The archer turned on her, ready to lash out, but froze as he saw who he was facing.

"Hooper?"

"Slowhand."

"How you doing?"

"Just for a change, working for the Final Faith. And so are you."

"Nice company," Slowhand said. He paused, then his eyes narrowed. "This is something to do with what happened to Makennon, isn't it?"

"Uh-huh. The Faith think their First Enemy is planning some kind of invasion."

"Him again? Who *is* this First Enemy guy?"

"The Pale Lord."

"Ah," Slowhand said. "Oooooh." He looked in Kali's eyes, then leaned forward to whisper in her ear. "Is he?"

"He's planning something," Kali whispered back, "but nothing about this feels right to me. Keep smiling, anyway."

Slowhand did. "So we need to sort this out, right? So where are we off? The Prison of Pain? Ranson's Remains? The Mound of Thunder?"

"Actually," Kali responded, "to the library."

"The library?" Slowhand repeated, not sure that he had heard right.

"We need to do some research."

"The library," Slowhand said again, deflated. "You know, one thing about working with this woman is there's never a dull moment."

Chapter Seven

The Hall of Proscribed Knowledge, the largest of the collections in the Final Faith library, was situated in a wing of the cathedral all of its own. The vast depository was packed with shelves towering as high as the ornate architraves and each shelf, in turn, was crammed to bursting with tomes of all shapes, sizes and provenance, the evident age and titles of many of which almost made Kali drool. The ones set in elven or dwarven script, particularly.

The books on the lower shelves were reached through a claustrophobic and labyrinthine network of narrow passageways which jinked left and right unexpectedly and along which two people could not walk abreast. These, however, were the more common tomes, and the loftier ones – literally and metaphorically – were accessed by a precarious and dizzying network of crooked and seemingly unlinked metal stairways that reminded Kali of a structure she'd struggled for weeks to scale in a recurring dream. As she had in the dream, she wondered quite how it was they managed to stay up. She doubted magic, because from the moment she and Slowhand had entered she'd sensed the library was somehow isolated from the rest of the cathedral, and whatever sorceries or technologies were in use elsewhere in the complex had no place here, lest they damage the tomes. There was probably even – under normal circumstances – a dampening field in place. The contents of at least some of these books also explained why so few people were present: a cardinal here, an eminence there, and white-gowned curators whom she presumed had been thoroughly vetted before being trusted with the information in their charge. This was a domain accessible only to the Faith elite, though Kali struggled to reconcile them with the term as over the sounds of scribbling and dry parchment pages being turned, there was the occasional consumptive cough, belch and blatantly delivered fart.

"As I said," Killiam Slowhand muttered, "never a dull moment."

"*Shhh!*" A voice admonished.

Slowhand stared at the white-gowned curator, a wizened little man about half the height of Suresight, who was as dusty as the shelves.

"Hey, I can mutter, can't I?"

"*Shhh!*"

Slowhand shook his head and pulled Kali aside. "I don't get it," he whispered. "Why here? Surely whatever we can find here, the Filth already know?"

"Maybe, maybe not," Kali whispered back. "I'm willing to bet there are thousands of books here that have been confiscated simply because they *could* be confiscated, and haven't been touched since. Hopefully we'll find something they haven't."

The archer looked dubious.

"Come on, Slowhand, how many people do you know who've read the entire contents of their *own* library?"

"You, for one."

"Yes, well..."

"And Merrit Moon," Slowhand said. "Well, all apart from –"

"The Flesh Rituals of Elven Slither Maidens? With pictures by P'Tang?"

Engines of the Apocalypse

"Oh, yeeeah." Slowhand looked at her suspiciously. "How did you know?"

"Because I was reading in the corner when you crept down and nicked it from his shelf."

"*Borrowed.*"

"A year ago. Frankly, I'd be amazed if you can still open the thing."

Slowhand coughed and abruptly paled. He hissed, "Wait a minute. You're not seriously suggesting we work our way through this entire place!"

"*Shhh!*"

"Will you fark off!"

"There is no need for –"

"Hey!" Slowhand shouted. He unslung Suresight from his back and mimed using the little man as an arrow and shooting him out a window. The curator scuttled off.

"Not if you know what you're looking for," Kali went on. She hopped up steps and plucked a pile of tomes, dropping them on Slowhand for him to read. "But it is going to be a long night."

Kali browsed more shelves for tomes for herself, and then she and Slowhand made their way to a reading table. Kali rolled her eyes as she flung her backpack onto the table. The bag clattered and there was a long sigh from beyond the wall of books.

They hadn't been working long when a shadow loomed over them.

"Need any help?" A voice asked and Slowhand looked up. Then he looked down, then up again, before stretching back in his chair, hands linked behind his head, beaming.

"Be our guest," he said, showing all his teeth.

Kali, too, looked Gabriella DeZantez up and down. The woman had washed off the dust of the trail and changed into a clean white surplice, its brilliance accentuating the subtle but powerful musculature beneath her bronzed skin. Kali pouted inwardly – she spent far too much time underground to get a tan like that. "You don't strike me as someone who has spent a lot of time with her head in a book," she responded, after a moment.

Gabriella smiled coldly. "You disappoint me, Kali. I'd have expected you of all people not to judge a book by its cover."

"Oh?"

"A girl from a backwater tavern with an over fondness for drink, an absolute disregard for authority and a tendency to repeatedly cross swords with the Final Faith? Hardly the kind of person you'd expect *them* to turn to for help."

"What can I say? We go back a ways."

Gabriella nodded. "I know, I've done some research of my own. The Clockwork King. The Crucible. Greenfinger's Wood. The Faith holds quite a file on you."

"You surprise me. That crack about 'sex occasionally' still in there?"

"The Anointed Lord's small attempt at a joke. She's human, too, you know, despite her calling from the Lord of All."

"Yeah, right," Kali spat. Then she apologized. What DeZantez had shown her earlier had proven that there was at least some basis to the Faith's beliefs, even if she remained convinced that their interpretation of it was deeply suspect.

"For the record," DeZantez went on, "I spent a good deal of my childhood in a place such as this. Not on the same scale, of course. My mother ran – still runs – the Faith archive in Andon."

Kali raised her eyebrows. "Marta DeZantez is your mother?"

"You know her?"

"Not well, but I've had... occasion to consult her records. She's a good woman – non-partisan."

For the first time DeZantez's smile warmed, and she nodded her acknowledgement, still a little uneasy.

"Listen," Killiam Slowhand said loudly, in an attempt to defuse the situation. "Seeing as we are all in the employ of the Fil – the Faith for the foreseeable future, what say we all be friends here?" The archer patted an adjacent chair. "Sit by me."

DeZantez stared at the proffered chair and then the archer, regarding him as she might a mollusc. "So you can pretend to read a book while you ogle my thighs? I don't think so."

"I guess she's read your file, too," Kali said.

"Uh-huh," DeZantez confirmed.

Slowhand did his best to look innocent, then attempted to change the subject. "Gabriella DeZantez," he said, with his best grin. "Quite the mouthful. How about I call you Dez?"

The swordswoman's eyes darkened. "Sure. How about I call you Slow?"

The archer's smile faded and it was Kali's turn to smile. She indicated a seat beside herself instead. "There's a lot to get through. We'd welcome your help."

Gabriella slid into the proffered seat. "Okay. What are we looking for?"

"Two things. Anything about the machines, their origin and history, but particularly any mention of how they are activated and controlled. Secondly, dates and details relating to the legend of the Pale Lord, known experiments and movements, anything that might cross-reference with the Engines or this 'pillar of souls.'"

DeZantez nodded. "Fine. Who's doing what?"

"I'll tackle the machines, with Dez," Slowhand volunteered.

"Nice, but how about you tackle the Pale Lord and Gabriella and I take the machines," Kali corrected. It had been a while since she had seen the archer go into a sulk, but he did as he was told, and a few minutes later three heads were buried deep inside books.

The hours began ticking by. Kali hadn't been wrong when she'd said it was going to be a long night, and the reading table was soon stacked high with tomes from all sections of the library. Most offered nothing, and a few gave snippets of information useless by themselves. Gradually, however, and after Slowhand had been kicked twice for snoring, some snippets began to correspond and a sketchy picture emerged.

It seemed that during one of the bloodiest times of their later history, having been routed by the increasingly powerful magic of their elven enemies, the dwarves had constructed a number of weapons or deterrents – the meaning wasn't exactly clear – said to be capable of nullifying the magic of the elves, effectively interfering with the threads manipulated by their song-magic. That interference, Kali guessed, had to be caused by the sound the machines emitted; it was possible that the sound could also interfere with other types of magic, including the barriers to the cathedral's railway tunnels, whose magical origins lay with the elves in the first place. One thing puzzled Kali, however. Although there were several references to the machines there was no subsequent mention of them having been used successfully against the elves. History, in fact, recorded that there was no such change of fortunes in the elf/dwarf wars and that they had soon after declared a truce that was to be the starting point of their third age of existence, where the Old Races had advanced their civilisations in peace. But if that was the case, one obvious question needed to be answered – *why* hadn't the dwarves used the machines it had clearly taken them a great deal of time and effort to develop?

It was Gabriella who found the answer. Or at least something that pointed to an answer. Records from around the time of the machines' development spoke of severe upheaval across the peninsula, of unnatural storms and quakes, and of coastal settlements being consumed by the sea. It didn't take much of a leap to imagine that perhaps the cause of these phenomena lay with the machines themselves – that perhaps they affected more than just the threads and the dwarves had inadvertently, created some kind of doomsday weapon.

The theory gathered credence when Gabriella came upon one further reference. It needed to be translated from the dwarven by Kali but this one gave the machines a name.

The Engines of the Apocalypse.

Kali sat back with a sigh. They had discovered what they were dealing with, but it was now all the more imperative they find out how these engines were controlled, and from where.

A further number of hours research produced little on the former, but eventually Kali lit upon, of all things, a number of dwarven engineers' requisition forms buried amongst other preserved papers. Sometimes it *was* the small things, Kali reflected. The requisitions were for heavy construction materials, all of which were to be delivered to a particular location. The materials by themselves were no proof of any connection but the fact that the location was smack bang in the centre of the three groups of machines and had, from somewhere, acquired the name 'the Plain of Storms' sounded somewhat more promising.

They were, however, not yet done. The more she learned, the more Kali became convinced that the Pale Lord had to be planning something other than a simple invasion of the soul-stripped. After all, what could he possibly hope to gain from a devastated peninsula inhabited solely by the near-dead? No, Redigor's use of the engines to take Makennon and the others as well as render their mages powerless against his army was part of a greater plan, she was sure, and anything they could find out about the man himself might have a bearing on it.

"Anything, Slowhand?" Kali asked.

The archer shook his head. "I've been through a hundred books and other than the usual guff about the Pale Lord being banished from Fayence for meddling with necromancy, then buggering off into the Sardenne to form his army of the soul-stripped, there's very little. But there is this one phrase that keeps recurring..."

"Oh?"

"Here they lie, still," the archer quoted.

"Here they lie, still?" Gabriella repeated. "Any idea what that means?"

"Reputedly, they were the last words spoken by Redigor before he entered Bellagon's Rip," Slowhand said, consulting a passage. "But who 'they' were and where they 'lie still,' nobody records."

"Could he have been referring to the engines?" Gabriella mused. "Maybe the dwarves moved them to the Sardenne? Their equivalent of decommissioning them?"

"Maybe," Kali said, biting her lip. "Anything else?"

Slowhand shook his head and thumped another large, dusty tome down in front of him. He had no sooner opened it, however, than he stopped with a start, his gaze flicking to Gabriella sitting opposite him. The archer coughed, squirmed slightly, then smiled and gave her a sly wink.

"Are you all right?" Gabriella asked suspiciously.

"Fine," Slowhand answered, squeaking and clearing his throat. He jerked his head towards Kali, occupied with a new book, conspiratorially.

"You sure?"

"Oh, I'm sure," Slowhand said, leaning forward and whispering in Gabriella's ear. "Only I thought you weren't interested."

"Interested?"

"Your foot," Slowhand breathed, "on my thigh."

Gabriella's eyes narrowed. "Mister, believe me, the only place you'll ever find my foot is *between* your thighs, but you'll be too busy peeling your gonads from the ceiling to enjoy it."

"Funny," Slowhand purred, "that sounds just like something Hooper would say."

"What sounds like something Hooper would say?" Kali joined in.

"Oh, nothing," Slowhand said. He turned to give Gabriella another knowing glance but she'd already stood to replace some of the books on the shelves. He glanced quickly under the table, where 'her foot' was still at work.

"Er, ladies..."

Kali glanced up, stood and pushed back her chair with a curse. Beside her, Gabriella unsheathed her twin swords with a metallic ring that echoed throughout the vast library.

"*Shhh!*" came an admonition from beyond the shelves.

Kali ignored it. "What the hells?"

The book which lay open in front of Slowhand, who was leaning well back and staring at it warily, was *exuding* something from its spine. A number of thin, black tapers were curling from the top and bottom of the book, growing by the second, one of them now fully curled around Slowhand's thigh. Multiplying and thickening, accompanied by a dry, sinister hiss, they were redoubling their interest in the archer.

"Hooper, one of 'ems heading for my –"

"Slowhand, get up slowly," Kali said.

"That might be a good idea," he responded. It took him a second to react, however, the tapers having a strangely mesmeric effect on those who watched them, and it was only when the taper made a sudden dart for his crotch that he stood and kicked his chair back with a "Whoa!"

It was, unfortunately, a little too late, and before Slowhand knew what was happening twenty or more of the things had wrapped themselves around different parts of his body and were holding him in their grip. The archer struggled against them but, with as echoing thud, they tipped him off his feet and slapped him to the floor.

"Mmf... ooper?" Slowhand said, his eyes wide, as one of the

tapers wrapped around his jaw. "Youf wanna helf me ouf here?"

"Hold on," Kali said, and attempted to tear the tapers away. "Shit," she shouted. "*Shit!*"

Not only were the tapers binding Slowhand as tightly as barrel hoops, but Kali's attempt to sever them prompted a backlash against herself. Suddenly they were far from mesmeric, a wild, thrashing mass that struck at her. She had no choice but to back off from Slowhand, and as the archer writhed helplessly on the floor, increasingly constricted, she adopted a defensive stance, gutting knife drawn in front of her.

"What are they?" Gabriella asked. She stared at the book's spine, which had thickened to accommodate the roots of perhaps a hundred of the tapers. "They look like some kind of..."

"Bookworm?" Kali suggested.

"I'm glad you said that."

"Hells, I call 'em as I see 'em."

Gabriella threw herself on top of Slowhand and, gripping him between her thighs, slashed at the tapers with her own twin blades, again to no effect. She, too, was forced back, Slowhand groaning in pain.

"There has to be something we can do." Gabriella said.

"Yeah, and fast. Before these things pop him out of his clothes." Gabriella looked at her strangely. "Trust me. It happens."

The Deathclaws, Kali realised. They might free Slowhand *and* prove to be a better defence. She leapt for the table where her backpack lay, snatched the blades from within and returned to slash at the tapers about the thrashing archer. They did the job, but the tapers had now multiplied to a degree where they were beginning to fill the entire reading area and, as Gabriella pulled Slowhand up and staggered with him down an aisle, Kali was forced to leap out of the path of the evil-looking mass and cling to the side of a bookshelf. At the same time she shouted to the curator who was approaching to see what all the commotion was about. "You! This book – where did it come from?"

"W-which book, Madam?"

Hanging there, Kali gave him her best, bemused look. "The one with the things growing out of it?"

"I d-don't know," he said, staring and stammering. "I'll need to ch-check the catalogue."

"*The catalogue?*"

The little man actually looked affronted. "M-Madam, there are over ten thousand tomes gathered in this library, subdivided into –"

"Just do it!" Kali shouted, slashing at the tapers with the claws. Severed sections spiralled away but more tapers darted in from her left and she threw herself from the shelf on which she clung to one on the opposite side of the aisle. "Because if you haven't noticed, things are getting a little out of hand here!"

The little man scuttled off and Kali found herself leaping from shelf to shelf as more and more tapers emerged from the book and snapped at her. The Deathclaws hummed in the air and the amputated tapers began to pile up below her, but there were always more, growing from the severed ends. Their tenacity was unrelenting and Kali wasn't sure how long she could keep up her defence. She saw one of the Eminences appear in the aisle, no doubt come to see what all the fuss was about, and the man stared in horror as a single taper shot out and punched into his chest. Kali actually saw it punch out of his back and then snap back, clutching his heart, leaving the dead man to slowly collapse to the floor.

"Keep back!" Kali warned as the curator returned, and it only took one look from the man to the still body of the Eminence for him to immediately obey. "Well?"

"This book and a number like it originated in the town of Fayence, Madam. They were acquired by the Hall of Proscribed Knowledge quite some years ago."

That sounded about right, Kali thought. "And their original owner?"

"A gentleman by the name of Bastian Redigor."

The name hung in the air for a second.

"The Pale Lord," Kali said.

The curator looked almost sheepish. "The Pale Lord," he repeated. "They were confiscated from his estate."

"Where the bastard must have trapped them before he was banished."

"Trapped?"

Kali sighed in exasperation. "Just what did you think we were dealing with here, Mister Curator? One of his collection of pop-up books?"

"No... I... oh, Lord of All, what do we do?"

Kali leapt from shelf to shelf again, veering mid-course so as not to bring the tapers that targeted her closer to the curator. He'd doubtless ask them to keep the noise down just before they ripped out his heart too. "*We* find a way to stop these things," she advised. "*You* get yourself and everyone else the hells out of here."

The curator looked non-plussed. "But my readers do not like their studies disturbed!"

Kali couldn't quite believe what she heard. Staring at the ever thickening spine of the book, she was about to explain that unless they all departed right now there was every chance they wouldn't be going anywhere, ever again. All of a sudden the spine of the book exploded and the entire section of the library in which they stood or clung was filled with a tree-sized growth of the things, thrashing toward the ceiling. The curator needed no more convincing and turned and ran, screaming to Kali to please, please, please not damage his books.

Kali flung a glance towards Gabriella, who stood with Slowhand, staring in horror at what had manifested itself, here, in the very heart of her faith. Kali understood, this was the same magic that had taken Makennon – something dark and very, very old that the Engines had not subdued like normal thread magic, that might even be related to the *black* threads that Aldrededor had seen while piloting the *Tharnak*. A magic that had no place in the Faith's or anyone's doctrine, and that was *unknown* to them all. The realisation only served to reinforce what she'd thought about the Pale Lord, that there was something much more to him, much more to this whole affair, than met the eye. It was also clear that Bastian Redigor would not have seeded the tome with such a trap if he didn't have something really interesting to hide. The only problem lay in living long enough to find out what that was.

Kali dropped from her perch and raced towards Gabriella and Slowhand, the roiling mass of blackness pursuing her, batting aside bookshelves as it came. They skidded into another passage as one, the tapers lashing at their heels.

"I'm beginning to think they've got something against us!" Slowhand shouted, ducking as more woodwork exploded all around.

"What the hells makes you think that?" Kali shouted back.

"So what do we do now?"

"I don't know!"

"There's something that might stop them," Gabriella gasped. She was staring up into the highest reaches of the library as she ran, above the precarious stairways, where a caged platform was visible. "The Dellendorf Scrolls."

"The Dellendorf Scrolls?"

"An archive of Old Race, perhaps *older*, scrolls – assorted incantations, enchantments, destruction spells and so on. They were found by an excavation team twenty years ago."

"What's the point?" Kali said. "Only Redigor's magic is working!"

Gabriella shook her head. "My guess is that the Engines interfere with the stability of current spells or the casting of new ones, but the magic of the scrolls is sealed into their parchment, *already cast*. All one of us needs to do is release it!"

And I wonder which one of us that's going to be? Kali considered.

She stopped and stared up at the scrolls' store. It certainly wasn't going to be easy; and between her and them, a veritable forest of tapers now thrashed, expanding into other passages, attempting to catch them in a pincer movement.

"We're trapped!" Slowhand shouted. The archer loosed a number of arrows at the nearest tapers but they were batted away. Gabriella slashed at the encroaching mass with her blades, but this time the tapers snatched her weapons from her hands, flinging them away over the shelves.

"Yeah?" Kali said, as her companions backed up. She leapt onto one of the walls of books enclosing them and slashed the

Deathclaws from top to bottom, landing back on the floor with a grunt. Slowhand stared at her, puzzled, until Kali booted the wall and the entire section tipped away before her, crashing into another shelf beyond it, starting a domino effect across the library towards the stairway.

"Neat," Slowhand observed.

"Take these and try to slice yourselves a way out!" Kali shouted. She stripped off the claws and flung them towards Gabriella. The Enlightened One plucked them neatly from their flight. She nodded to Kali and donned them.

"Hooper –?" Slowhand began, but Kali was already gone, leaping along the downed bookshelves, the tapers snapping at her from beneath and around their sides. Her alternative route seemed to have confused the dark magic strands, and Kali made it over several of the fallen shelves, but she saw that the tapers had extended ahead of her and were now punching in through a gap. She rolled, dodged and weaved, the stairs drawing ever nearer, until a taper managed to whip itself around one of her ankles and she found herself flipped high into the air.

After a moment of dizzying disorientation, Kali thudded to the floor beyond the final row of shelves and lay on her stomach, winded. To her right lay the base of the stairway she needed to reach, but to her left, hurtling towards her at a speed that in her state she couldn't hope to outrun, was a solid, seething mass of the black strands.

Kali struggled to her feet, looked for a way out, found none. She spun in a circle and punched shelves of books in frustration, furious with herself. A peculiar rumbling sound came from the direction of the stairs and she turned to face it, wondering what new threat she faced.

Her eyebrows rose. Gabriella DeZantez was racing towards her in mid-air, straddling two of the sliding ladders the curators used to access books on higher shelves. Between her legs, pushing the ladders as hard as he could, was a red-faced Slowhand.

"What, you think we'd let you do this alone?" He shouted as Kali ducked to let the ladders pass.

Kali watched their progress. Gabriella's hands blurred, the Deathclaws slicing constantly, the Enlightened One spinning and leaping between the two ladders in a dance that ensured not a single one of the tapers got near her or Slowhand. She and the archer cut a swathe through the mass, the black strands falling in their hundreds. The whole thing lasted no more than thirty seconds and, the tapers briefly repulsed, Gabriella leapt from the ladders and Slowhand released them.

"What are you waiting for?" She shouted to Kali. "Move!"

Kali didn't need telling twice. She ran for the stairway but, even as she did, more tapers lashed in from beyond the shelves, wrapping themselves around the lower risers, preventing her mounting them. This time Slowhand came to the fore.

"Hooper!" He shouted, and two of his arrows whizzed over Kali's head to embed themselves solidly in the wall. She leapt onto the first Slowhand had fired as another arrow struck the wall above her, feeling it snap under her but giving her enough upward momentum to carry her to the second, and then the third. Kali climbed Slowhand's makeshift staircase above the level of the tapers as he continued shooting, and threw herself onto the stairway beyond their reach. Her feet clattered on metal as she ascended, and the tapers raced after her, but Kali tumbled and leaped, leaving them behind as she negotiated the complicated structure. At last she reached the cage containing the scrolls, booted off the padlock and threw herself inside, slamming the cage closed behind her. The tapers swarmed about and rattled the metal enclosure but the mesh was too fine for them to penetrate. Kali let out a relieved breath.

Her relief was short-lived.

It was all right for DeZantez to say she could use one of the Dellendorf scrolls to blitz the tapers but, dammit, which one? There were hundreds stacked before her and, as far as she knew, the one she chose might make things worse, not better. It seemed, though, that whichever curators had been assigned to investigate these mysterious scrolls were possessed of frustrated egos and somewhat fanciful imaginations, and Kali found a clue to what she wanted in their attached notations. Quite clearly named after the curators themselves, the scrolls glorified in such names as Hamish's Wandering Eye, Charles's Dream of Domination and

Gleeson's Worrisome Whiff, and one which sounded as if it might be up to the job – Strombolt's Devastator. Yes, that sounded pretty unequivocal. Now, how was it Gabriella had demonstrated it should be used?

Kali took a breath and stood in the centre of the cage, sweeping her palm across the scroll she held. As she did, the script upon it – a strange collection of symbols unknown even to her – parted company with the parchment and flew out through the mesh of the cage. Nothing happened for a second, and then the floating symbols raced together and collided, forming a dense, pulsating cloud above the centre of the vast library. The air grew immensely heavy, the light dulled, and a charge in the atmosphere made Kali's hair stand on end. The last thing she thought as she wrapped her arms about her head was how the curator had pleaded with her not to damage his books.

The Hall of Proscribed Knowledge, all of it, detonated with an explosion so powerful that its walls buckled momentarily outwards, prompting screams and cries of alarm from outside. The stained glass windows lining its upper storey disintegrated, shards falling as a rainbow rain. The chandeliers were propelled upwards, bouncing off the ceiling and dropping broken metal and molten wax before crashing to the floor below. The explosion finished the job the tapers and Kali had started, smashing each and every piece of furniture – tables, chairs and bookshelves – against the walls, leaving them as a shattered tide washed against the hall's perimeter. For quite some time afterwards countless cream and white leaves – all that remained of the books that had crammed the shelves – fluttered to the floor. If there was any saving grace to what Kali had just unleashed, it was that the tapers had flopped to the floor, dormant or dead.

"Oops," Kali said as she picked herself up from the floor of the cage. She coughed and picked splinters from her hair. From far below she heard other coughs and looked down to see Slowhand and Gabriella emerging, battered and bruised but otherwise unharmed, from behind a heavy shelf that had miraculously landed at an angle over them. Gabriella backed cautiously away from Slowhand, looking puzzled and disturbed as to how the explosion, which left her relatively unscathed, could have blown him so neatly out of his clothes. Kali worked her way slowly down towards the pair.

"Well, that seemed to work," Gabriella DeZantez said.

"You know something?" Slowhand added, seemingly uncaring that he was naked, "I'm beginning to think we might make a pretty good team."

Chapter Eight

Slowhand had to hand it to the Final Filth – for a bunch of God-Botherers, they did military mobilisation rather well. Preparations for their response to the Pale Lord's threat were already well under way at dawn the next day, the sublevel a hive of activity as engineers and support workers prepared and supplied funicular trains while the men and women who would ride them gathered in ranks, waiting to board. The sides of the railway tunnels were packed with swordsmen, axemen, archers and lancers, many of them young and, considering what it was they were being sent to face, understandably nervous. Steadfast, if no less grim, were the hardened warriors draped in the livery of the Order of the Swords of Dawn, and mages – lots and lots of mages. Quartermasters and Enlightened Ones walked among them all, the former inspecting weapons while the latter blessed their bearers for the trials ahead.

Impressive as it all was, Slowhand frowned. The war council had convened while he, Hooper and DeZantez had been occupied in the library and had informed them of their decision when they had emerged. Despite Hooper's doubts about the Pale Lord's intentions – reinforced during their researches – the Faith remained committed to their belief that he planned a soul-stripped invasion. The plan was to establish a cordon along the length of the Sardenne after the last of the Pale Lord's strange army had filed in. The cordon was to be a defensive one – they at least had the sense to realise *offensive* strategies would be suicide while the Engines were active – and would only engage in combat if the Pale Lord made a move. Once the Engines were shut down and magic restored, however, they planned to advance on the soul-stripped – to go in, as it were, with all hands blazing. Of course, the Faith alone did not have the numbers for such a massive endeavour, which was why some of the trains were to remain empty for now. The Faith had arranged not only to second thousands of troops from the Vossian army, who would board at Faith 'missions' en route, but to enlist aid from the Pontaine militia too. Considering the attacks that had been occurring in their half of the world, Slowhand had no doubt they would agree.

Hence the frown. The Faith was, tactically, putting all the peninsula's eggs in one basket, an approach he had never been particularly fond of, and he could only hope the basket wasn't dropped somewhere along the way.

Slowhand moved through the frantic activity towards what would be his train. The fate of the Anointed Lord not forgotten in all of this, it had been decided that he, Freel, DeZantez and, of all people, Fitch – along with Hooper, when she returned from what she had to do – would not be part of the cordon but instead form a 'strike team' to infiltrate the Sardenne to try to find and rescue Makennon. As such, they were not to travel to the edges of the cordon, but to the main base camp – what had once been 'the pulpit.' To reach the pulpit meant they'd have to travel along the disused tunnel, where this nightmare had started and the thing that had taken Makennon had emerged.

Slowhand yawned. For what he'd expected to be, thanks to Fitch, a quiet night in the Faith's deep cells, things had turned out markedly different. Hooper's announcement that they were both temporarily seconded to the Filth had initially made him feel quite uncomfortable, and he had even felt slightly resentful that she had taken it upon herself to forge such an alliance on his behalf. Now, though, even though he'd slept little, spending what had been left of the night 'conferring' with Hooper and then fletching some special arrows for the rigours ahead, his discomfort had faded. As he moved towards his train he was actually beginning to find that the Filth's resemblance to an army on the move had instilled in him some of the feeling of his old, military days. It wasn't nostalgia exactly – he had seen and done too much for that, some still regretted – but there was a fondness for the sense of directed mass purpose that part of him still missed. Filth or not, it felt reassuring to be part of such a large force working together to a common aim, even if there were one or two tarnishes on the force's collective armour.

He could see tarnish number one ahead of him right now. The archer had hardly believed it when he'd finally been introduced to the man he'd be working with and, pulling the belt holding his special arrows taut across his chest, he nodded now to Jakub Freel. The enforcer nodded back noncommittally, the barest of acknowledgements and hardly the greeting of a comrade-in-arms. The atmosphere between the two of them had been neutral while Hooper had been around but distinctly cooler in her absence, each tolerating the other's presence only because they had little choice in the matter. Considering the loss they had both endured, and the circumstances of it, they were hardly going to become bosom buddies were they? He would have to keep an eye on him.

Tarnish number two was another matter. Standoffish in a different way and for reasons he was still struggling to understand, Gabriella DeZantez was perched on an upturned railway sleeper as he neared her, sharpening her twin blades on a stone and examining the results with a practiced, expert eye. A fresh surplice was bulked out with armour, gleaming beneath the cloth. She wore it utterly naturally, as comfortably as a second skin. Slowhand had come across a number of the Swords of Dawn in his travels – had even, on occasion, had cause to avoid them – but he could remember few, if any, who had looked so born for the role. What had caused her to relinquish that role until now, he didn't really know, but her reaction to him the previous night suggested that, one way or another, she had been badly hurt at some point in her past – the kind of hurt that could only have been caused by a man. Who that man had been, and where he was now, he couldn't begin to guess.

DeZantez glanced up at him as he approached, and Slowhand smiled rather than nodded. *What the hells,* he thought, it might be a fault of his but the woman had helped to save his life and he couldn't help still wanting to break the ice.

"I didn't get chance to thank you," he said. "For last night."

"You make it sound as if we lay together," DeZantez said, her attention having returned to her blades.

And he'd thought they'd worked together so well. "No, I didn't mean –"

"I know what you meant, Slowhand. It's just a little irksome when you couch everything in innuendo."

He found himself staring at the top of her head, and swallowed. "That wasn't what I –"

"As for the fact I saw you naked last night, don't make the mistake of thinking it has planted a latent seed of desire in me. It hasn't."

Slowhand tried a grin. "Most girls remember the sight, at least."

"I'm not most girls. And most men I've seen naked were wetting themselves or worse as they pleaded for their lives within the gibbet, which tends to temper any erotic aspect, believe me." She looked up. "Let's get this clear. We work together, that's all."

Slowhand's grin faded. "Look, is there a problem here? I mean, more than just me?"

"Your girlfriend is gone."

Ah, yes. That had been the other part of the plan. When it had been arranged for Hooper to leave to stop the Engines that morning, she was meant to have taken DeZantez along.

"I know. She gave me a goodbye kiss."

"She was meant to be in my custody. That was the deal I made with the Overseer."

Slowhand shrugged. "Yeah, she told me. Thing is, it's nothing personal. Hooper has a problem with authority. And she likes to work alone."

DeZantez made a particularly violent sweep along her blades with the sharpening stone, making Slowhand wince. "She isn't coming back."

"What? Of course she's coming back!"

"Then why did she sneak out of here before daybreak?"

"Because she could."

"Not funny."

"Not meant to be. But she left you these."

DeZantez looked up. The weapons she had returned to Kali after the library were being proffered to her once again.

"The Deathclaws?"

"The Deathclaws. She thought you might make better use of them than she could."

"But they must be priceless."

"Oh, they are. She asked me to ask you to consider them as bail. If she doesn't come back. To fix a church roof or something..."

DeZantez hesitated, then said in a resigned tone, "The City Watch reported her heading south-east, not due east towards the Plain of Storms. What's she up to?"

"Said something about having to make a house-call first. Don't ask me why because I'm always the last to know. It's what she does."

"Slowhand," DeZantez said after a second. "Do you trust her to get the job done?"

"With my life."

"That might come to be the case."

"I can handle myself."

"I don't doubt it. But I mean will she succeed, before the Pale Lord mobilises?"

"She said she'll rendezvous with us the day after tomorrow, at 'the pulpit.'"

"That doesn't give her much time."

"She'll make it. You might have noticed she has a rather unusual Horse."

DeZantez nodded then slid off the railway sleeper and sheathed her blades. She accepted the Deathclaws from Slowhand, attaching them to her belt.

"Then I guess it's time we got this show on the road," she said, and pointed.

Slowhand turned to see Jakub Freel striding along the tunnel past them, climbing onto the front carriage and waving back along the train's length. It was a signal to the gathered soldiers, and all along the tunnel they picked up their gear and boarded the carriages.

Slowhand stared at Jakub Freel. The enforcer was in command of this particular train and, as such, could have waved Slowhand aboard too. But he just stared as if he didn't care whether Slowhand boarded at all. The archer shrugged and grabbed a rail on the side of the last car, using it to swing up onto the train's roof where he had already decided he could serve the expedition best by riding shotbow. DeZantez mirrored his move, opting for the first car, as far away from him as she could get. It wasn't – he hoped – personal. Whatever the darkness that had come for Katherine Makennon was, for all they knew, it could still lurk somewhere in the tunnel ahead, and they would all need to be on the alert.

The train lurched beneath him and was off. There was a long journey ahead and Slowhand settled himself down into a cross-legged position, watching the curved, moss-covered ceiling of the tunnel roll by. It grew monotonous over the hours, the train seemingly limited by its funicular cable to trundle along at only a few leagues an hour.

Despite the danger of their situation, Slowhand found the rhythmic clacking of the train soporific and, tired from his almost sleepless night and lulled by the soft, warm breeze created by the train's passage, he began to nod off. Dimly aware that they were passing beneath the Anclas Territories right now and would, in an hour or so, be under the Pontaine plains, he found himself traversing them overland rather than underground.

He was flying above flowery, rolling fields, and in each field beneath him naked women danced from behind giant blooms to frolic and wave at him as he passed. Slowhand smiled, his clothes vanishing like thinning clouds, and saw he was over Miramas and Gargas, now. Their streets were devoid of naked women, but every bedroom window was flung wide, a happy, expectant trilling coming from within. Slowhand swooped down, but before he could pass through any of the colourful curtains that fluttered invitingly in the breeze, he became aware of something else – something beyond the towns – a great, dark mass on the distant horizon that swept to the east and to the west as far as the eye could see. It seemed that whatever worries were playing at the back of his mind wanted in – there was no escaping the Sardenne Forest and its appearance halted his reverie like a slap in the face. Literally.

Ow.

"Wake up." Gabriella DeZantez said. "We've got trouble."

"What kind of trouble?"

"The tunnel roof," the Enlightened One said. "Looks like the Pale Lord left a few of his friends behind."

Slowhand followed her gaze forward and upward and swallowed. *A few?* He thought.

Where the front of the train was nosing into darkness, the gently curving rock that they had been passing beneath seemed rougher somehow, and the reason could be made out as they drew close. Perhaps a hundred or more of the Pale Lord's soul-stripped were clinging to the roof of the tunnel like insects – blackened by tunnel grime, their whitened eyes their only distinguishable feature.

"Oh, crap," he said.

"My thoughts exactly." DeZantez responded.

Both she and Slowhand raced along the carriage roofs, shouting warnings to those within. There was little the occupants could do to escape the impending threat, however, and little room to use any of their weapons effectively. Their only real recourse was to steel themselves as best they could and raise shields at each car's entrance. Consequently, of course, any proactive defence of the train was left to those who rode on its roof, and Slowhand was actually quite pleased to see Jakub Freel climbing up from the driver's cab as the first of the soul-stripped dropped from the dark.

"Here we go," DeZantez said. Her jaw was set and her weapons drawn – the claws rather than her blades, Slowhand noted, if only because they were the only effective weapon against their current foes.

All he had was Suresight, but despite his trusted bow's failure – through no fault of her own – to halt the soul-stripped previously, he raised her anyway. The arrows would do little damage, he knew, but damage wasn't his intention. He let fly again and again, targeting the dropping soul-stripped half way between tunnel roof and train, aiming not for the vitals but for peripheries – shoulders, hips and thighs. Because the archer's intention wasn't to drop the soul-stripped as they landed, but to hit them before they did.

One soul-stripped, two, four and then ten were hit in mid air by his arrows, solid impacts knocking them sideways in their descent, away from the train. The soul-stripped spun helplessly, silently down to the tunnel floor on either side, hitting the sides of the tracks with a crunch of muscle and bone, twitching rapidly where they lay.

Slowhand couldn't get them all, of course, and inevitably many landed on the roof. Thankfully, most of those the archer missed were immediately intercepted by DeZantez and Freel in a blur of claws and chain. The Deathclaws were, as expected, singularly effective in despatching the cadaverous forms, slicing and amputating them at every joint, but Freel suffered the same handicap as he. But his whip lashed out to wrap around ankles and wrists, flipping the soul-stripped from the train.

But even all three of them couldn't handle everything, and those of the soul-stripped who escaped their triple defence began swinging themselves down into the cars below.

Orders were barked and what weapons could be used came into play, but the relentless and uncaring manner in which the Pale Lord's puppets threw themselves at their targets, scrabbling ferally, took its toll. Slowhand stared over the edge of the train at the warriors, young and old, being tossed to the tunnel floor, where he witnessed the true horror of the soul-stripped, the means by which the Pale Lord was building his pillar of souls. Each soldier who fell was instantly seized upon, drawn up into a lover's embrace as a cold mouth was pressed to theirs. They quickly surrendered to the Pale Lord's puppets, their eyes rolling back in their heads, their skin paling to a waxy sheen. For a few moments they lay still, before rising up to join their new brethren.

"They just keep coming," DeZantez said, suddenly next to him. The claws she wielded were ribboned with flesh. "How many more *are* there?"

"Let's find out," Slowhand said.

It had been his intention to save the special arrows he had adapted for use in the Sardenne but, of course, things rarely turned out as intended. He plucked one of his naphtha dipped creations from his belt and struck it against the flashpad he wore as a ring, igniting the arrow as it launched. The billowing projectile arced through the tunnel and illuminated the way ahead.

Freel was silhouetted in the heart of the fire, his squall-coated figure striding up the train, whip lashing left and right like something out of the hells. But beyond him were the hells themselves.

It hadn't been a one-off gauntlet they'd been passing through. Some few hundred yards ahead, there was another mass of them. Only this time the dark shapes didn't just cover the tunnel roof but the tunnel's sides, and thickly blocked the tracks themselves. The soul-stripped were everywhere and they went on for ever.

"Lord of All," Gabriella breathed, "the tunnel may as well end here. We'll never get through alive."

"We'll get through," Slowhand said.

Setting his jaw manfully, he smiled at Gabriella and raced for the train driver's cab, jumping in next to the man's sweating, but so far untouched, form.

"We need to use the train as a battering ram!" Slowhand shouted. "Can you crank it up to top speed?"

The driver nodded and thrust a lever forward. Slowhand was hardly rocked off his feet. They had gained maybe a third more speed. At a push. If this was the train's top speed, the only thing it was going to be capable of battering was a fish.

"What? That's *it*?"

The driver nodded again. He flinched as a number of soul-stripped crashed onto the front of the train and ripped at the metal cage that protected the cab. Though two of them tore their arms away in the attempt, the cage thankfully remained intact. "It runs on cables," he said through clenched teeth. "And the cables' speed is regulated by controls at either end of the line."

Slowhand shot an arrow into the eye of a soul-stripped who had worked out the cab had a side door, and booted it away. "Then what the hells does it need a driver for?"

"To flip the lever that moves the grip from the slow to fast cable!"

"The grip?"

"Under the train!" He stared at Slowhand as if the last thing he needed was an idiot. "The grip grips the cable and the cable pulls the train!"

Slowhand just stood there, desperately considering his options. Going back to DeZantez and telling her he'd set his jaw for nothing wasn't one of them.

Grip, cable, cable, grip, he thought – *come on, Slowhand, you're an archer, and cables are just like thick bow strings, right? Is there anything you can do with them?*

"What happens if the grip slips off?" He asked.

"The train stops."

"I mean, how do you put it *back on*?"

"There's an access panel under your feet."

Slowhand looked down, tore open the panel. The track below was hardly racing by but, this close up, it was a little unnerving. He fixed his attention on the cables instead – three of them, not two as he'd expected. "There's a middle cable here that isn't moving," he shouted to the driver. "What does that do?"

"It's the torque cable," the driver shouted back. "It regulates the tension in the other two."

"And if it severs?"

"What?"

"If it *severs*, what would happen then?"

"I don't know. I guess the other cables would snap and whiplash away."

"Like the one we're attached to now?"

"Yes but –" The driver paused. "Oh, no. No, no, no..."

"Bingo," Slowhand scrambled back up out of the cab. More soul-stripped had landed on the train's roof in his absence and he simply didn't have time for them. As Slowhand raced back towards the train's rear he aimed Suresight as he moved, loosing naphtha arrows with such force that their flaming shafts simply punched any attacking soul-stripped into the air, off the train, and out of his way.

He paused only once, grabbing one of the Deathclaws from a surprised DeZantez's hand, before reaching the end of the train and launching himself into the air.

Slowhand landed on the tracks behind, rolled, and swung the claw through the torque cable. It severed immediately and began to unravel, as did the one pulling the train. The archer grabbed onto its end, allowing the whiplashing cable to carry him into the air and back towards the train. It arced above the last carriage and he let go, crashing onto the roof, and immediately shouted a warning to DeZantez, Freel and all of those in the cars below.

"Hold on tight!"

Beneath him, the train, still gripped to the cable which was no longer restrained at one end, began to pick up speed, and Slowhand threw himself flat.

The front of the train ploughed into the wall of soul-stripped, bucking slightly on its tracks as it did. As always, there were no screams of cries of protest from those it hit, but a series of sickening fleshy crunches and a rain of dismembered body parts. The rattling and clattering of the train's wheels faded as the vehicle travelled not on bare metal but a thick layer of gore and blood. Slowhand cautiously raised his head and found himself staring into the blood-spattered face of Gabriella DeZantez. He offered her a hand up.

"You okay?"

"You know the personal motto of every Sword of Dawn. 'I always rise again.'"

Slowhand smirked. "I thought that was my motto."

DeZantez shook her head. "Quick thinking with the cable."

"I'm sure you would have thought of it yourself," Slowhand replied.

"Oh, I did. I just wanted to see how quick Slow was."

Slowhand nodded with a small smile, an acknowledgement that the prospect of their working together might not be as bad as it had seemed. He found himself staring up at Jakub Freel too, but the leather-clad man merely wiped a patch of gore from his cheek and slapped it to the train's roof with some disgust.

"It might not be over yet," he said, with no hint of gratitude. "We need to check for stragglers, any of them that might still be on or near the train. I'll check the front, DeZantez you get the sides, and Slowhand, you get the tracks to the rear."

Slowhand picked himself up, nodding as he wiped away gore. He made his way back down the cars and looked down. But other than the occasional piece of limb or bloody chunk of flesh being dragged along in their wake, there was nothing – the soul-stripped were gone.

Slowhand bowed slightly, placing his palms on his thighs and breathing a sigh of relief, when a hard shove in the small of his back sent him flying into the air.

He cried out in shock, twisting in mid air, and saw Freel standing on the lip of the last car. Slowhand fully expected to hit the tracks once more, but Freel's whip lashed towards him, coiling about him and slamming him against the rear of the train. Slowhand hung, dazed, and saw Freel glaring down at him, his teeth bared.

What the hells is this? Slowhand thought. *First the bastard shoves me off the back of the train, and then he catches me, and now he leaves me dangling here?*

This was about Jenna, it had to be. Freel was playing mind games, for sure.

The Faith enforcer stared down at him for what seemed an age, his face red, his eyes wide and wild, and then suddenly jerked the chain upward, bringing Slowhand with it. The archer clutched the lip of the car's roof and pulled himself up, and Freel snapped the chain off him, turned and walked away.

Slowhand stood, breathing hard and rubbing his wrists, staring after the man. His every instinct was to follow, to grab him and to sort the problems between them out right now, but somehow he didn't have it in him.

Instead, as the train sped inexorably towards the Sardenne he returned wearily to the cross-legged position he had adopted at the start of their journey, and once more his mind began to wander.

This time, however, his imaginings were not of naked women, of the rolling plains of Pontaine, or even of the Sardenne. Instead, they were of his sister's face, staring at him from the burning gondola of the *Makennon*. One word kept repeating itself, over and over in his mind. An order, delivered in his own, sure voice.

"Fire!"

CHAPTER NINE

It was said that a fistful of full golds could buy you anything in Fayence, but the bigger the fist the better the anything it bought. Not that any of the personal services of this town were in any way unsatisfactory. The local Lord, who maintained a fiscal and hands-on interest in them all, made sure of that. It was merely a matter of how long it would take to recover from the relaxations on offer, whether they were mental, physical, or both. Stimulation-wise, Fayence boasted it catered for all six senses, sometimes all at once, and it wasn't for nothing that the many hotels in the town were known as convalesalons.

Kali moved through a noisy crowd of the coming night's – or possibly week's – guests-to-be, many of whom, by the look of them, should have checked in some hours before. She was making her way along Fayence's main thoroughfare – known to one and all as Sin Street – and the air was a fug of exotic perfumes, stimulating massage balms and dreamweed clouds, the odours brushing off on Kali in the jostling melee. Though she knew exactly where she was heading, she found it impossible to get there in a straight line, the sea of revellers carrying her first towards Maloof's Erotivarium, thence the Palace of Pleasure and Pain and its patented 'Sinulator' by way of the Slither Baths and the Womb Chambers, the barkers in front of which deafeningly promised a sensory experience such that "you'll wish you'd never been born!" Kali knew that the so called 'Womb Chambers' were, in fact, the extracted bladders of globe toads from the Turnitian marshes but if the owners weren't going to tell the punters that little trade secret who was she to spoil their fun? You sure as hells had to admire the inventiveness of this place.

Not that Kali was *that* familiar with Fayence's attractions, she would be at pains to point out to anyone who asked – no, no, no, not at all. Slowhand, of course, had been badgering her to come here since they'd first become an item, but as that prospect was the equivalent of letting a very greedy little boy loose in a very large sweet factory, she had consistently denied him her company – and knowing she knew, he hadn't dared come alone. She smiled, thinking how galled he'd be if he knew she were here now. Even if she currently had only a passing curiosity in the establishments of Sin Street and was actually heading towards one of the town's more unusual attractions, a little more off the beaten track.

That was the thing about Fayence. It hadn't always been like this. For hundreds of years, in fact, the town had been the favoured home of those who studied the old Wheel of Power, and had once even been considered as a potential site for the Three Towers, the headquarters of the League of Prestidigitation and Prestige. That it had lost out to Andon in this respect had been an early blow for Fayence but one which had ultimately served it well. When their more conformist brethren had decamped to the north-west, the mages who subsequently came here – followed, in turn, by such complementary professionals as apothecaries, herbalists and suppliers of various arcane needs –shared a certain streak of independence, an *individual* approach to their studies that would have made it difficult for them to gain acceptance amongst their peers elsewhere.

They had their limits, however, and while many of their experiments might have stretched these to breaking point there were areas of their craft that, by general agreement, were considered too dangerous for exploration and, therefore, forbidden. Creation magic was one. Necromancy another. Thus it was that when Bastian Redigor was discovered to be waving his wand around in such murky waters – the specifics of which had not survived the passage of time – the man was banished forthwith from Fayence, never to return. It was at this point that the town's fortunes had begun to wane, not least because it was rumoured that with a wave of his hand upon his departure Redigor had left behind a legacy in the form of an incurable and agonising *taint* that quite literally consumed mages' brains, reducing the skull to an empty shell within a day.

Whether the rumour were true or not, one by one the mages died, and with them gone the livelihood of the apothecaries, herbalists and suppliers went too, and while a few remained to this day – albeit providing services for a clientele with more *intimate* requirements – Fayence was reduced to a little more than a ghost town.

So it remained for a number of years until the present Lord of Fayence, Aristide, inherited his position, whereupon he reinvented the town to reflect his own predilections, a change of emphasis he knew would be lucrative bearing in mind the amount of coin he himself had spent elsewhere over the years.

There was one area of the town Aristide did not change, however. Whether for fear of a return of the taint, or whether because the aura of the outcast who had become known as the Pale Lord still, after all this time, lingered there, it was left to rot, untouched, abandoned.

It was where the mages had died. They called it the Ghost Quarter.

Kali approached this forgotten part of town between the ignominious landmarks of a derelict comfort parlour called Whoopee Kushen's, outside of which an out-of-date courtesan swatted flies, and a grimy street stand trading in spit-roasted mool and bottles of thwack that gloried in the name *Abra-Kebab-*

Bar. It was doubtful if either enterprise was licenced by Lord Fayence, but they had attached themselves to the outer periphery of his salacious empire to engage in its spirit nonetheless. As Kali neared the latter, its proprietor – a huge, fat, greasy-bearded man three times the size of his stand who presumably was Abra – almost fell off his stool at the prospect of an actual customer. But his ear-to-ear grin faded as Kali nodded, smiled and passed on by.

"Girly, lady, madam, missus-woman," he protested as she passed, "I assure you, there is nothing for you beyond my small but perfectly formed establishment." He stroked his beard. "A little like yourself, if I may say..."

Kali smiled. "You can forget the flattery, Abra. I'm not looking for food or drink."

Abra coughed, and actually looked embarrassed. "Ah, I see."

The man's redness made Kali flush too. "No, no, not that either – not *anything.*" She resorted to her failsafe tactic when she found herself in an impasse situation. "Actually, I'm trying to save the world."

"The world?"

"Umm. Think so, anyway. Not quite so sure about what's going on this time."

"The world," Abra said again and then, aghast, "My advice to you is forget the world, save *yourself.*"

"Why do you say that?"

"Because if you are heading within, you must be heading for the Pale Lord's house yes? There can be no other reason to go there. I say do not do so, because those who do, they do not come back."

"*Other* people have gone there?"

Abra made a dismissive sound. "Oh, not often. The occasional mage or relic hunter, eager for a memento of our infamous son. Young, drunken couples with their underknicks already about their ankles, clearly acting upon a dare." He sighed and shook his head. "I do not see any of them again, other than as a stain upon a wall, a smear across a window, a splatter beneath my feet." Abra emphasised his point by suddenly squeezing a large dollop of kebab sauce onto the ground with a loud and flatulent plop, making Kali jump.

"I see," Kali said. Redigor had obviously trapped his old home the same way he'd trapped his books, which made her destination all the more interesting. "Thanks for the warning, Abra. I'll watch my step."

Abra sucked in an amazed breath. "You *still* go?"

Kali placed her hands on her hips in what she hoped was a heroic stance. "It's what I do."

"Then you are the loopo," Abra exclaimed, rotating a finger at his temple.

"That's what people keep telling me."

Kali moved on into the Ghost Quarter, shaking her head as Abra produced another sigh and flatulent plop. But she had soon left the *Abra-Kebab-Bar* behind her, Sin Street far behind her. The difference between the two locations could not have been more marked. Kali was now the only living thing in a warren of utterly silent streets, shattered glass cracking underfoot, the odd piece of rubble skittering away from her. There were no birds in the azure night sky, not even any vermin peering from the empty houses on either side – rich nesting grounds though they'd be. Lifeless and dark, the houses themselves were remarkably well-preserved, some even retaining the black 'T' daubed there long ago to warn others that their owners had succumbed to the taint. Kali was pretty certain that the 'T's would have served no useful purpose. The Pale Lord was powerful and, if his taint had your name on it, sooner or later it would have got you, no matter what.

The Pale Lord's home was the eeriest in the eerie warren of properties – a foreboding, rambling structure at the end of the street which, despite being long-abandoned, seemed to glow faintly of candlelight from within. Kali approached slowly, looking around to make sure she was alone, and climbed the step to the entrance. The door was half-obscured by thick cobwebs and half-hanging off its hinges and, when pushed, fell to the floor in a cloud of dust. Shadows danced slowly within. Kali eased into the hallway, and could have sworn she heard the sound of footsteps from the upper floor. She swallowed.

Disappointingly, though, as Kali cautiously began to explore, there were no ghosts – and very little of anything else – to be found. Apart from a couple of fairly obvious traps which she carefully defused, the house seemed exactly what it appeared to be: empty and derelict. For an hour, she worked her way minutely through all its rooms, finding nothing and ending up in the building's main parlour where, from the looks of what remained, Redigor had once kept his library and laboratory. But as elsewhere, there was little to see. What the passage of time had not rotted had been removed, most noticeably in the bookshelves lining the room. Even the laboratory was a disappointment. A dust-covered and vaguely horseshoe-shaped workbench occupied the heart of the room. Kali could imagine Redigor standing there conducting his 'unique' experiments, but the only evidence which now remained of them was the odd upturned belljar or shattered pipette. Kali pursed her lips. Not quite what she'd expected of an infamous necromancer's laboratory, it had to be said.

Still, though the dwelling seemed to offer her nothing, Kali couldn't shake the feeling that she was missing something. She had the feeling there was something *wrong* with the room that she couldn't quite put her finger on, something to do with space. For some reason, it felt bigger than it was, more open. Kali backed up to the door and studied it anew – nothing. Maybe she'd been wrong to come here after all, she thought, frustration flooding her.

It was in that moment, her mind returning to the bigger picture, filling with images of the Sardenne and what lay within it, that she stopped looking – and that was when she *saw*.

It wasn't much, like something in the corner of her eye *right in front of her*, but it was there. Something odd about the way the workbench curved, as if its relations with the rest of the room were oddly misaligned. She noticed then how it wasn't just the bench that appeared odd but the other trappings, too – bookcases, furniture, even the tiling on the floor. Where their lines should have been straight, they curved ever so slightly, and where surfaces should have been flat, they were very gently concave. The only comparison Kali could draw was that it was like looking through a very weak fish-eye lens, but what she saw was there – something bending the reality of the heart of the room.

Kali moved into the 'u' of the bench and waved her hand slowly back and forth where light seemed to bend the most. She felt a slight thickening of the air and, for a moment, her fingers brushed against something almost, but not quite, insubstantial. Dammit, she knew what this was now. It was a glamour field like the one she'd encountered at the Crucible, only in this case highly localised, highly concentrated. So concentrated it was able to confound every sense. To manipulate reality with such finesse would have taken great skill indeed, and such a degree of skill would surely only have been used if, as she suspected, Redigor had something very significant to hide.

Kali's elation was fleeting. The problem that remained was finding out what. Even though she *knew* there was something there, her perception remained too wrong-footed to tease it out into the open. Frustrated, she flopped down against a wall, clucking her tongue as she stared at the field.

Come on, Hooper! There has to be a way to work this, a way to skew my senses so that I'm not looking at what the field wants me to look at.

For a while no solution presented itself and then, slowly, she smiled. What was that old adage about mixing business with pleasure?

A moment later, Kali was out in the street, racing back through the Ghost Quarter to Abra's stand.

"Your thwack," she said. "I want it."

Shock at her sudden appearance mingled with surprise at actually making a sale. "H-how many bottles?"

"All of them."

"*All* of them?"

"And flummox. You got any flummox?"

"I – I think I may have a few bottles, yes..."

"Those, too. What about twattle?"

"*Twattle?*" Abra gasped. He glanced about himself guiltily. "I have one bottle. But it is deadly. And illegal. It is also very, very expensive."

Kali pulled a coinpurse from her pocket and emptied its golden contents into Abra's hands. "I'll take it. I'll take everything. The lot. But I'll need you to wheel it to Redigor's house."

The suggestion brought even more sweat to Abra's face than was already running down it but, as he watched Kali bite the cork from the bottle of twattle and down it in one, he realised she was not to be messed with. He had, after all, once seen a bottle of twattle make someone's ears drop off. Quickly, he began to unlock his stand's complex arrangement of brakes and supports. Kali, meanwhile, grabbed two armfuls of bottles and was gone.

Back at the house, she ploughed into the various ales with industrial zeal, popping out to Abra when necessary for more, and the wall where she slumped was soon stacked with a small mountain of empties. The booze hadn't yet achieved its desired result, however, her preternatural capacity for the stuff preventing her from getting drunk enough to loosen her hold on reality. Not that it wasn't having *some* effect.

As she once more sought out Abra for supplies she felt an overwhelming desire to tell him what a very nice fat man he was – no, no, *really*, Abra – and, on returning to the laboratory, she accidentally booted half the bottle mountain across the room. Kali hopped up and down flapping her arms, trying to shush them as they rolled and rattled everywhere, but the little farkers wouldn't listen, so she called them names instead.

She dropped to her knees, snorting, eyes moving in circles over her fresh supply. *Which to pick? Which to pick? Which to pick?*

Having decided that the fourth of the identical bottles was by far the prettiest, she stood precariously and raised it in a toast to the glamour field. There was still no change in its appearance but the small manoeuvre threw her off kilter and her feet momentarily forgot which of them was which. Kali staggered into one of the bookcases, bowed and apologised profusely, then soothed its hurt feelings by drawing shapes in the dust of one of its shelves. It was as she was doing this that she realised she could murder a kebab.

Kali staggered to a window and shouted to Abra at the top of her voice. As she turned back, it suddenly occurred to her that she had stumbled upon actually quite a cool concept, having food delivered to your door. Maybe she ought to jack in all the world saving stuff, go into partnership with Abra and open a home delivery shop. Hells, with Horse she could have the food anywhere in a five league radius in no time, still warm and at no extra charge. Now, what would she call it? Kebakali? Kalibabi? Kebabkalbulbu –

Pitsh!

There was something wrong with her lips.

The realisation suddenly struck Kali that for the last few seconds she'd been staring at a spiral staircase in the centre of the room. Mouth gaping, bottle dropping to the ground, she half walked, half stretched towards it, as if any sudden move might make it vanish once more. It didn't. It was there, all right, as real as everything else in the room, solid beneath her touch. Kali burped and pulled herself in, turning sinuously around its metal core like a dancer, head angled to peer up the spiralling steps into shadow.

"Boo!" She said suddenly, and giggled, blowing a hole in a thin blanket of cobweb, which dropped down onto her face like a flap of skin.

Kali puffed it away, peered through the hole and frowned. Even sobered up slightly. From what she could see through further cobwebs, the staircase went up high. Higher than the house itself. Maybe it was something to do with her pickled brain, or maybe it was because she had become used to such things, but Kali didn't find anything odd about that at all. Nor did she find its shadowed heights unnerving or daunting. Far from it, because she knew she was staring at a threshold that hadn't been crossed since Redigor had abandoned the house. This staircase was what he had been hiding, his little secret, and at its top she might very well find out just what the Pale Lord was *really* all about.

Did she go up or didn't she? Kali placed a finger on her lips. Difficult one.

Under normal circumstances, she'd have taken the spiral steps slowly, but, fuelled by booze, she raced up them as fast as she could - which was just as well, as they seemed to go on for ever. It was only after she had passed through the house's attic and found herself still going up that she began to slow, but this was more to do with the ever thickening cobwebs – almost like netting now – than any dwindling enthusiasm.

Becoming swathed in so much of the stuff that she began to resemble something bored of its sarcophagus, even Kali's boundless energy was taxed as she went round and round, but she found strength in the realisation that she had to be ascending some kind of magically constructed tower hidden from the outside world by the same kind of glamour that concealed its base. She found it slightly disconcerting that, in a sense, this meant she was climbing up into thin air, but the tower felt solid enough about her. Solid and *very old*. Old enough, in fact, to explain the preternatural thickness of the cobwebs: this, for some reason, was the growth of thousands and thousands of years.

The tower's top was becoming visible, now, and the shadows above lightened. Not much, the kind of illumination one might expect if daylight were projecting through a number of narrow windows, but enough to suggest the presence of a chamber above.

Kali didn't know what to expect up there. But it wasn't this.

Bastian Redigor waited for her at the top of the stairs.

"Shit!" Kali shouted, and almost fell back the way she had come. Saved only by a patch of the thick, sticky cobweb, she clung to the tower for a moment, fully expecting the clang of footsteps from above, but Redigor did not appear. Very slowly, she peered back around the last turn of the stairs. "Girl," she chastised herself.

Kali climbed into a chamber dominated by a portrait of the Pale Lord. It, too, was almost entirely obscured by cobweb, as indeed was the rest of the room, but the part she could see – *had seen* – showed the piercing black eyes, flowing raven hair and handsome, aquiline features she was familiar with from illustrations in books. Even represented in oils, Redigor had presence, and he wore expensive robes of a fashion not seen on the peninsula for a very, very long time.

Kali drew her gaze away from the portrait, turning her attention to the chamber, and tore away blankets of cobweb. If she had been looking for information, she guessed she could pretty much say she had found it.

A desk in front of her overflowed with books, journals, scrolls, notes and charts, most of which pertained to necromancy in one way or another. The assorted papers were not limited to the desk, either. The floor was littered with more of the same, the walls covered in diagrams and maps of every size and description, including, interestingly, one of the sprawling expanse of the Sardenne. Across this Redigor had marked in sweeping scrawl the location of Bellagon's Rip.

Kali sighed. What she needed was new information. It was here, she was sure of it, but she didn't have a clue where to start digging. She decided after a second to thrust her hands into a stack of papers to see what came out.

For the next few hours Kali ploughed through notes on anatomy, alchemy, conjuration, revivification, holding and other kinds of magical constraint. She flicked through sketches of Twilight and of Kerberos, and through diagrams of what appeared to be the pillar of souls she'd seen at Scholten. There were starcharts, too – in the kind of detail she'd heard only the Final Faith's astronomer had compiled – but she had no idea why. She had no idea, either, of the meaning of endless reams of calculus, columns of figures in their thousands, that Redigor seemed to have constantly annotated in his strange, sprawling script. One document did, for a moment, seem to bear out the Faith's theory that Redigor planned an invasion – a map of the peninsula overlaid with countless thin, sweeping lines – but unless the Pale Lord planned to despatch his soul-stripped on a thousand or more fronts, it made little tactical sense.

That was the problem. All this effort and the only conclusion she had drawn was that nothing here made sense.

Gahh! She needed a break.

Dumping a batch of papers, Kali strode to one of the windows that lit the tower, stretching, and froze.

Instead of staring out high over Fayence, she was gazing on a sprawling panorama of glistening towers whose architecture she had never seen but which, after her time in Domdruggle's

Expanse, was cloyingly familiar – architecture out of the distant past. Except that it *couldn't* be out of the distant past. It was new and thriving, figures moving along the streets below, sleek objects darting through the sky between towers, and between them a crystal clear river meandering into the distance.

It was a vast, Old Race city. An elven city. The warm breeze from it was fresh.

It was *real*.

The conclusion was inescapable. Somehow she and the tower in which she stood were in the past. It was incredible, not only the wonders she could see but the sorceries that must have brought it about. Maybe that was what Redigor had done with the tower, she thought. Maybe it wasn't concealed from Fayence with a glamour field because it didn't need to be. Maybe it projected itself further into the past the higher it rose.

My Gods, I'm there, she realised. The time of the Old Races. The temptation to climb out of the window, regardless of the insane height, was almost irresistible. But why would Bastian Redigor have done this? Why would he have expended the vast amounts of energy needed to stare out over a vista long gone? Maybe he just had a thing for elven architecture, she thought. Or maybe he couldn't stand looking out over the depravity in which Fayence excelled. Or maybe –

Maybe it simply made him feel at home.

Kali's heart thudded, and she spun back to face the inside of the chamber. *That* was what had been missing from all this, why she hadn't been able to make any sense out of what she'd studied, because all along she'd been trying to work out the plans of your average human, world-dominating necromancer. But there was much more to him than that, wasn't there?

Kali raced to the portrait, tearing away cobweb to reveal more of its detail. Of course. In pictures of himself elsewhere, Redigor had appeared as he wanted to appear, but here, in a portrait that would be seen by no eyes other than his own, he seemed almost to have taken pride in sweeping back his hair.

It was an ear thing.

Bastian Redigor was an elf.

Kali swallowed. It wasn't just the revelation that somehow this bastard had survived down the long years but what she saw in the rest of the exposed portrait.

The woman next to him bore a striking resemblance to Katherine Makennon. It wasn't her, of course, because even had she been alive when the picture was painted, there was no way Makennon would allow herself to be pictured garbed as this woman was – which was to say, in very little at all. That Redigor, smiling slightly, also held a fine chain attached to a collar about her neck, put paid to the possibility fully.

Kali's mind reeled. The woman was clearly *mu'sah'rin* – in human terms, somewhere between forced consort and slave – and that could mean only one thing. Redigor wasn't only an elf, he was Ur'Raney. The most misogynistic, cold-hearted, sadistic so-called 'family' of the elves there had ever been. The Ur'Raney were the same family who had relentlessly pursued and slaughtered the dwarves at Martak, who had brought both Old Races to the brink of war, and who, because of their gleeful, unremitting cruelty, were reviled even by their own kind.

Most contemporaneous texts had been of the opinion that Twilight would be better off without them.

Kali calmed herself. So, Redigor was an elf. The fact was, she couldn't say she felt *that* surprised, because something had occurred to her in Scholten that seemed to have been missed by everyone else. The Engines of the Apocalypse being what they were, lost to and forgotten by countless generations, should have been exactly that – lost and forgotten. Unless the Pale Lord had stumbled upon their control centre while out for a walk one day – an unlikely turn of events, to say the least – they had to have been activated by someone *old enough* to know it was there. Well, that was Redigor, all right. He had revealed his true heritage at last. But the question remained, what the hells was he up to?

Here They Lie Still.

Kali replayed the phrase Slowhand had quoted in the library through her mind, analysing it in a different light now she knew Redigor's true identity. As she did, she studied the assorted papers again, trying to piece together the jigsaw that was the Pale Lord's experimentation. Why should an ancient elf wish to unleash an army of soul-stripped onto the peninsula? What the hells was he going to get out of that? Unless, as she had suspected, that wasn't what he was planning at all. Her gaze rose back to the portrait of Redigor and the woman and once more she asked herself – what the hells did the Pale Lord want with Makennon or the other 'dignitaries' his soul-stripped had snatched from all over the peninsula? What was special about those thirteen people?

Another question. With so much power at his disposal, why had Bastian Redigor allowed himself to be banished? From what she had seen here, he could have wiped the floor with any mage on Twilight, and certainly the berobed fops and jesters who made up Lord Fayence's court wouldn't have stood a chance in the hells against him, and he could have taken the town any time he wanted. So why? Why move from what was clearly his home, as well as a well-equipped base, to the unforgiving wilds of the Sardenne? And just why did he already have a map showing the Sardenne and Bellagon's Rip?

Kali studied the map again. If she expected to see any previously unseen feature she was soon disappointed, but her eyes were drawn once more to Redigor's flowing script. Bellagon's Rip. It was written there as plain as day and yet there was something not quite right about it. She suddenly realised that her mind had been filling in the gaps and she was reading what she expected to read, because that was the name by which that area of the forest had always been known. But what if it was misnamed? What if some more modern cartographer had chanced upon some previously scrawled notation of Redigor's on some other map, and had misinterpreted it as she was doing now? Maybe this was a matter of perception rather than interpretation, because although Redigor had used human script on everything she had so far read there was still an elvish flourish to his hand that potentially gave a whole new meaning to what was written. Bearing that in mind, Kali reread the name, seeing each letter on its own rather than as a component part of a word, and gradually they began to flow together. That was *it*. It wasn't a name at all but an elven phrase. Not Bellagon's Rip but Bel'A'Gon'Shri. She concentrated hard, eyes closed, trying to pull together all the elvish she knew to make sense of the phrase, and her eyes snapped open in alarm.

Bel'A'Gon'Shri.

Here They Lie, Still.

Gabriella DeZantez hadn't been far wrong in her theory about its meaning. But the phrase wasn't referring to the Engines and it wasn't suggesting that anything was lying idle. It was suggesting that 'they' were lying where they'd lain for a long time and were *waiting*. And Kali suspected she knew who.

The charts, the maps, the diagrams, the calculations, they suddenly all made sense. Rather in the manner of an Eye of the Lord, she imagined herself descending from the sky into the map, the image no longer two-dimensional but a living canopy of trees through which she swept down, down, down. And waiting for her beneath was a structure of gothic horror overgrown with the vegetation of thousands of years, a structure that she knew was sitting deep in the Sardenne.

An elven necropolis.

An Ur'Raney necropolis.

Oh Gods.

The Faith, as she'd suspected, and as farking usual, had got it all wrong. There was going to be an invasion, all right, but not in the way they thought. She had to shut down the Engines of the Apocalypse and then get to the Faith, let them know what was *really* going on.

She ran for the stairwell, trying to ignore the staring eyes of Bastian Redigor, and heard a click beneath her feet. She looked down.

Trap, she thought. *Dammit.*

In her eagerness to leave she'd triggered something she'd missed, and as a result could already sense that something was coming. Something from outside.

Kali raced to a window, seeing the same wonderland as earlier. Now, thin, grey shapes were hurtling towards the tower through the sky. Whatever they were, they had the same aura about them as the death coach that had taken Makennon, as the tapers in the library, and had again to be born of the black threads. As Kali looked on in horror, the shapes resolved themselves into the figures of hags, skeletal things clad in translucent shrouds. Their talons were grotesquely overgrown, blurred streaks of things that seemed to stretch from this world into another.

Kali swallowed, knowing now what had caused Abra to see stains upon the walls, smears across windows and splatters beneath his feet, and she stumbled back from the window as the hags shrieked into the tower. They seemed, though, to have no interest in her, tearing around the circular chamber like a dark whirlpool. They moved faster and faster, Kali ducking under Redigor's desk, trying to work out what the hells was going on as a loud tearing sound rose over the creatures' shrieking. Kali looked out and saw flashes of sky. The hags' talons were slicing through the tower, not as the Deathclaws might slice through stone but seemingly through its very *existence*. Redigor had conjured the tower for his secret researches but must have booby-trapped it so that, if discovered, it would be obliterated.

The whole place was coming apart around her. Being erased.

Kali lurched from under desk, the flight of the hags – nothing more than blurs, now – whipping at her bodysuit and hair. She stared in horror as she saw great streaks of sky visible where, moments before, there had been a roof. Her heart began to pound as, around and beneath her, the walls and floor began to disappear slice by slice.

Kali dashed for the stairwell, hoping she would be able to outrun Redigor's trap, but then staggered back as the hags' talons eradicated the entrance to the stairs.

Oh, fark, that was not good. Not good at all.

Kali looked around the room in desperation, searching for an alternative means of escape, but the only one that presented itself was to jump. Despite the fact that was ancient sky out there – thousands of years before her time – it was better than the alternative of staying where she was and being sliced from reality. Hells, if by some miracle she survived the jump, she could leave the Faith a note and experience the wonders of the Old Races first hand.

She wasn't completely suicidal, though, and needed something to slow her fall. The rope in her backpack would be nowhere near long enough. There was only one other thing that she could see might work, even if it was one hells of a gamble. Moving almost in a blur herself, Kali spun around the remains of the chamber, gathering its thick and sticky coating of cobwebs about her body in layer after layer, then, when she felt she had gathered enough, turned to face the remains of one of the windows, took one deep breath and ran and leapt. The coating of cobweb wrapped about her body pulled masses of the stuff after her, almost stripping the tower clean.

Kali plummeted. And marvelled. As she fell, she travelled not only downward, but forward through the ages. In a flash, the elven city crumbled and disappeared, and clouds scudded across wasteland. The course of the river changed, twisting like a striking snake. Another city arose, then fell, and one after that, though none were yet Fayence. Faster and faster the images came until Kali could no longer keep up, each year, maybe even each century, a flash in the mind, gone before she could register anything she saw. The feeling was incredible, marred only by her sadness at falling through all she had ever wanted to know. Then, building by small building, Fayence appeared below.

Kali was keenly aware that the next thing that might flash through her mind could be the pavement. Though still distant, the ground was coming up fast and the cobweb wasn't yet slowing her fall. Just as she started to worry that her plan wasn't going to work, the thick layers wrapped about her jerked subtly and began to tear themselves away in ever increasing strips. That was it, cobweb's end, and all she could hope for now was that her descent would be slowed enough to negotiate some kind of safe landing.

What she hadn't counted on was that, as the strips tore away, they twined about and adhered to each other until they had formed a kind of elasticated rope. The only thought that went through her mind as she reached the end of her drop and continued on was that jumping from great heights attached to something that, if it didn't smash you into the ground, was going to snap you back into the air like a pea from a catapult, wasn't a pastime she could ever see anyone choosing to do for fun.

Unless she wanted to be on nodding terms with Kerberos, she needed an anchor.

And there was one, still distant but coming up fast.

"Abra!" She shouted.

"Yes?" A puzzled voice responded from below.

The fat man was waiting patiently at Redigor's front door, clutching an immense and, by now, stone-cold kebab. The vendor slowly rose before her, and, catching a glimpse of a pair of Hells Bellies' socks while thanking the gods that the cobweb seemed to have stretched its furthest, Kali grabbed onto his belt. Momentarily they were face to face – albeit with her upside down – and Kali stared Abra in the eyes and smiled. "Never mind," she said.

The pair of them shot into the air where, to his credit, Abra remained stoically silent, as if this kind of thing happened every day. He managed a weak smile.

The return flight reached its apex and they dropped again. Then rose. Then dropped. At last the cobweb seemed to recognise that enough was enough, and they ended up dangling a foot above the ground.

As the remains of the cobweb began to tear themselves slowly apart, dropping them towards the pavement, Abra coughed.

"Did you," he asked slowly, and with a crack in his voice, "discover what you needed to know?"

Kali stared back up at where the tower had been.

"Oh, yeah," she said after a second. "The Ur'Raney. He's planning to bring them back."

Chapter Ten

Head down, Kali rode hard and fast, pushing Horse to his absolute limit. The bamfcat was, as usual, loyal and uncomplaining, though he did seem somewhat confused at being unable to do what he normally would and shorten the journey. But he could not jump; for the last few leagues they had been riding across the Plain of Storms.

It was one of the peculiar features of the area. Surrounded by the temperate farmlands of mid Pontaine, the almost perfectly circular valley was a meteorological anomaly, prone to a stultifying heaviness of air and battered by constant electrical storms. Those who lived on the periphery of the area said that sometimes the catastrophic conditions on the plain affected other weather it had no business affecting, *pulling* at the northern lights and bending them toward the ground, or even snatching a maelstrom from the Storm Wall, far away on the coast, for a few hours. If this were true – and Kali had seen enough of the raw potential of Old Races creations to believe it could be – it was likely that the energies of the control centre for the machines, what she had nicknamed 'the hub,' were responsible.

In other words, she guessed she was in the right place.

Nearing the centre of the plain, Kali slowed Horse to a stop and stared into the rain-lashed, thundering vista before her. She dismounted, took her squallcoat from her saddlebag and slipped it on, fastening it securely. From there on in, she led Horse by the reins.

It was hard going, fighting the unnaturally heavy atmosphere and taking deep, grasping breaths as she went. Here and there, tornadoes whirled across the barren ground, threatening to pluck her up if she strayed too close. Not that it was much safer out of their path – where the whirlwinds didn't manifest themselves, Kali found herself having to dodge sudden bolts of lightning that struck the ground about her, leaving small, smoking craters where they hit. One or two almost got her, but she soon learned to anticipate their arrival, the dense air further thickening a few seconds before each strike, as if someone were pressing down hard on her head. No pitsing wonder the area was so desolate, she thought. Other than a few scattered hardy plants, tanglevine and redweed among them, it was like walking through a bad dream. No one had ever tried to fully explore, let alone colonise the region, but why in the hells would they?

Once again, she thought, to find the hub you'd have to know it was *there*.

And suddenly, unexpectedly, it was there. A dark cave mouth loomed before her out of a dust storm. Not just a cave mouth, though: the eroded rock still retained the faint remains of carvings chiselled into it millennia earlier, shapes Kali recognised as dwarven. The most obvious clue to its provenance, though, was that the cave mouth itself was the shape of one of the Engines.

Kali tethered Horse, moved to the mouth and paused. If this was indeed the entrance to the hub then surely it was once a prime target for the dwarves' elven enemies, and as such she'd have expected it to be protected by the usual array of dwarven defences and traps. There was no evidence of anything, however, and Kali wondered if perhaps the traps, like the mouth itself, had been obliterated by the ravages of the plain. She bit her lip, deciding all she could do was proceed with caution.

Kali entered the cave mouth, briefly disappointed. To be frank she had been expecting to find more than just a cave. But that was all she'd got. A plain tunnel sloped gently downwards, ending in a chamber devoid of features but for a large hole in the ground. Kali eased her way to its edge and peered down. While deep, it appeared, for all intents and purposes, to be simply that. A hole in the ground. Then Kali noticed that the floor of the cave leading towards it was scarred and grooved. Once upon a time heavy objects, and a good number of them, had been dragged towards that hole. She pictured teams of dwarves pulling their burdens on ropes and then –

And then what? She wondered.

Because unless she had been completely wrong about this being the hub and she had, in fact, stumbled across some dwarven landfill site, surely they hadn't simply been dumped down there? She looked around. There was no sign of any haulage mechanisms with which they might have been lowered. As far as she could tell there was also no sign of any mechanism which might raise an elevator from far below. Frowning, Kali conducted a thorough search of the surrounding rock, but nothing. It did indeed appear as if she had come all this way to be stymied by a hole.

Kali sat herself against the wall and made a flubbing sound. If she were going to make the rendezvous with DeZantez and the others, she did not have the advantage she normally might in such circumstances – to take as much time as she wished to ponder the problem. Frustrated, she plucked stones from the cave floor around her and began to lob them towards the hole. If she listened carefully, she might at least be able to determine how deep the farking thing was. It was then that she noticed two things – one, a thrumming from below that was barely audible over the lightning strikes outside and, two, the fact that the stones she had lobbed at the hole hadn't fallen in.

What the hells? Kali picked herself up and moved to its edge, leaning forward to grab one of the hovering stones from mid air. It seemed to contain metallic ore. As she leaned forward, she felt a resistance, placing her hand in a soft pillow, and stood back, her heart thumping. Did that mean what she thought it meant? That if she –?

Kali stripped off her backpack and threw it out over the seemingly bottomless drop, raising her eyebrows as it, too, bounced about as if tossed by currents of air. But this was not air she was dealing with – she felt nothing on her flesh, on her face, in her hair – it seemed instead to be something that *warped* the air.

Perhaps, even, the same force that kept the Engines of the Apocalypse aloft?

Okay, what's the worst that can happen? Kali thought. *If I step over the breach I end up hovering there and have to claw my way back.*

But what if the only reason that the rocks and backpack were hovering was because they were lighter than she was? What if this resistance, whatever it was, allowed the gradual descent of something with more mass – the objects that had scored the floor of the cave, perhaps? What if the strange force warping the air acted as some kind of invisible elevator?

Kali stepped forward, her foot wobbling slightly on the air, and then drew herself over the hole. She stuck her arms out straight like a wire walker and giggled as she floated. Then, very slowly she began to descend. Instinctively, Kali took a deep breath, but then smiled to herself. This wasn't water she was dealing with, this was something else entirely, and it had so far proved to be harmless, so she saw no reason why she shouldn't enjoy the ride.

Down she went, slowly down. At long last, Kali felt solid rock beneath her feet once more.

She stared at a solid rock wall. Disappointment threatened to overwhelm her once again. But then she turned around.

Kali smiled. *Hello, hub,* she thought.

Stretching away ahead of her, cut to the same dimensions as the vertical shaft, was a tunnel running horizontally through the rock, disappearing into the distance. Kali took a step forward, shrugged away a moment of giddiness, and waited while her eyes adjusted to the dim light of the underground.

The smooth, curving walls here were not bare rock, but lined with a softly-glowing metal, as was the floor, both inscribed over every inch of their surface with thousands upon thousands of delicate etchings. There were far too many of these etchings for Kali to be able to make sense of them as a whole, but they were undoubtedly dwarven in style and, what was more, of a kind that she had never come across before. The archetypal dwarven symbology was, of course, usually to do with war but Kali didn't see a single battleaxe, anvil or roaring dwarven visage. Instead, the fine etchings were flowing, swirling patterns – millions of them, perhaps – that reminded her of mathematical or algebraic symbols, all interlocking and sweeping in every direction and along the curving walls, combining as a whole into a thing of beauty. But were they just decorative or did they serve another purpose? Kali placed her palm on one small area of the etchings and immediately snatched it away, her flesh jolted, tingling and numb. Well, that answered that. Whatever they were, they were more than just decorative.

The answers lay ahead, they had to, and Kali began to walk the tunnel's length. She moved with caution, her concerns about the lack of traps playing on her mind. Again, though, there was no sign at all of anything threatening. The one thing that made her slow in her tracks turned out not to be any kind of hazard at all.

Lying on the floor of the tunnel, apparently torn apart, was the remains of some kind of machine. Multi-limbed, with appendages that resembled tools, it reminded her of some kind of giant spider.

Kali took a wide berth around it, just in case, and proceeded along the tunnel.

With all of her concentration focused on detecting traps she felt sure should be there, she found herself suddenly caught off guard, her progress impeded not by any trap but an unexpected wave of dizziness and disorientation that threw her off balance and sent her staggering.

"Whoa," Kali muttered.

Her head thumped, the passage seemed to spin about her, and she felt suddenly very hot with a wash of tingling saliva in her mouth, and a wave of nausea. Palms pressed against the passage wall, Kali swallowed and shook her head, feeling it buzz as she did and bringing a sudden stabbing pain behind the eyes. What the pits was going on? She suddenly felt as if she had the hangover from the hells. The previous evening had been a little heavy, even for her, but it felt all wrong. There was a throbbing heaviness of the head there, for sure, and an acid biliousness in her gut, but she knew what a hangover felt like and this wasn't it.

There was only one other conclusion. Something about – something *in* – this place was messing with her insides.

The sensation passed as she moved a few feet further on, and returned once more as she drew nearer to the end of the passage, before inexplicably disappearing again. Thrown, Kali continued, experiencing a few minutes of normality, before, abruptly, the debilitating sensation hit her once more. And if anything, it was worse than before. The resurgent feeling slapped her like a wave and, never mind her stomach, she felt as if her brain itself was sloshing about in her head. This time Kali buckled and actually did throw up and for a few seconds remained on her hands and knees, trailing spittle and groaning. She didn't want to get up but she knew she had to, that the sensations were connected to particular spots in the passageway and, perhaps by extension, in the whole place. Unless she wanted to suffer an ignominious death by a thousand heaves, she had to find a safe spot, and quickly.

Kali picked herself up, her vision wavering and blurring, and, her brain feeling like one of Slowhand's balloon animals, weaved like a drunk towards the end of the passageway. The current section seemed to have no safe spot whatsoever. She was dimly aware of passing another couple of the wrecked, spidery machines – in fact, almost tripping over one of them in her reduced state – and tried to think more about what function they might serve but found her concentration slipping away from her, unable to focus on anything but placing one foot in front of the other.

As bad as she felt, however, she could not help but react to what she saw as she reached the end of the passageway – even if for a second she thought it might be some vision induced by her delirium. Once more, Kali fell to her knees, not due to the disorientating effects of the place but because she was so staggered by the chamber she found herself in.

No, chamber was not a word that did this place justice. Spectacular as it had been, chamber was a word that described the lower level of Quinking's Depths, but this was...

Kali was kneeling on a platform overlooking a vast dwarven machine room, its metal-ribbed heights soaring as high above her as they plunged into the depths below. It was a vertiginous, spherical *world* of a place that made her feel as if she had stepped into the very core of Twilight itself. Great, irregularly-shaped metal objects rose and fell in the centre of the massive sphere, other smaller devices hovering around them like the satellites of metal moons. Other masses simply hung in the air, rotating slowly, while around the edge of the sphere, along its equator, a massive band of metal spun constantly, alternately clockwise and anti-clockwise, blurred by its speed – some kind of accelerator. And working on and around all of it – skittering on, about and around the devices – were spidery machines like the ones she had seen wrecked in the tunnel.

Kali couldn't take it all in, let alone make any sense of it, especially in the state she was in, and she crouch-walked along the platform until she found the blessed relief of a safe spot. Here, she felt able to crawl forward and peer down over the lip of the platform.

The machine room went far deeper than she had envisaged, burrowing down into the natural, rocky depths, so that the whole place was the shape of an upturned teardrop. Rising from that rocky depth was the reason 'the hub' had been built here, a narrow and tapering pinnacle of rock that disappeared into the confusion above, forming the centre around which they turned. The rock seemed, somehow, to be exerting an influence on the objects, keeping them afloat and in motion, and even from where she studied it Kali could feel the force it was emanating, as if she were leaning into a strong wind. She realised suddenly what it was she was dealing with here. The pinnacle of rock was an unimaginably massive lodestone – a giant, natural magnet –

and its satellites had to be magnets, too, repelling and attracting each other in a geological dance choreographed by unbelievably complex forces. By the gods, they said the dwarves were masters of the very rocks themselves but this... this was incredible. It was magnetism on a massive scale, a peninsula-wide field controlling the Engines of Apocalypse.

Kali shook her head, another wave of dizziness hitting her, and, as she did, she caught a glimpse between the gaps in the revolving magnets of something else – something perched *on top* of the lodestone secured by bent struts. Some kind of platform, with what appeared to be a control panel on it. There was something else on the platform, too, and Kali felt a knot of dread in her chest as, through increasingly wavering vision, she made out four of Bastian Redigor's soul-stripped, at their feet another wrecked spider. They had clearly been despatched to activate the Engines, and as far as she could see it would be impossible to access the controls without them detecting her presence.

But wait. There was something not right about them. The soul-stripped were less than animate when not under the direct control of the Pale Lord but these four seemed to be not so much standing at the panel as slumped there. But that didn't make sense. Wouldn't Redigor would have kept them alive to ensure the continued operation of the Engines, or at the very least to stop anyone coming along to turn them off? What, then, was going on?

Kali swallowed as the brief glimpses of the soul-stripped the revolving magnets permitted her revealed more about their state. The soul-stripped were not moving because they could not move. Each of them was quite, quite dead, rivulets of blood congealed beneath their mouths, ears and nostrils. Where their eyes had been were simply empty sockets still slowly oozing gore. It was as if some external influence had taken hold of their heads and squeezed until they popped.

Kali raised her fingertips to her own nostrils, and they came away red and wet. The dwarves had established no defences here because no defences were needed. The spider machines had been built to maintain the hub once it was running because the dwarves knew the overwhelming magnetic forces at play would prove deadly to any living thing, including themselves. While Redigor's puppets were no longer strictly alive, their bodies were still flesh and blood, subject to the same physical vulnerabilities as anyone.

Kali wondered if Bastian Redigor had felt the agonising pain that must have accompanied the soul-stripped's deaths. And she wondered, more resilient than most or not, how long it would be before she started to feel her own.

She had to reach the control panel.

Get the job done and get out of there fast.

Kali stood and found herself staggering, forced to steady herself on a nearby strut. Oh, that was just great. Under normal circumstances getting the job done might have involved a couple of daring leaps across the magnets and then onto the control platform, but in her current condition there was no chance of that. She had to find an alternative route.

Kali studied the chamber and its central platform. Once upon a time it had to have had some kind of access walkway but that had clearly been removed once the structure was finished, meaning there was no direct way to it. The pattern in which the magnets orbited it, however, did present one or two moments when protrusions of the rotating stones almost touched the platform. If she could get onto one she should be able to make the jump across. There was no way onto them from this side of the chamber, but on the other side one of the objects that passed near the platform also passed near the edge of the chamber, and that distance, too, looked jumpable. It sounded easy enough – A to B to C – but the only problem was that getting to B would involve having to hitch a ride on the accelerator. The very, very, very fast accelerator.

Kali looked down. There was some kind of access hatch beneath her feet and she bent and flipped it open, staggering back as a wave of velocity seemed to slam through the gap. The accelerator lay directly under the hatch, as she'd hoped, but there was no way she could drop onto it while it was in motion. Kali swallowed, watching it ram first one way and then the other, each transition marked with an almighty clang. Gods, it was fast – the moment in which it paused to change directions fleeting – and her timing would have to be perfect. She waited while it stopped once, twice, and on the third time dropped without hesitation, flattening herself and grabbing hold as tightly as she could before it started again.

Thankfully, the accelerator was layered with tiny ridges and these afforded Kali a better grip than she would otherwise have had. Even so when, a heartbeat later, the accelerator punched back into life, she was almost ripped from its surface like a leaf. Kali skidded backwards, grabbing at the ridges to slow herself, and heard herself screaming, partly in exhilaration, partly in shock. She felt her teeth bared, her cheeks flapping and the flesh of her face rippling against her skull as she was carried around the perimeter of the chamber at unimaginable speed, the room blurring. The ride was over almost in an instant, however, and Kali screamed again as she found herself flipped heels over head, her grip snatched away, skidding helplessly forward on her back. She had only a second to react and she clamped her fingers onto the ridges and, with a grunt, flipped herself over, grabbing them once again.

The accelerator punched itself in the opposite direction once more, and now Kali found herself travelling backwards, her bodysuit almost torn from her body. She suddenly hadn't a clue where in the chamber she was and, for a moment, nearly panicked. Then her eyes fixed on the central control platform, the only constant in an ever changing blur, and she kept her gaze trained on it, marking its position and the magnets around it each time the accelerator stopped. At least she was no longer being thrown, having splayed herself over the accelerator like a human limpet.

Kali had to endure another five of the sudden punches while she waited for the floating magnet to rotate into a position where she would be able to reach it. It was hellishly slow and, by the time it finally did come round, she felt as if she'd been locked in a stable with a rampaging bamfcat. She simply wanted to lie down and die. This was hardly the spot to do so, however. If she relaxed, even for a second, her only memorial would be a Kali Hooper shaped hole in the chamber wall which no living thing would ever see.

Kali rode the accelerator for what was hopefully the last time, slowly and very, very carefully lifting herself into a crouching position. With even her hair whipping at her, she was almost torn free before the accelerator even stopped – and in that position certainly would be when it did stop – but her plan was to make the leap between accelerator and magnet in the split second *before* it did, using the speed and angle to propel herself to the target. Despite her calculations, this was going to be a leap of faith and the last thing she needed was the sudden, dizzying pounding in her head. Kali didn't even have the strength to curse, and certainly not the strength to hold on any longer, so she simply allowed herself to be thrown into the air.

Impact with the magnet was, of course, potentially as lethal as impacting with the chamber wall, but somewhere within her throbbing world of pain Kali calculated just how much she needed to adjust her trajectory to lift herself above the magnet. It seemed to have worked because she wasn't staring at her own backside splattering the surface of her destination. She quickly scrabbled beneath her for the surface – all she was capable of doing, really – almost broke her fingers as they touched, and then grabbed. She was once again thrown head over heels, slamming hard onto her back, but roared with determination and clung on despite her arms being wrenched so hard she thought for a moment they'd been ripped off. Kali lay stunned for a second as the magnet rotated beneath her, her eyes beginning to bulge slightly, and groaned loudly.

Something tickled her feet. She looked up to see one of the spider machines poised over her legs, ready to sweep down with a blade that would have amputated them. *S*he was so thoroughly pitsed off that she just booted the maintenance machine off the magnet, sending it clattering into the abyss below.

More weary than she had ever felt, Kali picked herself up, waited for the slow rotation of the magnet to bring it into alignment with her destination and leaped.

She landed, at last, on the control platform and found herself among the collapsed remains of the soul-stripped who had been deployed there. She tried not to pay too much attention to them, to wonder who they might have *been*. She tipped their stiffened forms over the edge of the platform to tumble silently after the insect machine. Then she turned her attention to the control panel itself.

Oh hells.

Kali had lost count of the number of Old Race cryptograms, riddles, puzzles and traps she had been forced to decipher or solve in her time, but this one took the biscuit.

The panel was etched with a fine and impossibly intricate pattern of lines that glowed slightly and seemed to move, an optical illusion that didn't help her dizziness at all. The pattern was made up of circles, ellipses, ovals, plumes, radial spreads and whorls, all in various sizes and all overlapping. There were no other kinds of control mechanisms, buttons, levers or otherwise, and Kali felt her heart sink, wondering why for once, just farking once, the Old Races couldn't have designed something with a simple on/off switch.

Kali gazed at the panel woozily, and for a second thought she was about to make the task of deciphering the panel even more problematic by splattering thwack and kebab all over it. She swallowed the impulse down, however, and tried to ignore the pounding in her head. Each of the curving lines had to represent the line of a magnetic field, surely, so was it possible that somewhere in the pattern were also representations of what they affected? Working on that theory, she gradually began to discern three shapes that seemed static within the shifting of the etching, and guessed that these could be what she was looking for – the Engines themselves. The problem was that while the Faith had pinpointed the real locations of the Engines, their positions here, forming the three points of a triangle, seemed only symbolic, not relative to the sites they physically occupied. She was missing something, clearly – some term of reference that could relate how the magnetic fields interacted with the Engines in the real world – and without it she had no idea how they could be manipulated.

Suddenly, however, a thought struck her. Or rather, an image. She once again saw the map she had discovered in Redigor's tower – the one she had at first thought represented battle manoeuvres and had subsequently dismissed – and realised that it could be, after all, a vital piece of the jigsaw. If it *wasn't* battle manoeuvres it was illustrating, what if it were magnetic fields?

Kali once again shoved aside the pain in her head to concentrate hard, struggling to summon what she remembered of the map, its lines, and where they were positioned in relation to the coastline of the peninsula. She kept the image in her head and stared down at the control panel, trying to match up the slashes and curves. It seemed next to impossible, but she realised that all she really had to do was find the *first*. And there it was, a great sweeping line that ran from Scholten and across the Anclas Territories to grasp Miramas in its encompassing curve. Another ran across it, roughly paralleling the Territories themselves and was bisected by a third in the region of Andon. More of Redigor's smaller scrawls then became discernible, but they weren't really necessary. With their main counterparts identified, Kali was able to work out where on the control panel the coastlines of the peninsula lay, and with that knowledge the overall pattern laid out before her began to make a lot more sense. It really was quite ingenious the way every field of magnetic force affected every other across the whole landscape. What the dwarves might have accomplished had they survived could have been staggering. Now all Kali had to work out was how to ruin their achievement of a lifetime. To throw, as it were, a spanner in the works.

The problem was that there were still no visible controls and yet, clearly, the lines on the panel had to have been set somehow.

Experimentally, Kali moved her hand across the surface and nothing happened. She tried once more and still nothing. Then she looked up and realised that by looking at the control panel for changes to its settings she had been looking in the wrong place. Her gaze fixed ahead of her, she moved her hand experimentally once more, this time in a circle, and smiled as one of the magnets across the chamber rotated as it did, at exactly the same speed and for the same duration. She was onto something. Now all she had to do was work out how to get that magnet to interact with the others, from there determine how exactly they influenced the magnetic forces on the surface, and from there to determine a way to use them to disable the Engines.

For the first time in her life Kali began to regret dropping the moroddin lessons that Pete Two-Ties had once tried to thrust upon her, because the more she experimented with the controls the more she realised it was like playing some complex musical instrument. Still, she had to try.

Kali began to move her hands in a more relaxed manner, remembering Pete's words before she had aborted his teachings to *feel* the instrument in her hands, to let it be the guide, and as she did she found that she was gradually moving all of the magnets in the chamber at once, and not only that but managing to slow and speed up the accelerator as well. The whole process gave her an overwhelming feeling of power. If she weren't feeling so much like death, she might even have begun to enjoy herself.

The feel of the control panel much more familiar now, the magnets moving at her whim, Kali began to concentrate instead on the panel, which seemed to have warmed beneath her hands, so much so that she could feel the flesh of her palms beginning to tingle. Then she realised that it wasn't heat that was causing the sensation but the softest of magnetic pressures being emitted by the metal. As she moved her palms across its entire surface once more it was like moving them over a series of small, invisible hills and valleys – a miniature topography made of magnetism.

That was it!

Eager now, Kali placed her palms above the three spots that represented the positions of the Engines and there felt peaks of magnetic push far sharper than elsewhere on the etched map. As she began to gently manipulate them they actually began to soften in their resistance and began to *move*.

I have you now.

It would take a good deal of concentration and dexterity but, in theory, she should be able to move the Engines anywhere she wanted.

Kali set to work.

CHAPTER ELEVEN

Kali made the rendezvous that evening, helped along by three jumps from Horse, the last of which brought them atop an escarpment overlooking the dark border of the Sardenne. The forest stretched to the west and east as far as the eye could see, as did, about half a league back, the Final Faith cordon. Dotted by campfires along its vast length, it was as yet impossible to make out the individual figures waiting around them, but the numbers involved were staggering. Bolstered now by legions from both the Vossian and Pontaine militaries, the force represented the first time the two armies had come together since the Great War, and the first time ever that they had done so in peace. It was a reflection of the seriousness of the threat they faced. As Kali watched them from on high she felt almost like a party pooper knowing she had to tell them they had no choice but to stay their arms.

Her gaze rose into the azure twilight. As massive as the cordon was, the escarpment afforded a ringside view of something even more daunting – something now utterly unavoidable. The thick pillar of souls rising from deep within the Sardenne was now twice the height it had been when Kali had last seen it. A vertical maelstrom that swirled endlessly and chaotically and, whether it was her imagination or not, seemed to scream out at the darkening sky. Maybe the poor souls trapped within sensed their time was coming, Kali thought, because the pillar appeared, from her perspective, to be already piercing the outer layers of Kerberos, actually making contact with the gas giant itself. It wasn't – yet – but at the rate the pillar was growing she reckoned she'd been more or less bang on with the deadline she'd estimated.

Tomorrow was when it would happen.

Kali bit her lip and spurred Horse gently on, walking him down the hillside and to the perimeter of the central camp. Two Faith guards nodded in acknowledgement and parted to let her pass. She tethered Horse near a gathering of tents, clustered around a crackling campfire. A few acolytes were clustered around the fire, where Slowhand was fleecing them in a game of quagmire. By the look of his upturned cards, the archer had just stymied his opponents with a five-card plop and was raking in a handful of silver tenths.

"Hooper, how you doing?" He said casually as she approached. He nodded to the acolytes, a request for privacy, and they left shaking their heads and pulling less than pious faces.

"Oh, you know. Been introducing the pure of heart to the evils of gambling?"

Slowhand inclined his head to the east. "Didn't fancy a walk in the woods."

"Understandable." Kali sat herself down beside him and cracked open a bottle of thwack from her backpack, downing two thirds of it and heaving sigh.

"Introducing the pure of heart to the evils of drink?" Slowhand countered.

"Nope. It's all mine."

Slowhand smiled.

"Besides, there's no such thing as evil drink, only evil empty bottles." She took another swig and then upturned the one in her hand, scowling. "See."

"Rough couple of days?"

Kali shrugged. "No more than usual. Discovered Bastian Redigor is an elf, travelled a few thousand years into the past, give or take a teatime, almost got sliced apart by spectral hags, and then nearly turned into a doily by magnets the size of farking mountains."

"Right."

"Oh, and I had a kebab."

"Ooooh. There's that death wish again. But I take it the elf thing is what I should be paying attention to?"

Kali nodded. "I need to talk to the others."

"Well, Freel's patrolling the camp. Fitch is off somewhere, avoiding me. And Dez – sorry, *Gabriella* – is in her tent. I think she's... you know, the thing with the hands."

"Praying?"

"That's the one."

"For once, it might not do any harm. Which tent is she in?"

"The one behind you," DeZantez said. She was folding up a shnarlskin prayer mat as she exited, appearing casual, but by the look of her Kali had risen in her estimation for having returned. "Did I hear you say something about an *elf*?"

Kali stood. "I think you'd better get your people together."

Gabriella studied her, then nodded.

A few minutes later she, Freel, General McIntee, Fitch and assorted other senior officers were gathered in war council, listening to what Kali had to say. The relief of the magic users following their realisation that magic was, as it were, back on line, dissipated when Kali told them what she had discovered. There was almost universal silence, the only person to speak Gabriella DeZantez. And perhaps because what she heard conflicted so much with her own faith – everything she believed about the sanctity of souls and Kerberos – the only word she was able to utter was an incredulous, "What?"

"The return of the Ur'Raney," Kali said. "It's what the Pillar of Souls is for. To act as a conduit between Twilight and Kerberos, allowing the exchange of the human souls Redigor has taken with those of his dead elves. One for one, every one of his subjects reincarnated, right here, as an army, in the bodies of the soul-stripped."

"The bodies of farmers and their wives, their children?" General McIntee said doubtfully. "I do not see how they could pose much of a threat."

"I seem to remember them being pretty threatening under your cathedral," Slowhand countered. "To say nothing of the shit that's been hitting the fan everywhere else."

"Actually, the general's partly right, Liam. When the Ur'Raney inhabit the soul-stripped they will be alive again, and physically vulnerable as a result. But it's my guess that during whatever ritual Redigor is going to conduct he'll also transfer some of the *physical* essence of the Ur'Raney to alter the hosts." She turned to McIntee. "If I'm right, General, they'll be transformed, and you won't be facing farmers, their wives and their children, you'll be facing thousands of elven biomorphs."

"That's the bit I don't get," Slowhand said. "This necropolis you mentioned. It's got to be just bursting with pointy-eared stiffs, yes? So why doesn't Redigor just 'ritualise' the Ur'Raney back into their old bodies?"

"That, I don't know," Kali admitted. "Maybe it's just been too long."

Freel took a pensive breath. "You called them Redigor's 'subjects,'" he said. "Are you saying Redigor was some kind of elven king?"

"King, no. Lord, yes. The elves had no monarchy as such. What they did have were elven 'families' or courts – the Ur'Raney, Pras'Tir, Var'Karish and others – each autonomous but led by their Lord and twelve lieutenants who made up a kind of high council called the rannaat."

"Coincidence?" Gabriella pointed out. "The Anointed Lord and the other dignitaries who were taken by the soul-stripped?"

Kali nodded. "I think Redigor has them marked as hosts for his lieutenants."

"Except thirteen were taken," Freel pointed out. "Thirteen, not twelve."

"Yes, well," Kali said slowly.

She had her own theory on that particular discrepancy and her mind flashed back to the portrait in Redigor's tower. Makennon's resemblance to his one time *mu'sah'rin* must have seemed to him to be a gift from the gods or, at least, *his* gods.

Because, at one and the same time, the 'First Enemy' had the opportunity to behead the Final Faith of its leader *and* humiliate them in a way only the Ur'Raney knew how. The effort of reactivating the Engines of the Apocalypse might have been worth it to him for that alone.

"I think I can explain that," Kali continued carefully, considering the loyalties and sensitivities of the company she was in. "The Ur'Raney had little respect for the females of their court and I don't think Makennon has been taken to be one of his lieutenants."

"Then what?" Fitch queried.

"It's... difficult to explain. *Mu'sah'rin*. A kind of... submissive partner."

Slowhand almost coughed up his tonsils.

"Sorry," he said, after a moment.

The reactions from the others varied slightly. Freel took a second, then nodded. Fitch turned away to stare into the trees. Gabriella flared with anger and embarrassment. The only vocal reaction came from General McIntee.

"We order the advance immediately," he growled. "End this now."

"You can't," Kali said.

McIntee looked to the west and east, nodding to the ranks of soldiers and Swords of Dawn, and the mages amongst them. In an ever extending line in both directions, weapons were drawn and determined fists flared with fire, lightning and ice. "Oh, young lady, I assure you, we can."

"No!" Kali persisted, slapping a palm solidly on his chest as he moved to lead them. "That isn't what I mean."

The general halted, glaring. Freel stepped in to draw Kali's hand from his heaving chest, defusing the confrontation. "What *do* you mean, Miss Hooper?" He asked.

"Think about it, Freel," Kali said. "All along we've been assuming the soul-stripped are lost to us, dead, but if Redigor plans to use them as hosts for the souls of the Ur'Raney, there may be a way we can return the souls of our *own* people to their bodies."

Gabriella stared at the pillar of souls, thrusting into the night sky. "She's right, Enforcer. They haven't reached Kerberos yet."

Freel looked helplessly between the two women.

"Bring them back? Is such a thing possible?"

"Obviously Redigor thinks so," Kali said. "Right at this moment those soul-stripped are as much hostages as they are threat. Could you live with yourself if you at least didn't *try* to save them?"

"Madness," McIntee growled. "This might be our only chance!"

"You know what?" Kali shouted. "He's right. If Redigor manages to get his people into those bodies, they are going to march from the Sardenne and they are going to absolutely kick your arse. They drove an entire dwarven subrace to the point of extinction, for fark's sake. Clan Martak was helpless, utterly defeated, yet still they routed them, massacred them, drove those they couldn't kill into the sea to drown. Freel, your predecessor Munch himself told me - and believe me, that little bastard wasn't averse to a bit of carnage himself - they just never stop."

"We will hold them," McIntee insisted.

Kali slapped his chest again. "Are you *listening* to me? These elves were an Old Race who enjoyed rape, torture, pillage - even amongst their own kind. They sacrificed every tenth newborn to Yartresnika, their god of destruction. They added blood to their wine to make it *tastier*. Are you forgetting what happened when your lot first encountered The First Enemy? All you faced then was just one man. What happens when Redigor brings his friends to the party, eh? Thousands of them?"

"You seem to have defeated your own argument," Freel pointed out.

Kali shook her head. "Only if they're not stopped. Freel, let me ask you again - do you really want to slaughter thousands of your own, innocent people if it isn't necessary? Give me a chance."

"The girl was enlisted to shut down the Engines," McIntee said. "She's done that. Send her home."

"I was also 'enlisted' to save Makennon," Kali reminded him. "Let me try to do that. And the soul-stripped, too."

One at a time, Freel stared them in the eyes. His gaze, however settled on Kali.

"What if you fail?"

Kali faltered, swallowed. "Then you'd better hope your general here is as good as he thinks he is..."

"At least," Gabriella added after a moment, "you won't have the blood of your own on your hands."

Freel let out an exasperated sigh. The lives of thousands hung in the balance.

"What do you propose we do?"

"We go in as a strike team to find Makennon as planned. But with fifty mages and some Swords of Dawn, the best you have, as support. And while we're there, we do as much damage as possible to Redigor's ritual. Hopefully enough."

"Any ideas how?"

"One, but it's a long shot. I tend to work on the hoof."

Freel turned to Slowhand, the beginnings of an actual smile playing on his lips. "I heard a good way to deal with resurrectionists is to put an arrow in their head."

"Damn right," Kali and Slowhand said at the same time.

"There is one problem we still haven't resolved," Gabriella said. "If Fitch is right about the Pale Lord's eyes being everywhere, how do we bypass the soul-stripped?"

"With eyes of our own," Freel said. "I've already adapted an Eye of the Lord to make a low level reconnaissance and determine a safe, or at least safer, route through them."

"But wouldn't the Pale Lord still detect its presence?"

"I'm gambling his eyes can't be everywhere at once. There has to be some kind of trigger that opens them. Something *alive*, for example."

Kali nodded at Gabriella. "Makes sense. When can you send it in?"

"Right now. But before I do..."

Freel turned back to General McIntee, who seemed to have taken the reality of the situation facing his forces a little more on board. "Keep your people here," he instructed. "If this doesn't work, if we don't come back... just... do what you can do."

McIntee swallowed, and nodded. "Good luck, Sir." He turned to Kali, Slowhand, DeZantez – even Fitch. "Good luck to all of you."

The war council disbanded. Freel moved off to despatch the Eye of the Lord and, knowing once more that it would take some time to report its findings, to personally assign the mages and Swords Kali had requested. Slowhand decided to use the hiatus to fletch more of his special arrows and settled himself back before the campfire. Kali and Gabriella took up positions on the other side of the flames, giving him the room he needed to work. They sat in silence for a while, the Enlightened One regarding Kali carefully before she spoke.

"Why do you do it? What you do?"

Kali prodded the fire with her gutting knife, a fresh flare of flame illuminating her face. "What? You mean rub people up the wrong way?"

Gabriella smiled. "You know what I mean. Spend your life digging around in the dirt, trying to learn what's gone?"

"You admit finally that I was just looking for the Deathclaws? That I had nothing to do with the Engines?"

"Oh, I think you're pretty much off the hook. So why?"

Not so long ago Kali would have said to find out what happened to the Old Races. She hadn't yet even shared it with her friends, and she certainly wasn't ready to share it with DeZantez, but her goals had changed – to find out what had *killed* them, yes, but now also to find out what 'the Darkness' was.

"Urm, because they were there?" She said.

"And now they're not?"

"That's right. It's important I find out why."

Gabriella nodded, poked the fire again. "Did they leave much behind?"

Kali shrugged. "It varies from site to site. Most are empty shells, stripped by tomb raiders down the years, or by your mob, if they manage to beat me somewhere. But you're one of them, you should know that."

"I tend to avoid that side of the Faith's affairs. They... don't sit well with me."

Kali raised her eyebrows. She remembered their meeting outside Solnos, how she had felt that DeZantez was a lot like herself – following a calling, doing good, trying to help – but that somehow the world had changed beyond her control.

"The more inaccessible sites offer the occasional trinket," she continued. "And, every now and then, there's a special site that delivers something like the Deathclaws. Also those that promise much but usually – when you've worked your arse off for days trying to get into the thing – deliver bugger all. The Lost City of Fff, for one."

"The Lost City of Fff? You're making that up."

"I promise you, I'm not. Learned about it from the Followers of Fff at their annual Faff. Should have known better than to listen to people who Faff." Kali shook her head. "Treasures undreamed of, they told me..."

"And what did you find?"

"A chest full to the brim with crap."

Gabriella laughed, an actually quite embarrassing bass, guttural bellow, but the first genuine humour Kali had seen the Enlightened One display. Clearly, she needed the release that a little laughter brought but it soon faded, her smile dwindling until she wore her impenetrable mask of introspection once more. Her guard seemed to have lowered somewhat, though, and Kali couldn't resist asking the question that had been bothering her almost since they had met.

"The graveyard in Solnos," she said. "It's obvious you're not from the town but I got the impression there was –"

"His name was Erak Brand," Gabriella interrupted her. "He was the Enlightened One of Solnos before me. A kind, faithful man."

"You were close?"

"Erak and I were lovers. We were to marry."

"Gods, I'm sorry. What happened?"

Gabriella tensed and the stick she'd been about to throw onto the fire she snapped in half. "He was murdered. By a man named Dai Batsen."

"Why?"

"Batsen was a rogue shadowmage. A hireling of someone who didn't want us to discover an unsavoury truth."

"What truth?"

Gabriella let out an exasperated sigh that turned into a cracked, humourless laugh. "The truth is, I don't know. And now I doubt I'm ever going to find out..."

Kali frowned. "Rodrigo Kesar had something to do with this, didn't he? I saw your face back at Scholten when you learned he was dead."

Gabriella nodded. "And with him my chance to avenge Erak. May that bastard Kesar be burning in the hells."

Gabriella's cold ferocity took Kali aback, but more than that, it struck her that her companion meant exactly what she said. She wasn't speaking of the hells in any metaphorical sense, she was speaking of them as real places. It was clear she believed they existed as much as the Clouds of Kerberos floated above their heads. After what she had seen through the shard at the cathedral, it sent a shiver down her spine.

"Is there no other way you can find out what was behind Erak's death?"

Gabriella shook her head. "My position as Enlightened One of Solnos was only ever meant to be temporary. But I waited and waited and, as the months passed, no one came to replace me. Eventually I found out, from friends, that the Anointed Lord had arranged to have me watched – and then, simply, forgotten."

"You think Makennon was responsible?"

"I don't know. I don't think so. But I do know I seem to have little place in a changing Faith. I believed in their mission – *still believe* – to bring Ascension to the people, even if we have to purify some with fire. But after what happened to you with the Eyes of the Lord – seeing how they accused you and how they were *wrong* – I realised just how out of control they have become. The Faith threatens to become a dictatorship, ruling with an iron glove and I think something is rotten at its core."

"Can I take that as an apology for trying to burn me alive?"

"Kali –"

"Joke." Kali said. "But if you realise all of this, why are you still here?"

Gabriella stared at her as if the answer were obvious. "As a Sister of the Order of the Swords of Dawn, I remain sworn to protect the Anointed Lord."

"Now that's a joke, ri –" Kali began, but halted as Gabriella suddenly placed her palm on her forearm, beckoning silence.

At first she thought the Enlightened One had simply had enough of the subject but then saw that she was staring into the dark boundary of the forest, where Slowhand had wandered minutes before to collect wood to whittle into shafts. The archer seemed alone in the shadows but then she sensed another presence in the darkness, watching Slowhand from hiding. Kali stared at the spot, gradually discerning a shape, but she had difficulty making out what it was until there were two simultaneous flares about a foot and half apart at waist height. For a fleeting moment the flares illuminated curled palms, a dark-robed torso, and a white, cadaverous face, steadily regarding Slowhand with malignant intent.

"Fitch!" Kali said, starting to run. "One bastard who should never have got the magic back!"

Gabriella was up and by her side in an instant, the two of them pounding towards Slowhand, but the archer was hacking at vegetation, unable to hear their shouts. The fire in Fitch's palms, meanwhile, had transformed into crackling spheres of energy. As Kali and Gabriella watched helplessly, Fitch drew his palms back and threw the fireballs at the preoccupied archer. Luckily, Fitch's aim was slightly askew, and the fireballs impacted with a tree trunk next to Slowhand, knocking the archer off his feet. He scrabbled back in shock and raced towards his assailant, roaring as he recognised Fitch.

He suddenly stopped dead in his tracks and Kali saw the psychic manipulator smiling and weaving some distraction thread with one hand while nurturing a third fireball with the other. There was no question that this one would hit Slowhand full on and she and Gabriella were still too far away to do anything.

"You tackle Fitch!" Gabriella yelled, and then pounded toward Slowhand. Kali ran at the psychic manipulator along with Jakub

Freel, who had been alerted by the noise. As she watched the fireball grow all Kali could feel was the pounding of her heart, and the certain knowledge that the fireball was going to leave Fitch's hand before she or the enforcer reached him. She snatched a glance towards Gabriella and, like herself, the Enlightened One still had too much ground to cover.

Fitch launched the fireball and everything became dream-like and slow. Kali came to a faltering stop and tracked the crackling sphere of fire helplessly, her mouth falling open. As it passed the halfway mark between Fitch and Slowhand, she turned slightly, yelling to Gabriella to drive her onward. Ripping away her armour as she went, driven as much by momentum as muscle, Gabriella left the ground, throwing herself forward through the air, but it wasn't Slowhand she was throwing herself at, it was the fireball.

Enlightened One and fireball collided in mid-air and Gabriella DeZantez was consumed by the magic, disappearing inside an explosion of super-heated fire. The infernal heat it contained would, had she still been wearing it, have turned her armour red hot in an instant, roasting her inside, but with only her surplice she would likely suffer a quicker death than that. She had no chance of surviving, none at all, and so it came as something of a surprise to Kali when, as the fire blasted about Gabriella and then dissipated, the Enlightened One fell to the ground with her surplice burnt away, smoking and stunned, but otherwise apparently unharmed.

Slowhand looked about him in confusion. Fitch, meanwhile, stared at the recovering form of Gabriella DeZantez in disbelief. For his part, Jakub Freel covered the remaining ground between Fitch and himself where he flattened the psychic manipulator with a single punch to the face.

Kali turned her attention back to Slowhand. The archer had stripped off his shirt and was wrapping it about Gabriella as he lifted her slowly from the ground. The woman was clearly stunned, but there wasn't a mark on her, not a single blemish or burn. It was no time for questions, however, and Kali and Slowhand took Gabriella between them and slowly led her back to her tent. Slowhand paused mid-route and nodded to Freel.

"Thanks," he said.

"Don't mention it."

The Final Faith enforcer watched them depart with their charge. Neither of them noticed as, behind them, he hauled Fitch to his feet with one hand and roused him. Neither did they hear the words that passed between the enforcer and the cadaverous manipulator.

"I told you not to make a move," Freel said. "I told you that when the time comes, Killiam Slowhand is *mine*."

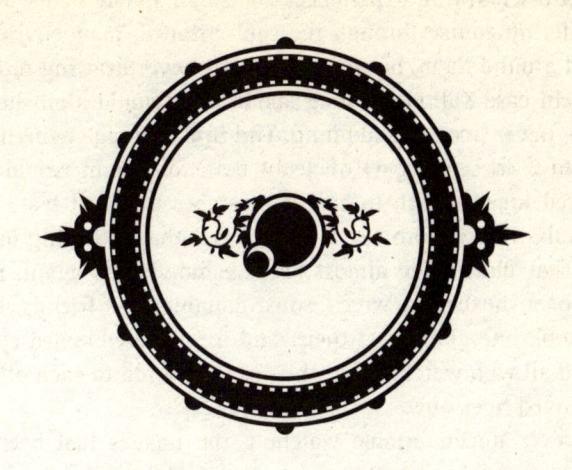

CHAPTER TWELVE

They entered the Sardenne at dawn, not that Twilight's distant sun ever made much difference in the heavily canopied forest. The first few yards of their ingress plunged them into shadow, the next few beyond that to a darkness equivalent to longnight, and with every step thereafter the ambient light lessened until, in parts, their surroundings were as black as a windowless room. To aid their progress, the mages in the party wove soft and subtle light threads that played about them like fireflies, not bright enough to attract unwanted attention but enough to make the individual members of the party aware of where they stepped and distinguishable from each other. Their beacon, albeit an ominous one, was the pillar of souls. The column of spiritual energy continued to grow, and offered a continuous reminder of why they were treading such dangerous ground.

They were amidst the soul-stripped now and followed the route that the Eye of the Lord had suggested was safest, though watching the images the device had returned to them had still been a discomfiting experience. The small sphere had woven a meandering course through the soul-stripped, manoeuvring up to and around them, between them, but never drawing too near and – in case Kali was wrong about what would alert the Pale Lord – never lingering too long. The Eye's passage nevertheless allowed it to see a level of detail that no human would have survived long enough to absorb, snatches of facial features of the soul-stripped – an ear, a nose, a mouth, a dangling lock of hair. That close, they almost became individuals again, might have been husbands, wives, sons, daughters or friends, but it only took one glimpse of their rigid forms or whitened eyes to remind all who watched that they were nothing to each other or their loved ones now.

However uncomfortable watching the images had been, the party's progression along the route mapped by the Eye was worse.

They moved in silence and almost in single file. Every breath, every footfall brought with it a palpable sense of fear. It seemed that each piece of tinder that snapped beneath a boot, each branch disturbed, would alert the soul-stripped, and that it was only a matter of time before one of them turned its gaze toward them. As a result, Kali moved everyone forward with great caution.

It had fallen to her – as one of the few, and certainly the only member of the current party to have ventured deep into the Sardenne and survived – to take point and in that role she had advised them of a few of the realities of the sprawling, ancient domain. The most important was that the soul-stripped were not the only things to be afraid of. The further they progressed into the forest the stranger and more dangerous the threats they might face. She had allocated everyone some floprat render, the olfactory camouflage she found worked best within the Sardenne, but some, the Swords particularly, wore the foul smelling substance awkwardly, as if they thought she was playing some practical joke at their expense. Kali's sincere hope was that they didn't have to find out otherwise. Familiar with the Sardenne's unnatural menagerie first hand, she doubted that any of the men or women present would believe her if she tried to describe some of the things she'd seen, so she didn't bother.

Oddly enough, though, there were none of the hisses, caws, growls, rumbles, rattles or shrieks from the surrounding undergrowth that she would normally expect to hear. She wondered whether the presence of the soul-stripped, or the aura of Redigor, had actually done their party a favour, driving the wildlife deeper into the forest and leaving the path ahead of them clear. They would only know the truth as they forged deeper.

Though their passage through the soul-stripped was tortuous and took some hours they miraculously avoided detection, reaching a point at last where the Pale Lord's puppets thinned. Soon after, they had passed beyond them completely.

It was at this stage that Kali instigated the second part of her plan to negotiate the Sardenne successfully. Her main reason for including the mages in the party was not for them to help tackle Redigor – five *hundred*, not fifty, would have been nearer the mark for that – but because she knew they did not have time on their side. Travelling in a normal fashion, it would take days to reach Bel'A'Gon'Shri, and the pillar of souls would have touched Kerberos long before that. But by using the mages to generate portals – effectively *teleporting* their way through the forest – they could reduce a journey of days to one of hours.

The ploy was not without its logistical problems, however. For one thing, the effort and energies involved meant that the mages would have to work in turns, and would only be able to move them a league or two at a time. For another, they would be teleporting blind. It was the reason they could not use the same technique to bypass the soul-stripped – the last thing Kali wanted was to materialise in the middle of a mass of them – and they could only hope that more of them, or other hidden hazards, did not lie ahead.

Slowhand looked uneasy as the first wave of mages began to weave the threads. They were helpless to sudden attack from the forest while the weaving took place, so the Swords stood vigilant around them.

"You've done this before?" The archer said to Kali.

"Sure. The old man and I travelled from Gargas to Andon during the k'nid invasion. It's what gave me the idea."

"And you arrived okay? I mean with... all your bits?"

"My bits? Gods and hells, Liam, is that all you ever think about?"

"*Did* you?"

"Of course I did! Stinking pits, I would have thought you'd have noticed by now!"

Slowhand faltered. "Oh. Right. Yes. They seemed okay."

"*Okay?*"

"Dammit, Hooper, you know what I mean!"

Before them, the mages had completed their weaving and the portal had formed, a shimmering circle that flared outward briefly before just hanging in the air a few inches off the ground. Slowhand swallowed as, with a distinct squelching sound, Jakub Freel stepped into it and vanished. DeZantez, Fitch and the ranks of the mages and Swords followed.

"Our turn," Kali said. "Want me to hold your hand?"

"I don't think so," Slowhand answered through gritted teeth. "Much as I love you, Hooper, I don't want us spending the rest of eternity as some three-handed, twenty-fingered *thing*."

"Be a bit more optimistic. We might end up joined at the groin."

"Yeah?"

"Dammit, we are *not* going to end up either way, okay?" Kali said, but Slowhand still seemed unconvinced. "Fine then. Go by yourself."

"If we end up on a different planet..."

Kali had had enough, and pushed him through the portal. She materialised beside the archer a second later, turning away quickly when she saw him looking down and squeezing himself unashamedly. She looked up; the pillar of souls was considerably closer. The portal had worked.

Spurred by their success, another portal followed, and another, and another after that, by which time the party had progressed so far into the Sardenne that Kali was certain she could smell the faint tang of the long burnt-out shell of the Spiral of Kos. The forest felt different from when she'd fled the explosions that had destroyed the Old Race site, however, wildlife still conspicuously absent. What had been a vital, if life-threatening, region of the forest back then now felt abandoned, as if every participant of its predatorial food chain had deferred to a far greater appetite and retreated into caves and broad burrows, or beneath large stones. Even those creatures who hunted not for food but fun had disappeared. The worst thing was, Kali sensed it was neither the soul-stripped or Redigor that had caused this, but something else.

She had to admit to being quite relieved when Gabriella DeZantez joined her at the front of the ranks. The Enlightened One was fully armoured once more and recovered from Fitch's attack. They walked together in silence for a while, but then Kali found herself broaching a subject that just had to be broached.

"That fireball thing last night. You feel like telling me what *that* was about?"

"I wondered how long it would take you to ask."

"Well, hey, a fireball brushed off as easily as a nibble from a worgle? People tend to notice such things."

"Does anyone ever interrogate you about the things you can do?"

"Things?"

I saw you in action in the library, remember? And some of the eye witness accounts of your exploits in your file – well, let's just say they raised eyebrows."

Kali faltered. "Generally I try not to show off."

"Show off what?"

"I wish I knew."

Gabriella seemed genuinely surprised. "You don't know?"

"Hells, no."

"And yet you always seem to show up where your abilities are most useful. Almost as if it were –"

"Don't say it," Kali interrupted. "Predestined? Well, if it is, I wish to gods someone would tell me, because believe me, all I do is make it up as I go along."

The two of them lapsed into silence again. But only briefly.

"It's happened before," Gabriella admitted. "In Solnos. A fireball full in the face and... and nothing. There was another time, too, when I was a child, in some ruins south of Andon. We... that is, my friends and I, used to play there."

Kali's eyebrows rose. "The Seventeen Steps? Every level is an inaccessible deathtrap."

Gabriella nodded. "Because of the Dust Curtains."

"So named because they strip to the bones anyone who comes within fifty feet. I've been trying to crack them for two years."

"Not me."

"I'm sorry?"

"The Dust Curtains. I walked right through them." Gabriella took a slow breath. "My friends didn't react well to that and it wasn't long after I signed up for the Swords of Dawn."

Kali felt her heart thud. After all her efforts, all she *should* have wanted to ask was what lay beyond the Dust Curtains but what DeZantez had just admitted to her was a revelation that made the secrets of the Seventeen Steps utterly insignificant. She turned to face Gabriella, and grabbed her by the shoulders.

"Are you trying to tell me you're immune to magic?"

Gabriella swallowed. "I guess I am."

"Hells."

"*Hells?* That's all you have to say?"

"What do you expect me to say or do?" Kali hissed. "Abandon you like your friends – turn you into some kind of freak, outcast, pariah? We're more alike than that, remember?"

Gabriella stared at her, then nodded. "And I'm not sure we're the only ones."

"What?"

Gabriella sighed, but it seemed a relieved sigh because she could finally talk to someone about what she knew. "I told you I sneaked a look at your file in the Faith record but what I didn't tell you was that next to it I found one on me too. And two others."

"What the hells are you talking about?"

"Two other files, each relating in some detail the strange abilities of their owners. A thief based in Turnitia, by the name of Lucius Kane. And another, a mariner called Silus Morlader."

"Kane?" Kali said. "I met him. He was something more than your average thief."

"Exactly. And from what I read, this Silus isn't your average fisherman, either. You heard anything about him?"

Kali shook her head.

"Apparently, he now commands a ship by the name of the *Llothriall*. A ship stolen from the Final Faith. What's more, the *Llothriall* is an –"

"Elven ship," Kali finished.

Gabriella shrugged. "I suppose the clue's in the name."

"Not really. I found the plans for it." Kali sighed. "This world gets smaller every day."

"I don't understand."

Kali paused. "What if I told you that a year or so ago I had an encounter with something beneath the waves? Some form of water dweller, who spoke to me in my head. Mind to mind."

"Water dweller?" Gabriella said.

"Water dweller," Kali repeated. "Most of what it said was couched in riddles, about it being part of the Before, the After. But it also spoke about a group of people known as 'the four'."

"The Four?"

"'Four known to us. Four unknown to each other. Four who will be known to all.' That was what it said."

"And you know what that means?"

"Haven't the remotest idea. But it's one pretty big coincidence, don't you think?" Kali paused, frowned. Despite her reservations about discussing the subject with Gabriella, the situation had clearly changed and she deserved to know something more. "In fact, it's two."

"Two?"

"Tharnak, the dwelf creature I encountered in the Crucible, also spoke of 'four.' In his case, of four humans who were being prepared to travel to Kerberos – alive, that is."

"In that ship you found? But why?"

"To save the world, I think. The point is, these four had been changed, altered, somehow physically manipulated so they could survive the journey. Their abilities had been *enhanced*."

"Surely you're not suggesting..."

"Gabriella, I'm not sure what I'm suggesting – but what I *know* is the Faith is keeping files on you, me, and two others. Four. The question is, why?"

The Enlightened One was silent for a second, then said, "Maybe the person who holds the halo versions of the files has the answer."

"Halo versions?"

"Faith security classification. Halo files contain additional information. More *sensitive* information. The locations, for example, of supporting physical evidence on their subjects."

"Who has these files, do you know?"

Gabriella nodded. "But you're not going to like it when I tell you."

"*Who?*"

"Querilous Fitch."

Kali stopped dead. Without a word, she turned and began to push her way back through the ranks to where Fitch, avoiding Slowhand, trailed at their end. Gabriella followed, ignoring the confusion on the faces of the archer, Freel and others who had been pushed aside, catching up to Kali as she neared the psychic manipulator.

"Lord of All, we're in the middle of the *Sardenne*. Are you always this impulsive?"

"Yes."

Kali was almost in Fitch's face now, his features all the more gaunt in the wan light. He started slightly but smiled coldly, as if knowing what Kali had just learned and knowing, too, that he held all the cards.

"You –" Kali was about to say, "have got some farking explaining to do!"

But she had barely formed the first word when a massive shape swung into view between them, brushing by her and Gabriella and dashing them to the ground. Fitch was not so fortunate. Struck full on, his cadaverous form was sent hurtling away through the trees with a shrill scream – gone, just like that.

Kali and Gabriella scrambled to their feet, trying to adopt a defensive position, although they had no clue what they were defending against. As they did, the shape swung again, and they ducked. Whatever the hells was coming at them, it was huge; the Swords charging, weapons drawn, into its path had no chance against it. Kali heard the crunch of metal and bone and dimly registered their broken forms flying into the undergrowth. She and Gabriella stared at each other, horrified, and rushed for cover. Others nearby were not so well practiced and, as the massive shape swung back for a third pass, another four Swords shrieked as they were knocked away by the impact.

"What in the name of the Lord of All?" Gabriella breathed, and a great, primal roar erupted from the darkness above them, sending those below into a panic, colliding with each other or freezing on the spot.

Kali wanted to shout to them to *move, move, move*, but she was desperately trying to process what it was they were dealing with. She remembered many things about her last visit to the Sardenne, but none were stamped quite so indelibly on her mind as the one she was remembering now.

It had occurred during her desperate flight from the Spiral of Kos when, with vast swathes of the forest lit by the detonations behind her, the creatures who dwelled within had flocked to her. As she and Horse, bless his bacon-lardon-loving heart, had galloped towards safety, they had been assailed by the full spectrum of nightmares that called the forest home, wooden things and armoured things, things of bone and of things of blood, things of moss and mud and stone. But there had been one creature, felt more than seen – a giant fist, registered fleetingly as Horse pounded along, swinging down at them from behind the trees. It had impacted with the forest floor with such force that Horse had momentarily lost his footing and she'd almost been thrown from his back. Naturally, they hadn't lingered to meet its owner, and Kali had no idea of what kind of creature it was, but it had to be the same creature that was attacking their party now.

"Move, move, move!" Kali shouted, but the command would do their ranks little good.

She stared up into the trees, trying to make out the creature that was attacking, but could see little. In truth, she didn't really *need* to see it. It was obvious that for every hundred yards their people could run, a single stride would bring their attacker back into reach. Gabriella DeZantez made the same assessment and unsheathed the Deathclaws in a determined, if futile, attempt to defend herself.

Nor was she the only one. Amongst the group – most of whom were torn between running or standing their ground and fighting – she saw Slowhand flip Suresight from his back and unleash a volley of arrows into the trees above, and Freel snap his whip from his side, eyes narrowed, scanning for a target. Some of the Swords, who had at last pulled themselves together, unsheathed their weapons as the mages unleashed bolts of fire or ice or lightning. Many still panicked or blundered around. The attack had come so suddenly, so unexpectedly, that with the first swing their battle readiness had been reduced to a complete and utter shambles.

The fist returned, and while the soldiers were ready for it, throwing themselves out of its path in a clattering of weapons and armour, a second fist slammed down on the spot where they moved. There was an explosion of weaponry, bone and gore and the unfortunates were crushed like bugs. Now the creature's feet pummelled the ground too, stomping onto a growing carpet of crushed bodies. The survivors were not idle, however, Slowhand having fired at least twenty arrows into one of the feet as soon as it appeared, and Freel having lashed out at the wrist of one of the hands with his whip. Neither seemed particularly effective, though. Freel found himself being swung through the trees as the creature tried to rid itself of his weapon. Gabriella, too, was moving, racing at the behemoth to slash at its exposed flesh with the claws, using the corpse of a soldier as a springboard to launch herself into the air, twisting her body as she flew to slash through a briefly exposed forearm and bring forth a rain of blood.

Green blood, Kali noted with horror.

Few creatures that had ever stalked the peninsula had green blood, and there was only one that she knew of that was this size, and it had been extinct as long as the Old Races, primarily because it had been *created* by one of the Old Races and used as their pet. *Gods,* she thought, could that be what they were dealing with here – an elven juggennath? Had it somehow survived here in the Sardenne for all of those countless years? The juggennath was a relentless, all-but-indestructable killing machine without emotion or mercy, and it absolutely would not stop in its efforts to crush them beneath it. They had to get out of here and right now.

It was easier said than done and Kali had difficulty reaching those she needed to warn.

The wound inflicted by Gabriella seemed to have opened an artery in the giant's arm – serious but not serious enough, apparently, to slow the bastard down – and as it swept back and forth once more, its blood soaked the vegetation and defending ranks, obfuscating and adding to the chaos and carnage unfolding before her eyes. DeZantez wasn't to have known but one of the more unpleasant aspects of juggennath blood was its corrosive nature, burning and mutilating those it struck. Kali could do little to help those caught in the heat of battle, but grabbed those she could and flung them towards cover. She shrank back from a soldier who wheeled on her, clutching his face, smoke pouring from his helmet as he collapsed to his knees.

"Liam!" Kali cried, "DeZantez, Freel!"

No response came and, having rescued all those she could, Kali leapt into the fray herself, aware of how pitiful her gutting knife was. All she could hear was the shattering of limbs, the clatter of blades and arrows. But despite all these efforts, there was no respite in the assault at all.

A cry of frustration drew her attention. Gabriella was attempting to pull an injured Sword out of harm's way, and was too preoccupied to notice the giant hand swinging towards her. In the instant before it struck, however, she saw Kali racing to help her, and for the briefest of moments their eyes locked.

Thanks for trying, DeZantez's expression seemed to say.

Kali felt each impact of her feet as they thudded onto the forest floor, her legs dragging beneath her, bringing her to a skittering halt, and as a cloud of leaves thrust up in her path she could only cry out and look on in horror at what unfolded.

Gabriella had turned slightly, attempting to throw herself away, but it simply wasn't enough, and the juggernnath's swipe caught her on the side. The cracking of bones echoed in Kali's ears like the shattering of wood. As Gabriella was hurled into the air, Kali heard her armour crumple beneath her surplice. She sailed towards the edge of the glade and slammed into the base of a tree. The Enlightened One's body crumpled, folding into a grotesque distortion of the human form.

At that point, at last, things seemed to quieten. The ground shook as their attacker retreated into the forest, and the frantic sounds of battle were replaced by the wails and pleas of the injured or dying.

Kali looked slowly around. Though there was no sign of Slowhand or Freel. Gabriella remained where she had fallen and Kali moved to try to help her. The last thing she remembered before rough hands bundled her away was Gabriella's face, blood trailing from her mouth, staring at her once more.

But this time the Enlightened One's head lolled to the side and her eyes grew dim.

CHAPTER THIRTEEN

Godsdammit, godsdammit, godsdammit!

Kali hunched in the roots of the bajijal tree, hugging her knees, sucking in deep breaths. She ignored the look from Jakub Freel, the only other survivor of the assault and the one who'd pulled her from the melee. Now here they were beneath this overgrown pot plant – hiding, dammit, *hiding* – and while Freel's look was concerned rather than accusing, as far as Kali was concerned it didn't matter an ogur's turd. The Faith enforcer had enlisted her to help him sort out this whole mess and instead she'd managed to turn it into even more of a mess, and people were dead as a result. There was no two ways about it. Freel had put his trust in her and she'd farked up badly.

Pits, she had been *stupid*. Fitch, Gabriella and, gods knew, even Slowhand. How many had died in the last hour? How many more lay maimed in the undergrowth, never to be found again or, worse, found by something they couldn't imagine in their darkest nightmares? Gods, she had become embroiled in this whole affair because, for just a while, she had wanted to forget about how she'd endangered the lives of Dolorosa, Aldrededor and the rest, and now she hadn't just endangered lives but *ended* them. Oh yeah, 'stupid' was the word. Stupid to expose the uninitiated to the Sardenne. Stupid to have become self-obsessed and let her guard down. Stupid to have thought she could even start to second guess an elven psychopath who had been preparing for these moments since the towering trees about her were striplings.

"Your friend the archer said there is usually a moment like this." Jakub Freel said.

"What?" Kali asked, without much interest.

"Crisis. Doubt. A stage in every one of your adventures when you feel you have failed and let down all who placed trust in you. A moment when you freeze, impotent, scared, feeling like a lost little girl..."

Kali flinched, Freel's words hitting close to home, but looked up indignantly.

"Slowhand's been *talking* about me?"

"I asked him whether he thought you were truly capable of doing this. He answered."

Kali bridled. "You sought me out. I guess you must think so."

"Oh, I do. But it isn't what I think – it's what your *friends* think."

"Slowhand might be dead, for all I know. Does it matter anymore what he thinks?"

"I think so. Especially when he says that *after* moments like these you invariably pick yourself up, dust yourself down and... make it up as you go along."

"Make it up as I go along," Kali repeated, looking to the skies. "Not a phrase that inspires much confidence today, is it?"

"Maybe not. But doing so, I am told you almost always succeed." Freel sighed. "Tell me, Miss Hooper, are you going to make a liar out of your friend?"

Kali stared at him. *What is it about this man?* She wondered. She'd seen from the start how different he was to Konstantin Munch, but it was more than just the way in which he approached the job he'd inherited. There was a confidence about him, a way with words, a bearing that made him difficult to dismiss. In a way she wasn't surprised that Slowhand had opened up the way he had.

"Are you playing mind games with me?"

"Is it working?"

Kali bit her lip. Things so far had gone badly against plan, but there were always other possibilities that might yet succeed, and didn't she owe it to the dead to see if they did?

"Freel, do you truly understand what we're up against? Things could get ugly."

"Miss Hooper, 'ugly' is my middle name."

Kali laughed, despite herself. "That sounds just like something Slowhand would say."

"Maybe he and I are more alike than you think."

"Opposite sides of the same coin?"

"Precisely."

Kali raised her eyes to Freel's, half expecting to see a smile. But if there had been one, it had already faded. Her gaze returned to the enforcer's hand, and she drew in a deep, shuddering breath, and then slapped her palm solidly into his, allowing herself to be hauled to her feet.

"For Slowhand," she said.

Kali and Freel were no sooner upright than they froze again. While they had been talking, a number of shapes had detached from the roots around them, Kali didn't need to hear the dry cracking of their joints to recognise some of the forest's nastier progeny. Her heart lurched as the stick-like predators unfolded, drawing themselves up to their full height, and the cracking came, like the breaking of baby's bones, from six of them in all.

"What in the name of the Lord...?" Freel breathed.

"They're called brackan," Kali said. "They're tough, fast and –"

Kali didn't finish. Three of the brackan hurled themselves at her and three at Freel, though one was instantly decapitated by his chain whip. As its body flailed blindly in the confines of the bajijal roots, the enforcer yelled at Kali to duck and spun in a full circle, scything over Kali's head and slicing two more of the brackan in half. The remaining brackan slammed into the pair of them, flattening them to the ground. Kali and Freel struggled beneath the creatures, rolling from side to side to dodge their sharp, pointed, jabbing limbs, and trying to ignore the fact that the brackan Freel had already incapacitated were even now splintering and regrowing.

"You were trying to say?" Freel growled.

"A pain in the arse," Kali growled back. She stabbed at her attacker with her gutting knife.

"Not much help," Freel went on. He gasped in pain as the brackan broke through his defence, gouging a thick red runnel down his cheek. "They must have a weakness!"

"Oh, they do, they do," Kali gasped. "Unfortunately, we're a little out of –"

"Fire?" A voice said.

Two flaming arrows thudded into the backs of the brackan and suddenly the things rolled over, desperately defending. Not that it did much good, their panicked flailing setting fire to the others in turn, transforming all of them into thrashing torches. Kali and Freel booted the brackan off them and backed out of the bajijal roots, soot-streaked but otherwise unharmed. Their weapons remained cautiously trained but the brackan began to break apart, collapsing into a pile of burning wood. Kali and Freel watched as a dishevelled, tall, blond figure walked to the fire's side, sat, and casually began to roast a chunk of meat skewered on the end of a dagger.

"Hells of a morning," Killiam Slowhand said.

"Nice shots," Kali responded. "Is that *breakfast*?"

"Mmm. How you doing, Hooper?" As an afterthought, he added, "Freel."

Jakub Freel waved away the offer of a piece of meat which Kali then took and devoured.

"You two don't seem particularly shocked to see each other," he commented.

"Oh, you'd be surprised how we keep popping up together."

Freel's expression became more serious. "Other survivors?"

Slowhand looked up, swallowed, and shook his head slowly.

The gesture might have seemed casual but there was pain in the archer's expression.

"Guess it's time for Plan B, huh?" Slowhand said.

"Plan B," Kali said. "The three of us finish the job ourselves."

She stared up through the dense forest canopy, which, while it defeated most attempts by daylight to brighten the murk, could not fully obscure the brilliance of the pillar of souls as it lanced into the sky.

"We're close enough to the necropolis to make it without portals now," Freel observed. "But we still have a journey ahead of us."

Slowhand stood and snuffed the remains of the brackan with his boot. "Then the sooner we get started..."

They moved on into the forest, trying not to think of the dead they were leaving behind. For some hours they worked their way through the treacherous terrain, which grew still denser as they neared the necropolis. The vegetation was changing, from the vines and sub-tropical plants Kali associated with the Sardenne to thick patches of dry scrub and coarse, thorny bushes. They felt wrong somehow, tainted, and the further they moved, the more hostile the plants became, until at last there was little doubt that they formed a defensive barrier around Bel'A'Gon'Shri, likely conjured by Redigor himself. As Kali and the others hacked their way through she reflected that the Pale Lord had missed at least one trick by not infusing the vicious barbs with poison. Still, knowing that bastard, she supposed there was time yet.

Kali approached Slowhand and spoke quietly.

"What were you doing, talking about me to Freel?"

Slowhand looked surprised. In truth – considering what had happened on the train and all – he wasn't really sure.

"What? Hey, it was a trek, Hooper, and you and Dez were busy with girly talk."

"*Girly talk?*"

Slowhand nodded. "Nothing wrong with that. Nice to see you making a friend." He paused, smile fading. "Kal, I'm sorry she didn't make it."

"Me, too. Don't change the subject."

"What is the problem? I'm willing to bet you talk about me, don't you? Don't you?"

"Actually, no. What would I tell people? About the collection of underknicks pinned to your bedroom ceiling? Or how a girl would be lucky to get through a first date without your clothes falling off?"

"Hey, I took the underknicks down, didn't I?"

"*Pshyeah*. And then kept them labelled in a drawer. How *was* Luci Lastic, by the way? Or Nikola Start? Those *were* their names, ri –"

Slowhand suddenly slapped his palm over Kali's mouth, and her eyes widened in shock and rage. She was about to pull free, demand to know why it was she couldn't get a *full farking sentence* out today, when the archer nodded between thorn bushes, at a feral shape moving towards them fast.

Breaking apart, he and Kali readied bow and knife while Freel dashed into cover, his whip to hand.

A second passed and something wild-eyed, torn and filthy burst into view. But rather than some slavering denizen of the Sardenne, it was human. Garbed in the shredded remnants of a green robe and considerably older than any of their party, however, he wasn't one of their own.

The man collapsed at Kali's feet. "Help me. Lord of All, help me, please."

"Where the hells did you come from?" Freel breathed.

"The Lord... the Pale Lord," the man gasped, pointing back through the thorns.

"Easy," Kali said, kneeling. "You've come from the Pale Lord?"

The man nodded, taking slugs of water from a skin Kali handed him. As he drank, Freel studied him warily. The man was terrified, but beneath the dirt and sweat he was well-groomed. He did not belong in the Sardenne.

"Be careful," Freel suggested. "This could be Redigor's doing."

"No, wait a minute, I know this guy," Slowhand said. "We've met before."

"Before?" Freel queried.

"It doesn't matter where."

"*Yes, it does.*"

"Fine. In court, if you must know. He gaoled me for a longnight for... well, let's just say I know what colour sheets cover a lot of beds in Kroog-Martra." He stared at Kali. "And before you say a word, Hooper, it was a bet and I had no *time* to collect their underknicks, okay?"

Kali gave Slowhand a weary shake of the head. "This is the magistrate of Kroog-Martra?"

"Yeah. A magistrate in the middle of the Sardenne. A fat lot of use he's going to be."

"Liam, hang on. If you're right, this guy is one of the twelve taken for Redigor's High Council. He might know something about what we can expect at Bel'A'Gon'Shri." Kali took the magistrate by his shoulders, forcing him to look at her. "How and why are you here? Did you escape? Did you escape the necropolis?"

"Kroog-Martra was attacked. By things hardly alive. Something came. A coach as black as night. Brought me to that place. Oh, Lord of All, that *place*..."

"Hey, *m'lud!*" Slowhand pressed. "The lady knows that, okay? You maybe wanna cut the pie and get to the meat?"

"In the depths," the magistrate went on. "Tombs. Vast, cold tombs. There they lie, still. The elves." He struggled in Kali's grip, remembering, suddenly desperate to get away. "But they're coming back. Lord of All, they're coming back!"

Freel strode to the magistrate and gripped him by the head. "*How did you escape?*"

"The Anointed Lord," the magistrate said, flinching. "She was taken with myself, the others. The Pale Lord took something from us, everything seemed like a dream, a nightmare. But the Anointed Lord she fought him... she was defiant... she was *strong*."

"Makennon escaped with you?" Kali asked.

"Makennon?" The magistrate repeated, and shook his head. "No, no. But while the Pale Lord fought to bring her under his control, I felt his magic weaken. Not much... not much at all... but enough for me to run, to flee the Chapel of Screams."

"The Chapel of *Screams*?" Slowhand repeated "Oh, the day just keeps getting better and better."

Kali sighed, looked up at Freel. "I think he's telling the truth."

Freel nodded. "The Chapel of Screams sounds like where the ritual is going to take place."

"The ritual," the magistrate said. "Yes, yes, the ritu –"

He stopped abruptly, eyes widening with fear. The forest had begun to resonate with a slow, bass tolling.

"The ritual begins," the magistrate said. "The Time of the Bell."

"Time of the Bell?"

"The *summoning*."

Freel snapped Kali a look. "Does that mean we're too late?"

Kali bit her lip. "I doubt it," she said, although in truth she wasn't really sure.

The magistrate had said *it begins*, and if her calculations were correct they had some hours yet, so likely the Bell was only the start of a ritual they should yet be able to stop. She was about to question the magistrate further when he at last managed to break from their grip and run. Slowhand leapt after him, but halted as he saw countless soul-stripped heading towards him. Slowhand, Kali and Freel stared at the approaching horde open-mouthed, as they passed through the thorns – and through *them*, too – insubstantial and translucent, leaving them with a feeling that somebody had walked over their graves.

"What's happening to them?" Freel asked. "They're like ghosts."

Kali had wondered how Redigor intended to bring the soul-stripped to Bel'A'Gon'Shri across the sprawl of the Sardenne. And now that she knew, she didn't like it one bit.

"He's using a different plane of existence to phase them to the necropolis," she said.

"But if he has the power to do that, with such numbers?" Freel calculated. He did not need to voice the next question for Kali to answer.

"Once he brings his people back, he can send them anywhere, right across the peninsula."

Freel kicked a tree-root. "The bastard's one step ahead of us all the time! Tricked us into forming a line at the Sardenne. And for nothing. Miramas, Volonne, Andon, Fayence, and Vos beyond – they're all but defenceless. We'll never make it back in time."

"Then we'd better make sure we get to Redigor in time," Kali said.

Slowhand and Freel stared as she stepped into the stream of spectral figures and, absorbed by the mist-like cloud wreathing the figures, began to walk amongst them.

"Hooper, what the hells are you doing?"

"Going along for the ride. Can you think of a better way of getting where we want to go?"

Freel smiled and joined her. "This, I take it, is the 'making things up as you go along'?"

"Aha. But be careful. We'll be in direct contact with the Pale Lord and he could sense us, so try to empty your mind."

The pair concentrated while Slowhand, too, stepped into the stream.

"Empty your mind, Liam."

"Done."

"What?"

"Mind. Empty. Done it."

"Are you taking the pits?"

"Hooper, I'm *ready*, okay. Now are we doing this thing or not?"

They did the thing, now reduced to phantasms, staring at each other in wonder as they moved. Whole swathes of the Sardenne, including the thorn barrier, passed in instant blur as they, along with all the soul-stripped who had no choice in the matter, were drawn ever closer to Bel'A'Gon'Shri.

Redigor's enchantment did not take them right to the necropolis's door, however, but to a deep, creeper-lined gorge on the approach to it, and there the soul-stripped began to return to corporeality. As they did, some turned to stare curiously at Kali, Slowhand and Freel.

"Redigor's getting his eyes back," Kali warned.

"Then it's time to break ranks," Freel said.

Kali and Slowhand trailed the Faith enforcer as he walked to the side of the gorge and took cover behind a dense wall of creeper. From there, the three of them watched the soul-stripped file in, emerging only when all of them had finally passed by. Then, after waiting a few more seconds, they followed some distance behind.

"Oh, crap," Slowhand said.

Freel stared. "Lord of All."

Carved out of the gorge's end, soaring above them, was the entrance to Bel'A'Gon'Shri. A threshold of utter blackness punctuated only by the occasional circling, cawing shrike. It wasn't the entrance itself that was disturbing but what surrounded it. Angled away from her, rising up on either side of the blackness to the twin horns tolling the Time of the Bell, great rock ramparts had been sculpted into a grotesque statuary which, decrepit and strewn with creepers, loomed malevolently over everything below. Great, winged creatures – the hags Kali had seen in Fayence – thrust stone claws at the world, while sweeping carvings of the black coaches that had come for Makennon and the others raced around and between their malformed limbs. Most unnerving were the screaming faces that covered every remaining space on the ramparts, which whispered as the wind blew past them, murmuring half-heard warnings not to approach, to leave this place while they still could.

"Bloody hells," Kali said at last.

"Not exactly welcoming, is it?" Freel added.

"It's going to be less welcoming in a second, if we don't move it." Slowhand nodded towards the top of the threshold.

While the three of them had been examining the necropolis, the ranks of soul-stripped had continued to file towards it, *into it*, and now the very last of them were being absorbed by the blackness within. The entrance began to seal, a mountainous stone slab rumbling slowly down. The three of them were still some two hundred yards away from it.

"Shit!" Kali cried, and began to run, Slowhand and Freel hot on her heels.

Negotiating the tangled floor of the gorge at speed was not easy, however, and the entrance was half closed before they had covered a third of the distance.

Kali continued to pound along the gorge, shouting to Slowhand and Freel to *move, move, move!* The two men were already slowing behind her. Kali struggled for a few more steps before she, too, was forced to accept that the attempt was hopeless, and she roared in frustration. As the last of the soul-stripped vanished, the slab closed with a rumble of ground-shaking, deafening finality. She pounded on the door as the others caught up.

"Hooper, it's useless..." Slowhand said.

Kali continued to pound, staring up at and around the slab as she did. "Dammit, I will not be stopped now!"

"Miss Hooper, I fear the archer is correct."

"No! There's a way. There has to be a way."

Slowhand slumped with his back to the slab. "Well, we're open to suggestions..."

Kali stared at him, hot, angry, and breathing hard. She was about to bite his head off when she suddenly turned away from the slab, staring back down the gorge, toward the forest.

She began to stomp off, Slowhand giving her a curious glance.

"Hooper, where the hells are you going?"

"Redigor's not going to stop me now," Kali reiterated. "You two stay here, do what you can."

"And you?" Slowhand shouted after her.

"Plan C!"

"Which is?"

"We have a locked door, right?" Kali yelled. "Then what we need is a key!"

Chapter Fourteen

Slowhand and Freel watched Kali work her way back down the gorge and into the undergrowth with a mixture of puzzlement and concern. The archer thought he caught sight of her a few minutes later – of all things, *climbing trees* – but he couldn't be certain and his attention was caught by Freel, anyway. The Faith enforcer had been studying the huge, statue-covered frame of the slab, apparently working out a way to climb the incline. Now he seemed to have decided where to start and lashed his whip upwards so that it wrapped around one of the lower statues, then, with a grunt, began to pull himself up towards it.

"Where the hells are you going?" Slowhand said.

"Doing what I can. Looking for another way in."

"Hooper will get us in there, Freel. Trust me."

"I believe she will *try*. But in all truth this whole operation has been a disaster so far, though through no fault of your Miss Hooper. And now she's out in the Sardenne, alone. Face it, archer, there's no guarantee she'll be back."

"*She'll be back.* She always comes back."

"And if she doesn't come back this time? Like Jenna didn't?"

The question completely threw Slowhand. "I –"

"I knew Jenna had been assigned to the Drakengrats," Freel said. "And I didn't know why, or for how long. But you sense, somehow, when it's been long enough, and then you start to wonder. I wondered, in fact, until Makennon summoned me, with news. The news came from the one survivor..."

"Freel..."

"You love her, don't you?"

Slowhand hesitated, momentarily unsure whether Freel meant Jenna or Kali, until he realised that he'd spoken in the present tense.

What had brought about these sudden revelations, he wasn't sure, nor why he was about to again be so candid with the man. Was it because of what had happened to Jenna at *his* hands? Did he feel the need to justify himself, giving Freel the full picture of the circumstances, and his place in them, that had brought about his sister's – and Freel's wife's – death?

"Sometimes I love her. And sometimes she annoys the fark out of me. And sometimes I wonder whether I'm in way out of my depth. I'd follow her anywhere and do anything for her but one thing's for sure – she isn't the innocent tavern owner and sometime adventurer she was when we first met. Something's *happening*, Freel, but whatever it is, she won't let me anywhere near it."

Freel nodded. He lashed his whip around a second statue now, and began to haul himself up. "You coming?"

Slowhand looked back down the gorge, but if he had indeed seen Kali she was now gone. He nodded and, without hesitation, unslung Suresight, attached one of his whizzlines, and fired it towards a statue above Freel. A second later he had hoisted himself to a position where he waited for the enforcer to catch up.

"Useful toy," Freel commented. "But this isn't some kind of competition..."

"I know. I'm just trying to get the job done."

Now that they had bypassed the initial lip of the slab's frame, where the statuary was sparser, there was no need to continue using the whip or Suresight, and the pair were able to pull themselves manually from one statue to the other. The going was slow. Some of the grotesque figures were unstable in their settings, and needed to be negotiated with the utmost care. When, finally, they reached the halfway point of the incline, the men paused, breathless and sweating.

"How did you meet?" Freel asked. "You and Miss Hooper."

Despite himself, Slowhand smiled. "On the Sarcre Islands. I'd bought passage with a pilot named Silus. He, in turn, had been hired to pick up a female passenger from one of the outlying islets – but I don't think he knew what he was going to get. Hooper came running at us out of the jungle, down the beach, dropping ancient artefacts as she ran, she was trying to carry so many. She yelled at us to rig for top knots, and a mob of angry natives poured out of the jungle after her. All of a sudden about a thousand fire arrows came arcing through the sky and Silus had no choice but to get the boat out of there. I was pitched overboard and ended up on the beach, with Hooper, surrounded by the natives. Turned out what she'd thought was an Old Race site was actually a temple to their fertility god... Rumpo-Pumpo, or something." Slowhand paused and shrugged in the manner of someone convinced the name couldn't be quite right. "Hooper was new to the game, then."

"You obviously lived to tell the tale."

"Just. The two of us ended up stripped and dumped in a pot to be blanched for the native's supper, jammed together thigh to thigh. Only got out when I told them we had the hic."

"That would do it. You actually sound as if you enjoyed yourself."

"Ohhhh, yes. Took Hooper back a year or two later when the natives had started dabbling in tourism. Room with a hot tub. Wasn't my fault the native eldress recognised us. Hooper almost got stuffed and I... well, I was cursed."

"Cursed how?"

"Something about me always being dressed for dinner. Never could work it out myself."

Freel looked at him sceptically. He'd read the report of the number of times Slowhand had been arrested for losing his clothes, so it was either an astounding set of coincidences or the man was in complete and utter denial.

"Let's move on," Freel said.

He grabbed the base of the next statue and heaved himself upward. Slowhand was about to follow when, with a crack, the statue broke away from its base. Freel tried to throw himself free but was snagged in the statue's hands and found himself tipping over the edge of the buttress. The statue dropped another foot with a sharp jerk and the remainder of its base began to crumble. Slowhand steadied himself and thrust out a hand but couldn't reach.

"If you're thinking of making a rope out of your clothes, don't," Freel growled through gritted teeth. "I'd rather take the fall."

Slowhand studied the crumbling statue. "Fall, then."

Freel snapped a look upward, glaring at him. And the statue jerked again.

Slowhand's jaw pulsed. "*Fall.*"

A strange expression crossed the enforcer's face – disappointment, perhaps? – but there was no time to work it out as the statue came free of its base and began to fall, Freel still trapped in its grip.

The moment it did, Slowhand snatched Suresight from his back, primed an arrow and aimed it at his falling companion. But he didn't fire. Not yet. Instead he waited while the falling statue impacted with the incline of the entrance slab, breaking apart. His eyes narrowed, picking out Freel's flailing form amid the cloud of debris. Suresight moved infinitesimally but, again, Slowhand did not release his arrow until his aim was true.

The arrow flew through the coils of chain whip at Freel's waist, and ricocheted off the entrance slab beneath to wrap around the neck of one of the statues further below. Freel came to a sudden stop, bouncing on Slowhand's rope, and looked up at the archer calmly securing its other end. He blew out a relieved breath.

"I thought you were..."

"I know what you thought," Slowhand said. The archer climbed back down a number of statues and thrust out a hand, which Freel grabbed.

The remainder of the climb was laborious but uneventful, and at last Slowhand and Freel pulled themselves up onto the necropolis roof. A slight mist curled on its lip. They walked forward between the towers of the Time of the Bell, mouths agape at the pandemonium beyond.

Both men swallowed. On reaching the roof, they had, of course, expected to see the pillar of souls, for it was now originating from beneath them, but neither had given much thought as to how it might be rising from Bel'A'Gon'Shri. Through some kind of dome, maybe, or perhaps even just a channel in the rooftop. But ahead of them there *was* no rooftop. They faced a surreal, broken landscape that seemed half part of reality and half not. It looked as if the entire top of that part of the necropolis had exploded upward and, moments after detonation, frozen, component parts suspended in a slow-motion limbo. A gently rotating jumble of bricks, lintels and stones dangling the moss and detritus of ages, starkly illuminated by the blazing pillar.

The pillar itself was a screaming, roaring, constantly whirling maelstrom of ghostly forms and presences, these once human manifestations, thousands of them, writhed and churned about each other, even tore at each other, as they sought release. Stripped from their bodies as they had been, drawn inexorably into this insane captivity, it must have seemed to them that they had been condemned to the hells themselves. As Slowhand and Freel moved closer, they found themselves recoiling as the desperate souls tried to punch through the surface of the maelstrom – a horrifically distended eye here, a screaming mouth there, half a face or a spasming, clutching hand on the end of an arm made of spectral bone. Nor were these horrors occurring only before them. The pillar of souls was so vast that the victims passed out of sight in all directions. They craned their necks to try and see the distant top of the pillar stretching out to Kerberos.

"Not something you come across every day," Slowhand shouted.

"True," Jakub Freel agreed. His jawline throbbed as he regarded the morass with a steely gaze. "The Pale Lord will answer for this."

"Come on. There might be some way we can get down into the necropolis."

The two men picked their way onto the floating masonry at the pillar's periphery, taking care to avoid stones whose orbit took them too close, lest the grasping maelstrom pull them in. Hopping slowly from stone to stone, they caught glimpses of the necropolis' interior between the jumble of tumbling rubble. Hair and clothes whipping about them, they found themselves a relatively stable platform and stared down onto a floor they guessed was a few hundred yards in from the necropolis' main entrance. At the base of the pillar of souls, the chamber could only be one thing.

The Chapel of Screams.

Their position, in truth, did them little good. Despite Slowhand's best attempts to find an anchor for a whizzline, there was no way down. All the pair could do for now was reconnoitre from here and then look for another route.

The Chapel of Screams was blood-red. Arranged around a central aisle were tombs, six to the left, six to the right, and before each but one stood a rigid figure, but who these figures were was impossible to tell. At the end of the aisle, the Chapel widened into a huge circular chamber, and a raised stone platform overlaid with a complex magical circle. This was the base of the pillar of souls, and its screaming captives, for the most part, obscured it. All that could be made out with certainty was that the patterns were not carved, because they pulsed and shifted occasionally, darting about the circle like angry snakes.

Or perhaps threads. Black threads.

Standing before the platform, dwarfed by the pillar of souls, were two more figures, one as rigid as those by the tombs, the other, much taller and with a mane of flowing hair, thrusting his hands high into the air, as if summoning the gods themselves.

Bastian Redigor. The Pale Lord.

Slowhand shifted towards the edge of the platform they stood on, and Freel held him back.

"What are you doing? We already decided there's no way down."

"I'm not going down," Slowhand said, pulling Suresight from his back. "I'm going to end this thing right now."

Freel stared at the distant figure of the Pale Lord. "In these conditions? Impossible."

"Yeah?"

Slowhand notched an arrow and aimed directly at Redigor's forehead, right between the eyes. The shot wasn't impossible, but it was challenging, even for him. There were a number of factors he had to compensate for – the height, the movement of the platform beneath him, the disturbance from the pillar of souls – but doing so was just a matter of patience. Unfortunately, patience wasn't only a virtue, it was time-consuming, and by the time Slowhand had locked his aim, the platform beneath him had begun to move again, rotating about the pillar of souls.

It became suddenly like finding a target through a kaleidoscope.

Slowhand narrowed his eyes, unfazed, and loosed his arrow. The tip raced unerringly towards the Pale Lord and would, a second later, have punched directly into his brain – but the arrow stopped dead in the air, an inch from his face, and dropped to the floor. The Pale Lord looked up, directly at Slowhand, smiled, his mouth widening into a razor-toothed maw.

"We're out of here, now," Freel said, and pulled Slowhand up by the shoulder. He bundled him across the floating stepping stones.

"Dammit, Freel. I can take another shot."

"To what end, Slowhand? You saw what happened."

"I'm quicker than he is – I'll get an arrow through!"

"Really? How exactly? By making it up as you go along?"

"What the hells is that supposed to mean?"

Freel span to face him. "That sometimes you have to think about things. Maybe if you'd thought about things a bit more at the Crucible you could have avoided a confrontation. And maybe my wife might still be alive."

Slowhand stared at him. *Is this it?* He wondered. *Is this when it all finally boils over?*

"Jenna intended to blow us out of the sky," he said, more calmly than he felt. "And without that ship, the k'nid would have obliterated the peninsula."

"The Faith would have found a way to combat them. *I* would have found a way."

"Are you *sure* about that, Jakub? It was, after all, your wife – my *sister* – who could have avoided a confrontation. But that doesn't seem to have occurred to you, does it – it never does in the Final Filth."

Freel's grip tightened about the stock of his whip but he made no move.

"Face it, Jakub. Jenna became a puppet. The Faith's puppet. *Your* puppet."

Freel roared, raced at him, and the archer was winded as the enforcer piled into his stomach and threw the two of them back over the floating stones.

Slowhand found himself with his head only yards from the pillar of souls, but his greater concern was Freel's hands, slowly tightening about his throat. For a second the two men stared at each other, faces red and taut with strain, before Slowhand found enough strength to growl, "Is this it, then? Where you kill me?"

"Kill you?"

"Like on the train? What stopped you, Freel? That DeZantez would be a witness? Or was it just what it felt like – some kind of warning, a game?"

"What the hells are you talking about?"

"The shove in the back? The almost but not quite death on the tracks? The whip?"

Freel's eyes flickered over him, as if suddenly shocked to find someone in such a helpless position beneath him and he snatched his hands away. He rolled onto his back and snorted. "I guess working together finally got to us both. I wasn't trying to kill you, you fool! That cable you cut came lashing back, almost cut you in half. I was pushing you out of the way."

"Bullshit."

"Why on Twilight would I want to kill you? I helped save you from Fitch, remember? Even went so far as to steer him away, told him you were mine."

"And just why would you do that?"

Fitch laughed, rough and guttural.

"Has it ever occurred to you that we are, in fact, brothers-in-law, you and I? That out of all the people on this godsforsaken world we are the only ones with something unique in common? Someone we loved?"

"Jenna," Slowhand said. "No... no, it hadn't." He shifted uneasily. "Even so, I find it hard to believe that an agent of the Final Faith would let family get in the way of removing a thorn in their side."

Freel paused. "Let me ask you something. Were you to work in a tavern, would that make you a drunk? If you yanked teeth for a living, would you necessarily like causing pain?"

"I've known a few in both cases. What's your point?"

"Simply put? That the job doesn't always make the man."

"You work for the Filth. You're their chief enforcer, for fark's sake. I'd say that was more vocation than job, Jakub."

"So much so that I almost never pray."

"Come on. I'd have thought that was mandatory."

Freel shrugged. "Abstinence is a privilege of the position."

"Wait a minute," Slowhand said. "Are you telling me that while you're an agent of the Faith, you're not *of* the Faith?"

"What can I say? I prefer a choice of Gods myself."

Slowhand blew out a breath. "Oh, this day is just full of surprises. Then *why*, Freel? Why do what you do?"

"Let's just say that certain... factions in Allantia have growing concerns about the Faith's ultimate mission here on the mainland, because Allantia is not so very far away. And that the demise of Konstantin Munch provided them with an opportunity to place one of their own in a position of some seniority – and perhaps influence, if and when needed. Thank you for creating the vacancy, by the way."

"You're a spy."

"More of an observer."

Slowhand said nothing for a second.

"Jenna. Did she know?" He asked at last.

Freel shook his head. "I couldn't take the chance that she'd reveal what she knew under Fitch's influence. But I like to think that the man she fell in love with was the real me."

"I always thought..."

"What? That our marriage was a forced one? Decreed by Makennon and orchestrated by Fitch? No, Slowhand, we loved each other. And she, in turn, loved you and me both."

"Then why in the hells didn't you get her out of there?"

Freel smiled, though it was tinged with sadness. "I had been making plans for her removal after the Drakengrats. A disappearance – a convenient death – during a mission arranged by me. She would have been free."

Slowhand looked up at the enforcer.

"Gods, I'm sorry."

"Don't be. You did what you had to."

Finally, Slowhand heaved himself to his feet. "The tension of these last few days. From you. It struck me as pretty genuine."

"Oh, it was. I didn't know you, archer – as you didn't know me – but I knew your reputation. Since then I've learned more about the man you are. I needed to be sure that this, all of it, including Jenna's death, was more than a *game* to you."

"Oh, it's no game," Slowhand said. "Not any more."

Freel regarded him steadily. "So... what say we get on with it?"

"What say we do."

Slowhand held out a hand, and the enforcer took it.

"Tell me one thing," Slowhand said. "Why since your first question to me have I been unable to keep my mouth shut?"

"Ah, that," Freel said. He ran his hand down his squallcoat. "This whole thing is stitched together with mumbleweed."

"Mumbleweed?"

Freel leaned in almost conspiratorially. "I'd have thought you'd have come across it in your travels. It relaxes people's inhibitions. Very handy when you're a spy."

The two men turned, distracted by a noise from the forest. They leapt from the stones and returned to the roof's edge. Something big was approaching through the trees, and approaching fast, and it made even the temple roof pound like a drum skin beneath their feet.

Freel looked at Slowhand.

Slowhand looked at Freel.

The two men turned and ran, almost falling over themselves in their efforts to shield the other and push him away, and they cried out in unison.
"*Ohhhhhh, shiiiiiiiiiiiiiit...*"

Chapter Fifteen

Kali grunted, pushing her boot against the tree trunk as she pulled the vine taut and knotted it in place. It was the fourth time she had carried out such an operation, and the fourth time she wondered just what it was she was getting herself into. As usual, she decided her plan didn't bear too much thinking about.

She slapped the vine to test its tension, and dropped from the tree and moved on. More coils of the stuff were slung over her shoulders, and they would all be used. For once in her life she didn't resent the number of times she had needed to bail Red, her adoptive father, out of trouble – both financial and physical – now that the time she had spent with the old poacher was at last coming in useful. He had a way with traps, did old Red.

Kali ducked as a flock of shrikes burst from the thick branches above, but ignored them. The wildlife had returned to the forest since she, Slowhand and Freel had reached the necropolis, which was an added complication, but she frankly didn't have the time to be bothered with it. It had taken some effort to renegotiate the thorn barrier. If she had to hide every time she had a close encounter with the forest's denizens the Pale Lord's plan would be done and dusted before she got anywhere. Even so, she wasn't stupid, and had taken added precautions to conceal herself from the creatures around her. Having decided that floprat render alone might not be enough to confuse predators' senses, she had trapped and butchered a yazuk, stripping the flesh from the creature and draping it about her like a cloak.

It stank to the pits but, once more, thank you Red.

Amidst the noises and movement of the forest were the sudden, horrified screams of soldiers and mages who had survived the juggennath assault. She had no time for them either, but each time she heard them she closed her eyes and bit her lip. They may have been why she had made it so far without being attacked but she could not be grateful for them. There was nothing she could for them other than to will them not to run, to panic, to stay still, to *pray*, but she knew, ultimately, it would do no good. If she were in their place in this godsforsaken hellshole wouldn't she do the same?

A young, sweating Sword suddenly crashed through the undergrowth before her, falling to his knees on the forest floor. He spotted Kali and stared at her imploringly, shouting "Help me! Help me!" but it was already too late. The tendrils coiled about his ankles snapped him back in an instant. The sounds of his thrashing struggle – and screams – continued for several seconds before they were abruptly silenced by a gelatinous *gloop*.

Kali kept moving, not even looking back, and chose another tree.

Once more she lashed vines about its trunk, stretching their length in a tense line to another opposite, where she climbed and lashed them tightly again. She repeated the procedure two more times, with trees further ahead and hundreds of yards apart, and at last seemed satisfied that all she could do with the vines had been done.

Girl, she thought, *you've taken risks before but this time you've got to be mad.*

Kali negotiated her way further into the forest, fighting a growing sense of isolation and wishing she had Horse by her side. The area she was entering was where she and the first Horse had almost given up on their search for the Spiral. Yes, there was the acrid stench of the Spiral's ruins and there was the mix of odours – metallic, biological, faecal – that meant the juggennath was still nearby. She had successfully made her way back to its stomping ground.

Stomping ground. Never was a phrase more appropriate, because Kali felt her prey before she saw it, vibrations in the forest floor that resonated in her bones.

Kali moved forward cautiously, weaving her way through the undergrowth. The trees thrashed and snapped back and forth, as if caught in the throes of a violent storm, but the sky above was clear of clouds. Abruptly, the air was split by a series of angry, deafening roars.

She eased her way to a clearing ahead.

Kali had been presuming that the creature that had attacked their party had been a juggennath, she had been calling it a juggennath, and it certainly smelt like she imagined a juggennath should smell, but it was only now, setting eyes fully upon on it that she really appreciated what a juggennath was.

Legend had it that the elves had grown six of these creatures in huge vats. They were unnatural, undying behemoths nurtured of thousands of gallons of offal, sinew, hide and bone, the mashings of huge creatures, individually terrifying, who roamed the peninsula long ago. Elven alchemists had grown them with one purpose – to empty the battlefields of the dwarves they had fought in the oldest of the wars. It was said that the six could reduce a line of ten thousand men to a bloody smear. Armoured in spiked metal plates, shaped over vast anvils, and armed with stone hammers hewn in blocks higher than a man, they were said to be unstoppable, and only by choosing their battlefield cleverly – in a place known as the Hollow Fields – had the dwarves eventually rid the world of their destructive blight. The abyssal caverns of the Fields, lying beneath thin layers of topsoil and roots, had swallowed even the juggennaths whole, and the dwarves had given those caverns a name, too – in dwarven, Yan'Tuk – which in human speak meant something roughly along the lines of 'Up Yours'.

Okay, Kali had never been sure about that last bit. But she liked it.

Clearly, though, one juggennath had survived. The thick, heavy mass that blocked her view was its *legs*. She craned her neck as far back as it would go, past legs the width of redwood trunks and a torso the size of a small hill, to a head and shoulders as high as the treeline, if not above.

The only thing that Kali could think was, *no wonder the dwarves wanted rid of them.*

Well, that was precisely why she was here, wasn't it? But before she made a move she needed to work out a route.

Kali studied the juggennath further. On a colossal scale, the creature resembled the primates of the higher World's Ridge Mountains – the ogur, for example – and was covered almost entirely in hair, muscular arms and legs concealed by the thick and straggly coat. In places jagged sections of rusted and tarnished metal clung to its body, some pieces still bearing the remains of the spikes that had once covered it. They would come in handy. The remains of some of her party were strung and slung about its massive frame, at least thirty men and women bounced lifelessly against the juggennath as it shifted, and whether they were worn for decoration or for food, Kali almost turned away seeing the state they were in.

She had seen what she needed, and was ready. All she had to wait for now was for the juggennath to move again.

It did so, the trees and branches about it thrashing and breaking as a wave of shrikes and razorbeaks circled its head, at least twenty of them taking it in turns to dart at the giant figure as it flailed against their attacks. The giant batted them out of the air but there was no way it could stop them all, and they dived for its flesh, returning with chunks of bloody flesh and matted hair held in their beaks. The juggennath roared in irritation and frustration, the wounds insignificant, but the attacks had clearly been going on for some time – and the reason that they had commenced them was, she believed, the same reason that the rest of the wildlife had emerged from its cover in the forest. For the first time in its impossibly long life, the juggennath had been injured – slashed by Gabriella DeZantez and the Deathclaws – and the great beast that had so far held dominion over them had seemed weak, as they had smelled its blood.

Kali almost felt sorry for the ancient creature, the bemused beast once king of its domain, but there was little she could do to help it. Wouldn't have helped if she could, in fact. She was banking on the distraction to make the next part of her plan easier.

She had to act quickly.

If the juggennath decided to flee its tormentors, went pounding off deeper into the Sardenne, she might never catch it again.

It was time to hitch a ride.

Kali burst from the treeline and raced across the glade. She made it with only a couple of minor scratches into the shadow of the juggennath itself. Only one, particularly persistent brackan tried to take a slice out of her, but with a running twist she managed to manoeuvre it into the path of a hackfire toad and, with a cheery wave, it was goodnight stickface. This done, she threw herself upwards with a grunt, grabbing two fistfuls of the matted hair on the giant's legs. She hauled herself up onto the limb proper and took as firm a purchase as she could, the giant pounding about the glade in its efforts to defend itself, and was flung to the left and the right like a small doll, but she gradually scaled the phenomenal creature. Kali doubted that the giant even recognised her presence.

Kali rose higher and higher, aiding her climb with a couple of somersaults from spike to spike, and at last she found herself on its shoulder, headed for the neck and clung onto the nape as she might cling to an exposed rockface. There, she took a breath.

Before she could move further, Kali found herself snatched from the juggennath's neck by one of its giant hands, swung around to the front of the creature and held before its face. If, that was, it could be called a face. She had never actually considered what a juggennath saw if it shaved in a morning. There was no nose or mouth as such, only a twitching orifice where both should be, and above that a single, bar-shaped eye that stretched almost across its forehead from left to right, giving it a perpetual frown.

"Gods, you're ugly."

Kali struggled in the giant's grip as she stared into its looming eye, and wondered why everything had gone suddenly quiet, the attacking shrikes and razorbeaks gone. Then she realised that the eye, previously a feral brown, had become as white and dull as those of the soul-stripped, so that she felt as if she were held before a cold, snow-filled sky. Whatever intelligence the juggennath possessed – and Kali suspected it wasn't much – seemed to have been replaced by another.

The fist of the juggennath tightened ever so slightly around her.

"Who are you, girl?" A voice boomed. "What are you doing in my forest?"

The voice was arrogant, cold and cruel. Bastian Redigor, it seemed, was introducing himself.

"Hello, Baz," Kali said. "You don't mind being called Baz, I hope?"

"I asked you a question. What do you want?"

"Er, world peace? A cure for the hic? No – how about an all-over tan?"

The fist tightened.

"Okay, okay, just breaking the ice." Kali leaned forward and peered into vast orifice. "Dark and smelly in there, huh?"

"I am not here, stupid child. This beast is but a means of communication."

Kali rolled her eyes and tutted. "Farking hell, I know that, elf. I should have known the Ur'Raney would have no sense of humour."

Redigor laughed. "So you know who I am. Would it surprise you to know that I, in turn, know who you are... Kali Hooper?"

Actually it did, but Kali didn't let it show. Maybe there was something in what Fitch had said about Redigor's gaze being so penetrating it could read minds. She concentrated on keeping her true thoughts – and plans – to herself.

"I see the little girl, wide-eyed with stories that I would come for you," Redigor went on. "I sense the fear, the desire to run and curl beneath the bed..."

"Forget it, Redigor. I wasn't afraid then, I'm not afraid now."

"I would not say that. I can feel your sweat leaking onto this creature's pores."

"You sure it's my sweat?" Redigor's laughter was a rumble this time. "Listen, Puce Lord or whatever your name is, I've been in tighter spots."

"Really?"

The juggennath's grip tightened suddenly, not enough to crush her but enough to squeeze all of the breath from her lungs. She had no doubt that Redigor *could* have crushed her had he wished, but was enjoying playing with her. Knowing his predilections she wouldn't be surprised if the immense fingers of the giant he controlled soon started to peel away her clothes.

"I ask you again," Redigor's disembodied voice said. "What are you doing in my forest?"

"I've come to stop a dirty old man returning his perverted rule to my world."

"Bel'A'Gon'Shri is sealed and the exchange will soon begin. And I hardly think you are in any position to stop it."

"No? You don't know me very well, do you?"

Kali suddenly rammed her gutting knife into the tender flesh of the juggennath's palm and, with a roar of pain, the creature opened its hand. She had gambled on the fact that, even though Redigor was ostensibly in control of the mammoth creature, its reaction to pain would remain instinctive. Of course, she'd hoped that the giant's grip would simply loosen enough to allow her escape from it, and hadn't expected to be dropped.

Time to improvise.

As the juggennath's other hand swept around to swat her from existence, Kali twisted in mid-air, booting herself away from it, and once more found herself heading towards the hairy hide of the beast, somewhere about its midriff. She struck, clung, and began another slow climb.

She didn't want to know what it was she was climbing up and as she ascended the thick, matted hair she instead concentrated on what mattered – that it was getting her where she needed to go. One way or another she had Bastian Redigor by the short and curlies, and when she had finally returned herself to the juggennath's neck she told him so, whispering into the beast's ear, "Redigor, I'm coming."

Kali heaved herself up on top of the living mountain, avoiding its hands. She leaned forward, holding her gutting knife in both hands, and plunged it viciously into the creature's eye. Vitreous humour spurted forth and the creature reacted once more as she had hoped.

Roaring and slapping at the eye, the juggennath staggered forward in the direction from which the pain had come, seeking out the cause and attempting to crush it. There was, of course, nothing there, and Kali had already flipped herself away. She dangled, now, on a length of hair by the left side of the beast's head, and after a few seconds kicked herself around and delivered another blow with her knife, this time to the juggennath's cheek. Again, it roared, turning to identify its new attacker, but once more there was nothing there. As the beast lurched forward, she did a quick calculation, working out that only one more application of the knife would be needed to get the creature to go where she wished it to go, and then she could effectively sit back and enjoy the ride.

Kali returned to its head and this time used the fringe of the beast to drop herself down until she dangled directly in front of its eye. The blinded eye had reverted to a natural state, a sign that Redigor had departed his host, most likely in response to the pain. That suited her needs perfectly. Glancing behind her to double check that she, and more importantly the creature itself, were on the course she wanted, Kali rammed her gutting knife into the eyeball once more.

The creature roared louder than ever, scaring away those of its predators that still remained in the nearby undergrowth, and charged through the forest, swatting its great hands before it as it did, trying to locate and remove its tormentor. Kali, however, was once again, gone, perched now just above the beast's forehead like a driver. From that position she occasionally jabbed her knife into the wrinkled flesh of its brow, reminding it, when needed, of where she wanted it to go. Then the first of the traps she had laid became visible just before its stomping feet, and just before the rampaging beast triggered it, Kali wished herself luck and hung on tight.

The trap caused the beast no pain, of course, but it roared anyway, this time in confusion, as Kali's meticulously arranged vines wrapped themselves around its feet, throwing it off balance. The trap was not enough to bring it down, of course, but it *was* enough to send the giant stumbling blindly and out of control further through the forest and towards the second trap she had laid. This one was strung at a different height to the first, and this time the tension in the vines turned it as well, sending it careening to her goal. Kali tightened her grip on the giant's matted hair as it slammed through the trees surrounding it. She could make out the remaining traps ahead of them and, beyond those, the gorge that led towards the necropolis.

She couldn't help but yell out loud – "go, boy, go!" – as the juggennath impacted with her next trap, this one designed to catch the giant at the waist, throwing off its centre of gravity.

Kali suddenly found herself atop a rampaging mountain that could not stop itself from flailing forward, a victim of its own momentum. The last two traps she had lain came into their own now. As the giant stumbled into the complex arrangement of crossed vines, breaking each with a sound like a musket shot, the branches and, in one case, log that Kali had secured in place sprang from their lairs and struck the juggennath full on, slapping it forward. The giant roared in protest and confusion, brain unable to register what was happening in such swift succession, flailing all the more.

Perfect, Kali thought from her position at the creature's summit. All she needed to wait for now was the final trap and she could be off, leaving nature – and gravity specifically – to take its course.

The Juggennath broke through the thorn barrier surrounding Bel'A'Gon'Shri, and was in the gorge leading to the necropolis's front door. From her height Kali could actually see the stone slab ahead of them. She encouraged the Juggennath once more, ramming her knife into what remained of its eyeball. As the giant beast roared in pain she saw two tiny figures on top of the necropolis – Freel and Slowhand – turn at the sound.

The Juggennath staggered forward and Kali counted down the seconds until it triggered the trap.

If she did say so herself, there was no doubt that she had saved the best for last.

As the two tensioned vines stretched across the gorge floor were snapped by the Juggennath's staggering feet, a complex series of weights and counterweights were set rapidly in motion, and the two overhanging trees that Kali had tied back using ropes and pulleys sprang out from the gorge wall and slapped it hard in the back, somewhere in the region of each shoulderblade. Flung forward, the Juggennath roared and swung its mighty arms, trying to regain its balance, but its enforced momentum had already tipped its centre of gravity, and its mass was far too great to recover from such a complication in time to save it from its inevitable fall. It careened forward head-first, the heavy and uncontrolled pounding of its feet travelling up its body and shaking Kali to the bone, and she knew it was time to leave. She turned away from the eye and began to scramble down the back of the beast's neck, then unexpectedly flipped forward with a yelp, suddenly halted in her flight.

What the hells? She thought, and twisted her body, struggling to look above and behind her.

She saw that her foot had become entangled in a knot of the Juggennath's hair and she was now dangling from it like some kind of decoration.

Oh, that was great. Just great. Just farking great. How many seconds did she have before her plan came to fruition? Three? Two? One?

Roaring herself now, Kali flipped herself upward, tugged at the constraining mass of hair and then, realising she could not get free, instead heaved herself around the side of the Juggennath's neck as far as she could go.

One, in fact.

The last thing she saw with any clarity were the figures of Slowhand and Freel on the upper lip of the sealed entrance to

Bel'A'Gon'Shri, their mouths agape. Then she saw the two of them throw themselves out the way.

By an odd coincidence, her cry echoed their own.

"*Ohhhhhh, shiiiiiiiiiiiiit...*"

The Juggennath struck the sealed entrance to the necropolis like a battering ram, cracking the thick stone. For a moment it seemed that that might be it, that the slab would give no further, but the Juggennath's vicious spikes had embedded themselves in it. Clinging still to its neck, having at last managed to kick loose from its hair, Kali felt the Juggennath strain and lurch as the spider-web cracks widened and the slab crumbled before it. The Juggennath let out a last great roar of pain and protest and fell through the gap, hitting the floor with a force that rocked the very foundations of the necropolis. The Juggennath tried to pick itself up, but the remnants of the broken slab broke free and crashed onto its helpless form. It seemed unlikely that it would rise again.

A dusty, coughing figure picked itself up from next to the crushed, bloodied mass and stared into the darkness ahead. It wasn't exactly how she'd planned to make her entrance admittedly but, what the hells, the end result was the same. She'd promised Redigor she was coming and here she was.

"Knock, knock," Kali growled.

CHAPTER SIXTEEN

The first thing Kali noticed as she moved into Bel'A'Gon'Shri was how *old* the necropolis felt. It wasn't the usual sense of age she experienced when finding Old Race sites, but a feeling that she had somehow stepped backwards in time – not into the past exactly, but certainly out of the present. It was as if, when the place had been built, it had somehow clung onto its time and never been willing to let go.

Her world seemed suddenly far away and she was therefore grateful to see Slowhand and Jakub Freel silhouetted in the entrance, descending together on one of the archer's whizzlines. The pair climbed over the debris to join her.

"Quite the entrance," Freel commented.

"That?" Slowhand countered. "You should have seen how she got into the Hoard of the Har'An'Di."

"The lost artefacts of the forgotten tribe? I'm sorry I missed that."

"Don't be," Kali said. "They collected thimbles."

They fell silent as the dust settled. A vaulted corridor stretched away into the distance, as high and as broad as the massive door itself, and lined with carved representations of those in whose honour it had been built – statues as high as a house.

"The Ur'Raney, I take it," Freel said.

"The Ur'Raney," Kali repeated.

Freel nodded. "Nice."

In every case, the statues depicted the Ur'Raney inflicting some kind of torture or pain on helpless victims, ranging from dwarves to ogur, humans to fish-like creatures. The carved victims were shown as far smaller than their torturers. Freel slowly unwound his chain whip, keeping it at the ready, as they moved on through the avenue of horrors. He had a point, Kali and Slowhand realised, and unsheathed their own weapons, gutting knife and Suresight alike.

The silence that had met them at the entrance gave way to an unsettling chanting in the distance, that sounded as if it were coming from human mouths yet did not chant human words, and a chorus of agonised and desperate cries that could only be coming from the Chapel of Screams – the same tormented sounds that Slowhand and Freel had heard on the necropolis's roof, here amplified by its stone corridors until the whole place seemed to be suffering.

As they moved along the corridor no horde of soul-stripped came to meet them. Bastian Redigor did not stand threateningly in their way. The business now occupying him, it seemed, was being conducted deeper within. Their only company the leering statues, they came at last to an ornate double door and Kali halted them.

"Trapped?" Slowhand wondered.

"Can't see anything," Kali said, scanning the door and its frame.

"Maybe Redigor put all his faith in the slab back there," Freel guessed.

Kali nodded. Tentatively, she pushed the massive golden door with her fingers and it opened with ease.

The path became a bridge beyond the door, crossing a vertiginous chamber carved wholly out of some substance that looked disturbingly like bone. From the floor of the chamber to the ceiling on either side – and it was a long way up and a long, long way down – the frontages of countless tombs could be seen, each of them inscribed, in elven script, with the name of its occupant. Kali tried to count them but gave up after the third ledge of tombs, but there were thousands here. These were Bastian Redigor's people. This was the final resting place of the Ur'Raney.

But there was something wrong with the whole picture. Kali couldn't immediately put her finger on it but something was very wrong. Straining to read the script on the tombs, for the most part ignoring the names, her eyes flicked from one to the other until what was nagging at her clicked into place.

It was the dates accompanying the names. They were all the same.

"Yantissa 367, Interlude Third," she whispered to herself.

"Something wrong, Miss Hooper?" Freel queried.

"Yantissa 367, Interlude Third," Kali repeated more forcefully. "It's elven chronology. According to these tombs, all of these elves, thousands of them, died on the same day."

"So?" Slowhand said. "I thought it was generally accepted that the Old Races were wiped out in one go. Maybe that's when it happened?"

Kali pondered. "If it was, I'd be ecstatic, believe me, because we'd be able to pinpoint the end day exactly. But I don't think this date has anything to do with that."

"Why?"

"Think, Liam. If that was the day the Old Races were wiped out..."

"Who buried them?" Jakub Freel finished.

Slowhand looked from one to the other. "Redigor?"

"One man, all this?" Kali mused. "Even with an eternity to play with, I don't think so."

"Okaaay," Slowhand said. "So maybe Yantissa 367, Interlude Third isn't a day. I mean, I know your elven history is better than mine but as you admit yourself, you've still a lot to learn. Maybe Yantissa 367, Interlude Third refers to a *period* of time, and maybe it took the Ur'Raney a while to die out?"

Kali stared at the archer. "You know, Slowhand, that's not bad. Not bad at all."

"Hey, I'm not just a pretty face..."

"Completely wrong, mind. Because it still doesn't make sense." She indicated the tombs and structure around them. "Think about it. If the world was falling apart around you, would you take the time to build *this*?"

"I wouldn't," Freel said. "But if it wasn't the end day that killed them all, what did?"

The question was momentarily forgotten as Slowhand pointed. "Hooper, Freel, look."

Above and below the bridge they were standing on, obscured in the shadows of the huge chamber, other, smaller bridges crossed the bone chasm. Each of these bridges led to one of the ledges of tombs, and each was filled with slowly filing figures. The soul-stripped who had been phased through the Sardenne, all chanting that strange, elven chant, were making their way to the fronts of the tombs and, one after the other, taking up positions before each of them, simply standing there, staring blankly ahead.

"It's as if they know which tomb to go to," Freel whispered, for fear that his words might alert the soul-stripped to their presence.

"Redigor knows," Kali said.

"And it strikes me," Slowhand offered, "that he's the only one who can tell us what happened on Yantissa 367, Interlude Third."

The party crossed the bridge, casting wary glances about them as they did, and the wailing, haunting, tortured cries that had been audible since they first entered the necropolis grew louder with every step, reaching a deafening pitch as they reached the door at the far end. A door which could only lead to the Chapel of Screams.

Again, Kali scanned it for traps and pushed it open. Before them was the tableau Slowhand and Freel had caught glimpses of from the roof, only the Chapel seemed much bigger, stretching away before them, the figures barely discernible at the far end. Behind them – silhouetting and warping their outlines with its churning, chaotic energy – was the base of the pillar of souls.

It was, of course, from here that the screams were emanating and, again, as Slowhand and Freel had seen on the roof, souls captured within struck and writhed at the surface, giving the occasional close-up glimpse of a struggling form or tortured face, even the odd hand outstretched in pleading to be pulled from the turmoil. The proximity of the pillar of souls – its sheer size and power – seemed to be of no concern to the two figures, however, presumably because one was the Pale Lord himself, the master of all he had conjured, and the other, under his control, was Katherine Makennon.

They walked down the central aisle of the Chapel of Screams, Makennon's fellow abductees lining the Chapel on either side of them like a guard of honour. The tombs were far more ornate than the masses they had passed on the bridge. The eleven men and women had been stripped of their own clothing and garbed in uniform, flowing robes, making them look like sacrificial victims – which for all intents and purposes, of course, they were. There was little doubt that those who lay in the tombs behind them were the individuals for whom they had been hand-picked to become hosts – Bastian Redigor's Ur'Raney High Council. As they passed between them Kali recognised the faces of Kantris Mallah, the mayor of Gargas, Thilna Pope, Volonne's Ambassador to Vos, and Belf Utcher, Thane of Miramas, among others – though, of course, none of them recognised her in return. Redigor, it seemed, had not soul-stripped the hosts for his most important returnees as he had the masses outside, but it was clear from their haunted, staring eyes that neither had he left them entirely intact. The expression in their eyes begged her for release from bodies that had become prisons.

There was nothing Kali and the others could do for them. Yet.

The three of them, Slowhand and Freel walking either side of Kali moved on up the aisle, coming at last to stand before Bastian Redigor and Katherine Makennon. Despite herself, Kali faltered slightly. The portrait she had seen of the Pale Lord in Fayence did not, in reality, do him anywhere near justice. He soared above both Freel and Slowhand, a tall, gaunt, angular figure with flowing black hair who should have seemed cadaverous but who radiated an aura that Kali had to admit made her go weak at the knees. The man – the *elf*, she corrected herself – was sheer presence, more magnetic even than the hub, and she could see how he had become lord of his people. Bastian Redigor stared down at her, smiling coldly, and for a few seconds she found she could not draw her eyes away.

She kept telling herself how much of a bastard he was and, with this mantra, dragged her gaze to Makennon, and the sight of what he had done to the Anointed Lord quashed the elf's glamour.

Redigor had wasted no time in preparing Makennon for her role, stripping her armour and clothing and dressing her in a diaphanous shift that fell loosely from her shoulders to her ankles and did little to conceal her nakedness beneath. A high, stiff collar had been placed around Makennon's neck, thrusting her jaw upwards; a *zatra*, a collar of obedience whose prime purpose was to denote the status of a woman as a pet. Kali's eyes travelled down her body, noting the recent bruises, and then back up until her gaze met Makennon's. Though Kali had little time for the woman, her eyes teared at what she saw – fury and frustration at what had been done to her, yes, and shame and utter humiliation that she should be paraded in this way, knowing that all *knew* the indignities she must have suffered. Kali tried to offer her some look of reassurance but wondered whether anything could offer solace for what had happened, and after a second she was forced to turn her gaze away. She looked at Slowhand, but even the normally libidinous archer was staring at the floor, unable to look up.

"Proud of yourself, Baz?" Kali queried, snapping her gaze back to the Pale Lord. "Is this what we're to expect when the Ur'Raney return?"

"This, and more," Redigor replied, his smile widening. He turned to look at Makennon and then back at Kali, his eyes widening in anticipation. "Perhaps when I tire of her I shall take you as *mu'sah'rin* in her place. I sense in you a stamina that I think will be able to satisfy even my demands."

"You keep your slimy elven hands off her," Slowhand threatened, making a move forward, but Kali placed her hand on his arm, stopping him. Redigor might be dripping sleaze but she could feel his raw, unadulterated power. The reason there had been no traps on the way in was that Redigor didn't need any. Slowhand would have no chance against him.

"In your filthy, farking dreams, pal," Kali said to Redigor. She motioned to Makennon and the others. "At least give her the dignity of oblivion. Why must Makennon know what's happening to her? Why must any of them?"

Redigor smiled. "It is necessary that I retain some of their knowledge of the leaders of your civilisation, such as it is. Their familiarity to their people, superficial as it might be when the ritual is done, will be of some advantage. It will make our transition to power... less bloody. It also makes things so much more *fun*."

"Since when did the Ur'Raney care about spilling a little blood?"

"We don't. In fact, we intend to spill a lot of blood. But that," he added with a sigh, "will come later."

"I hate to point out the obvious," Slowhand said, "but this High Council of yours, you're one missing."

"The magistrate of Kroog-Martra," Redigor said. "Convenient, then, that you saw fit to include a replacement in your party."

"What the hells are you talking about?"

The Pale Lord waved a hand and the whip at Jakub Freel's waist suddenly took on a life of its own, uncoiling from his side and wrapping itself around his neck. As it lifted him from the floor, Freel had the presence of mind to react quickly, to jam his fingers between chain and flesh to prevent himself being hanged. Even so he gagged and choked as, with another wave of his hand, Redigor manoeuvred his floating body into position before what had been the magistrate's allocated tomb. Freel dangled there, his legs kicking, his eyes bulging as he stared down at Kali and Slowhand.

"Hey," Slowhand said. "It was me speaking. Let him down, take me instead."

"*You?*" Redigor boomed. "Why should I wish a bedraggled commoner when I have Prince Tremayne of the Allantian First Family?"

Both Slowhand and Kali turned to look at their helpless comrade.

"You didn't *know*?" Redigor said.

"Prince Tremayne?" Slowhand said. "My sister married royalty?"

"Indeed. So you see why I have absolutely no need of riff-raff such as yourself."

"Yeah?" Slowhand challenged. "Well, let me show you what riff-raff can do."

The archer released a clutch of arrows at the Pale Lord in blinding succession. Redigor managed to deflect four of them but two breached his defences, embedding themselves solidly in his right thigh. Redigor gasped and stared down at the protruding shafts in incredulous fury and waved his hand again. Slowhand was propelled violently backwards along the length of the Chapel, impacting with the wall above the entrance with a bone-cracking, sickening thud. The archer slumped there, held by an unseen force, one arm dangling at an unnatural angle through Suresight's string.

Kali stared at her helpless lover and swallowed, then turned back to Redigor.

"Nice party tricks. But when do we get to the main event?"

Redigor raised an eyebrow. "You seem strangely eager."

Kali shook her head. "Nope. But if we've a few minutes, I wouldn't mind the answers to a few questions."

Redigor steepled the fingers of both hands, intrigued. He nodded for Kali to continue.

Kali again looked at Slowhand and Freel. The questions she had in mind, she would not normally have raised in anyone else's presence for fear of burdening them with what she had learned at the Crucible, but both men had lapsed into semiconsciousness. Still, she wanted to take no chances, and spoke to Redigor in elvish.

"Now that we're alone," she said. "What's this all about, Baz?"

"What? You are trying to buy time, child. You know this already."

"Of course I know you're bringing your people back. What I'm asking is, why now?"

"Now?"

"I saw the charts in your tower in Fayence, and I know the intellect you possess. You know as much as I do that a darkness is coming – the same darkness that obliterated the Old Races – so why would you want to resurrect your people when the world's about to come to an end?"

Redigor stared at her and burst into laughter, as if she were a child who had said something profoundly foolish. Kali frowned and pouted.

"Forgive me," Redigor said at last, though his tone still quaked slightly. "Forgive me, but I believe I have overestimated you. All you know is that the darkness is coming, isn't it? But you don't know what the darkness is, or why it comes. You don't know *anything* about it."

Kali felt her heart skip a beat.

"I'm willing to learn."

"An exercise in redundancy, believe me. There is nothing you can do."

"No? Then what did your people do, Baz? They all died at the same time, I know that, but no other member of the Old Races – elf or dwarf – had the luxury of his or her own tomb. They were just... gone."

Redigor's lip curled in amusement yet again. "Your point being?"

"That somehow your people survived the darkness. That somehow they –"

Kali stopped, something in Redigor's expression and something in her own head making the truth click into place.

"My Gods, they didn't survive, did they?" She said. "They died *before* the darkness came."

"All of them on the same day," Redigor confirmed. "Thousands of Ur'Raney ascending to Kerberos to wait for this moment, the moment of their return. It was glorious."

Kali felt suddenly, intensely cold. "You killed them?"

"They died at my behest. A subtle, mostly painless poison."

"A suicide pact?"

"A *survival* pact, child!" Redigor's eyes flared as he spoke. "Though even in their tombs I knew they would not be safe.

Still, I knew the darkness would find them, ravage their physical remains, reduce them to husks. Only I remained whole. I, their guardian, their leader, their lord, curled like a babe, cocooned deep beneath the surface, swaddled in the thick, protective wraps of magic older than time. Only in this manner could I conceal myself from what came."

The thought of even someone as powerful as Redigor having to *hide* chilled Kali to the bone. But a question nagged at her.

"Why kill your people? Why didn't you just let the darkness take them and then restore them from Kerberos?"

Another laugh bubbled up from the Pale Lord.

"Because, child, when the darkness takes you, your soul does not *go* to Kerberos."

"What?" Kali said. "What is it, Redigor? What is the darkness?"

"The Hel'ss."

"The Hells?" Kali said.

"The antithesis of Kerberos. The Other."

Kali staggered with the sheer weight of the revelation. But whether what Redigor seemed to be telling her – that the fundamental beliefs of Twilight's religions were correct and there *were* two places to which souls went, Kerberos and the Pits, or in other words, the Hells – was true or not, another question nagged for an answer.

"But if it's coming again, how do you intend to survive it this time?"

Redigor shook his head almost sadly.

"We do not *have* to survive it this time, child, because this time it does not come for us."

"What? What are you saying?"

"That the last time it came for the elves and the dwarves. And this time it comes for you."

"Humans?" Kali gasped. "Are you saying it *chooses* what it wipes out?"

"I am saying that there is an order to these things."

"So that's your plan, you bastard? To get your jollies from enslaving us humans before inheriting what we leave behind? You disgust me. You're vultures."

Redigor smiled. "No. Vultures are creatures of instinct, their pickings what they find. We, on the other hand, are creatures of refinement, and the pain we shall inflict upon you will be exquisite. Think of it, child – as the darkness comes and the screams of your race echo across the land, we shall *thrive*."

"Not if I can help it..."

Kali roared and leaped for Redigor, unsheathing her gutting knife as she did, but her hand was caught in a vice-like grip and Redigor's eyes stared down at her, wide and wild.

"What is it you are trying to do?" He said, almost compassionately.

"You said it yourself, Redigor," Kali gasped as she twisted in his grip. "There's an order to these things and you've had your turn. The Ur'Raney don't belong here any more."

"And you intend to stop me how? By scratching me with your knife?"

"I'll stop you, you bastard."

Redigor released his grip, but Kali found herself frozen before him. The Pale Lord gazed at the pillar of souls and took a deep, satisfied breath. "This isn't a time for weapons, child, this is a time for celebration. Dance for me."

"What?"

"*Dance for me!*"

Kali didn't do dance, she didn't like dance, she didn't understand dance, but she danced. Danced for the Pale Lord. Spasming and twitching at first, trying to resist, her feet began to tap the floor, and then she began to spin, moving away from the Pale Lord, down the aisle, her body whipping around again, and as much as she wanted to, she couldn't stop – couldn't stop, didn't stop, until she reached the far end of the Chapel of Screams. She slammed into the wall beneath Slowhand with numbing force and, her dance done, slumped to the floor.

"Did you really think you would be able to make a difference?" Redigor asked.

Kali shook her head and wiped a slick of blood from her face. She realised it was dripping on her from the archer suspended helplessly above her. *Oh gods, Slowhand,* she thought as her head spun. What was it she had gotten her lover into? What had she gotten them *all* into?

Kali struggled to rise, staggered, retched, intending to go for the Pale Lord again. It was only as she began to weave between the tombs that a whisper from the helpless Slowhand halted her in her tracks.

"No, Hooper... no, it's too late..."

Kali turned to look up at him, but focused again on the pillar of souls spearing the Chapel roof. It was impossible from where she stood to see the top, but she didn't need to see Kerberos to know that it had at last been reached. The pillar of souls suddenly pulsed brightly, its helpless captives rushing up, and a second later pulsed again, this time downwards. The pillar of souls darkened as if flooded by a rush of arterial blood. Not so dark that Kali couldn't see what was within, though, and she drew back as the base of the pillar struggled to contain a miasmic wave of grasping, clutching, spectral forms, tearing at their own and screaming so loudly it seemed to pierce the very fabric of her ears.

One triumphant cry could be heard above the screaming; Redigor, his hands held high.

"They come!" He declared, laughing. *"They come!"*

Chapter Seventeen

Kali had wondered how exactly the final exchange might take place – how Redigor's *delivery* of the Ur'Raney back to Twilight would occur – and as she staggered back she got her answer.

The expansive, seething, screaming base of the pillar of souls filled and bloated, and exploded, dazzling those present. As Kali watched it through her fingers it blasted harmlessly through her and the wall of the Chapel behind her, towards the tombs. It *wasn't* harmless, though, was it? It was deadly, conjured across the millennia to be as insidious as anything could be. At least to those who had been chosen to be the recipients of what it contained. Kali could not help be awed by the sight, but knew full well that, within the next few seconds, it was going to end the existence of countless innocents who, through no fault of their own, had become caught up in the schemes of a madman who had plotted against them almost since before the human race had been born.

How would they end, though?

Despite herself, Kali couldn't help but ask the question. She pictured the soul wave expanding rapidly through the tombs, individual tendrils of it darting into each of the thousands of ancient resting places like snakes before snapping back out, carrying within each of them the physical essence that had been preserved in the remains of the Ur'Raney. Then, perhaps with a violent spasm from each of the soul-stripped assembled before the tombs, these snakes would strike, darting into necks, eyes, mouths, preparing to infuse themselves into the horrible emptiness from which the true inhabitants of these bodies had been so cruelly torn.

It sickened Kali – the awareness that somehow these things had to *know* which tomb to seek out, which body to violate, and they would move to them as unerringly as salmon returning to their spawning ground.

This, though, was all her imagining, and by the time she could see the Chapel once more, she realised she might never know.

Those souls belonging to Redigor's Ur'Raney Court had already found their homes, slipping into the bodies of Katherine Makennon and the other dignitaries as easily as worms into soft soil, and the effects on their hosts was immediate. Soft groans escaped each of them. Their eyes widened in response to the intrusion, then took on a peculiar blankness. This faded away, to be replaced by *new* eyes that took in their surroundings first with an almost childlike innocence, then a growing curiosity, and then a hunger unlike any Kali had ever seen.

They began to metamorphosise – ever so slightly but enough – taking on the slightest sharpening of their physiognomy, a subtle elongation of the ears, and the lightest of green tints to their skin. Kali could also have sworn – but this may only have been because of the manner in which they carried themselves – that they grew taller.

With almost reptilian twitches of their necks, each of the Ur'Raney *rannaat* sighed and, as one, turned to face Bastian Redigor. Their Lord stood smiling at them, a welcoming smile, his *mu'sah'rin* already draping herself languorously about his neck.

"Hooper..." Slowhand's voice said weakly from above Kali. "This might be the time for that 'long shot' you mentioned to Freel."

Kali said nothing.

"Hooper, the long shot?"

This time, Kali bit her lip.

"Hooper, you *do have* a long shot, right?"

Don't ask me that, Liam, don't ask, Kali thought.

What was it she had said to Freel, back in the Sardenne – I tend to work on the hoof? Well, she wasn't on the hoof now, was she, she was on her backside, collapsed helpless against a wall, and it didn't look like her long shot was going to be materialising at all.

"Sure, Liam. I'll ask Baz to stop, shall I? Get him to send his people home to Kerberos?"

A drop of blood fell from the archer, and he spoke slowly, quietly. "They have no home other than the hells, you know that. They don't belong on Kerberos and they don't belong here. Hooper, *come on*, you always have something up your sleeve..."

"Not this time. I'm sorry."

"Kali..."

"*Not this time!*"

Shocked, Slowhand stared down at her. But Kali was not looking up and all he saw was the top of her head.

"Kal," he said. "We've all lost people close to us, and we know how much that hurt. Now that's about to happen again, only on a massive scale. As I see it, as soon as that pillar disappears, they've lost their loved ones for ever, but so long as it's *there* we have a chance to bring them back... somehow."

Kali's eyes slowly rose to the base of the pillar of souls, still emptying itself of the last dregs of Ur'Raney souls. What the archer said was true – while that pillar still existed, there might still be time to save them somehow, to bring them back, for *something* to happen – no matter how much of a long shot it might be.

"Hooper," Slowhand said. "You're the only one who can do this..."

"I know," Kali whispered to herself.

"What?"

"I said, I know!" Kali shouted, picking herself from the floor. Between her and Redigor, the *rannaat*, who were just about to move away from their tombs, turned at her defiant cry. She uttered a primal roar as she ran along the aisle to launch herself at the Pale Lord. The *rannaat* looked almost amused, and looked to their Lord for guidance. Redigor, looking less amused, shook his head.

Kali pounded towards him, beads of sweat falling from her.

"Enough," Redigor said. "You are a meddlesome pain, child. I could easily strip your soul and take your body for my collection, but I do not believe I wish to keep either."

Redigor's arm shot out and he curled his fingers. Kali found herself halting in her tracks and collapsing to her knees with a cry of agony as something seemed to close around her heart and pull. She looked down, her mouth falling open in shock and pain. Whisps of light were being drawn from within her. As he had with so many before her, Bastian Redigor was extracting her soul – and doing so, it seemed, in as slow and as agonising fashion as he could.

"Hey," Kali uttered between clenched teeth, "that just isn't fair..."

"And since I do not wish to keep your soul, child," Redigor continued, ignoring her. "Why don't I simply tear it out?"

The elven sorcerer jerked his outstretched hand again and Kali wailed with pain. Though she remained on her knees, she was bent backwards, her spine and neck arched like a bow, throat taut, mouth stretched open as far as it would go. The light poured from her and across the Chapel to Redigor's fingertips. There the Pale Lord breathed in deeply and with satisfaction, as if he were drinking her.

Kali groaned. The more her soul was drawn from her, the more agonising it became. She was struggling desperately now to hang onto the last of her being, but she was fighting a losing battle. Her vision darkening, her thoughts dimming, feeling as though she were adrift in some dark expanse, she was only peripherally aware of a shape that staggered into her distorted vision, and then of two blurry flashes that sliced through the air before her. Through the air and through her departing soul. Kali screamed in agony as the whole of her self suddenly snapped back in like an elastic band, and she bucked on the floor taking deep, gulping breaths.

In that instant she realised that Redigor's grip was gone, and that she was whole again.

Whole, and not alone.

"Stay behind me," Gabriella DeZantez said, wielding the Deathclaws. "I guess what they say about these things slicing souls is true."

What? Kali thought. What they say about the claws is true? But Gabriella has the claws and Gabriella is dead... she died.

Gabriella was dead... she had *seen* her die in the Sardenne, at the hands of the juggennath. But at the same time here she was.

Kali shook her head and saw Gabriella, pulling her to her feet. The Enlightened One was scarred and battered, her armour crushed and misshapen beneath her torn surplice, and a dark rivulet of blood leaked from the side of her mouth, but she was there. And behind her, staring with a strange mixture of curiosity and rage, was the Pale Lord.

"No, no," Kali said to Gabriella, trying to push her away, "he's too powerful. Get out of here, get out of here now."

Gabriella grabbed her by the shoulders. "It's *all right*, remember."

"All right?"

"Yes, all right! Now, stay behind me."

Kali nodded, not really understanding. And then she began to remember. Remember because Redigor was attempting the same trick on Gabriella that he had tried on her, but with absolutely no effect at all. Gabriella, in fact, still had her back turned to him, and she hadn't even *noticed* what he was attempting to do. Then – Redigor still trying without success to rip out her soul – she turned and began to limp slowly up the aisle towards him, drawing Kali in behind her.

From over Gabriella's shoulder Kali saw the Pale Lord hesitate.

"What is this?" He said. "Some kind of resistance? Who are you, girl?"

"My name Gabriella DeZantez. I am a Sister of the Order of the Swords of Dawn."

The Pale Lord's eyes narrowed. "And pray, Sister, what brings you here?"

"I come to smite thee."

The Pale Lord looked, for a second, amazed, and – as Gabriella and Kali continued their approach. But then his face reverted to its usual arrogant mask and he raised his arms towards Gabriella. Kali knew what was coming and it was clear that so, too, did Gabriella.

The Enlightened One's fingers curled into the top of her breastplate, ripping it away, and she drew in a deep, preparatory breath.

"Bring it on, you unholy bastard!"

Bastian Redigor's lip curled.

"Very well. We shall see how strong you are."

Lightning burst forth from his fingertips, smacking Gabriella directly in the chest. It had no physical effect other than to slow her slightly, discharging in bright arcs and cracks about her shoulders as she pushed against it. Redigor loosed another bolt, equally ineffective, and his eyes widened. He thrust his arms forward once more and this time a plume of fire lanced towards Kali's protector, bursting about her body. Kali ducked, but still Gabriella moved forward.

Now Redigor tried ice, and the crackling, steaming bolts of magical energy slammed into Gabriella with a serpentine hiss but, again, only slowed her in her tracks. It was like struggling forward against a strong wind, and this was exactly what Redigor tried next, summoning a gale to pummel Gabriella that, while it set every loose object in the Chapel flying, she strode through as if it were an inconvenient breeze.

The pair of them were halfway up the Chapel's aisle now, nothing stopping them reaching Redigor.

The Chapel was filled with shrieking hags as phantom horrors materialised out of every corner and swept at Gabriella, threatening to tear her apart. As they came, so too did great, writhing snakes whose wide, fanged maws bit down on her.

Nor were they the last of what Redigor had to offer. Spectral daggers hurled themselves at her in wave after wave, fist-sized explosions detonated about her body, and stone barriers assembled themselves out of the floor, only to crumble before Gabriella's determined march. The Pale Lord actually looked visibly shaken now – was perhaps even becoming drained – but rather than feel a sense of impending victory Kali felt increasing concern for Gabriella. It was true that the Enlightened One seemed unstoppable in her progress, but Gabriella seemed at last to be weakening before it.

She moved more slowly now and, above the noise of the assault, Kali thought that she even heard Gabriella wheeze with strain. She wanted to say *stop now, that's enough, you've done what you can,* but she knew she couldn't. If Gabriella gave up now the two of them would be dead, and any chance of stopping Redigor gone for good. Suddenly all of Kali's attention was focused not on Redigor's continuing barrage but on Gabriella herself.

A great, unremitting river of destruction poured from Redigor's fingertips, slamming relentlessly into Gabriella. No one, however gifted, could withstand such destruction for much longer, and Kali's heart sank as Gabriella at last began to falter. She felt the sheer impotence of her own position, the fact that she couldn't help the woman at all. Knowing that she would be inviting instant obliteration if she stepped from behind Gabriella's protective guard, all she could do was will the Enlightened One onwards despite her mounting pain.

And more than pain.

At first Kali wasn't quite sure what she was seeing, but Gabriella's muscles were now less pronounced than before, and somehow deteriorated. Her skin had lost its golden sheen, becoming less vibrant. With horror Kali realised that this wasn't simply a reaction to the suffering Gabriella was enduring; she wasn't just weakening before Redigor's onslaught, she was *aging* before it. Kali placed a hand on her shoulder, felt bone rather than muscle beneath her fingers.

Oh gods, what's happening to her?

The answer seemed clear. As immune to magic as Gabriella had announced herself to be, she might have had the ability to spend her entire life shrugging off any one of the Pale Lord's individual attacks – of anyone's attacks – and somehow recovered. But what she had suffered from Redigor collectively in the space of minutes was *already* a lifetime's worth. She had been drained of everything she had in attempting to save her, in attempting to save *everyone*, and Gabriella DeZantez's life was ending right before her eyes.

Redigor's barrage continued and Gabriella, having almost reached him, faltered, staggered, and crumpled to the floor, more bone than flesh.

Redigor lowered his arms and looked down. His eyes widened and he bent and plucked the Deathclaws from Gabriella's twitching hands.

"Ah," he said, "I've been looking for these for a long, long time."

Kali's rage was incandescent as she stood before him, but she could do nothing. If she made a single move, the elf would reduce her to dust.

"Now," Redigor said, "wouldn't you agree that was just a waste of time?"

Kali's eyes rose to him, but the Pale Lord was calmly looking at her, awaiting an answer to his question. He *wanted* an answer, Kali realised, so that he could bask in his supremacy, and, in all honesty, she wasn't sure that she wouldn't have to give the one he desired. But not yet. Not yet. She looked slowly around the Chapel of Screams, at Slowhand, at Freel, down at Gabriella DeZantez, and then up at Makennon, from whose eyes a stranger stared haughtily down. She hoped that they understood she'd tried her best, and that this time her long shot hadn't paid off.

Her eyes returned to the Pale Lord. As they did, she heard something that the Pale Lord hadn't yet picked up on. It was a sound that she had been hoping to hear almost since she'd arrived at the Sardenne, a sound that when she had first heard it had filled her with dread, but which, now, buoyed her heart.

That was the thing about long shots, she guessed. Sometimes they took a while to arrive.

"Actually, no," she said to Redigor, "I wouldn't agree at all. What Gabriella did wasn't a waste of time, it *bought* us time."

Redigor looked up, now recognising the disturbance in the air above.

"That's right, Baz," Kali said, springing up and hissing in his ear. "Remember those?"

Redigor stared through the shattered roof of the Chapel of Screams, his face twisted with anger. Three massive machines hove into view, and whether Redigor had personally set eyes on the Engines of the Apocalypse before or not, there was no mistaking the immense cones for anything other than what they were. But if any more proof were needed, the sudden blare of their positioning sirens as they began to spin above the necropolis was more than adequate. Redigor snapped his gaze from them down to Kali and then to his *rannaat*. The twelve-pseudo elves looked at him with pleading, but already their features were reverting to human, his hold over them disappearing.

His hold over other things was disappearing, too. At the far end of the Chapel, Slowhand fell from where he was pinned against the wall, crashing to the floor with a thud. He picked himself up, his expression dark, and, clutching his broken arm, began to weave his way down the aisle towards Kali.

"No," Redigor whispered.

"Yes," Kali corrected. "That's right, Baz. That old black magic is going away. Quite ironic, don't you think, since that's how this whole thing began?"

"Impossible!" Redigor protested. "The Engines are designed to negate only elven threads, and my magic is... is –"

"The dead bits in between?" Kali said. "What remains of dragon magic, perhaps?" Kali shrugged. "Under normal circumstances, yeah. But, hey, you know, if you twiddle the dials, turn everything up to eleven..."

"*No!*" Redigor cried.

His voice echoed throughout the Chapel of Screams and he raised his arms, trying to propel Kali and Slowhand back along the aisle. Only Kali staggered back, and only because he physically shoved her. Redigor threw his arms wide, somehow finding the reserves for one last outburst of energy, trying to infuse his people with his own essence, to slow their reversion, but the energy fizzled even as it began to spread, dissipating into a cloud of nothing, and Redigor collapsed to his knees, spent. He stared in disbelief and could do little but watch as the whole sequence of soul exchange reversed itself before his eyes, the souls of the Ur'Raney pulled from the bodies of their hosts and back towards the pillar, and the pillar, in turn, brightening with the return of the human souls from Kerberos. Kali doubted that Redigor felt the same but the whole process was quite magical to watch, the whisps of humanity slowly twisting and twining throughout the Chapel, finding their rightful homes first in those who had been doomed to be the High Council and then travelling further afield, to the general tombs, to reinhabit those who waited there.

The exchange complete, both Kali and Slowhand stared up at the pillar of souls. The essences of things still writhed within it, still sought somehow to escape, and perhaps even to snatch at those whose flesh they were now denied, but there was one important difference – these souls were Ur'Raney, and they were going back where they belonged.

The pillar of souls disappeared and Kali and Slowhand found themselves staring at the looming masses of the Engines, still rotating above.

"Hooper, I thought you said..." Slowhand interjected.

"Sorry, Liam. For one thing I didn't know if I had programmed them correctly but, more importantly, I couldn't even think about them in Redigor's presence. He'd have sensed it, stopped them somehow..."

"You worked out a way to bring them all the way here?"

"Made it up as I went along," Kali said, smiling.

Their smiles faded as they heard Katherine Makennon groan and were reminded of the ordeal she'd been through. Slowhand was about to offer aid, but Kali placed a hand on his arm, holding him back, allowing the Anointed Lord to emerge from her nightmare by herself.

Her gait stiff, her head erect and proud, Katherine Makennon moved slowly from the altar by the kneeling Redigor to a slab where her clothing, armour and weapon lay neatly folded and stacked. For the moment, she ignored the garments, regarding them curiously, fingering them, but nothing more. Instead, she took the shaft of the battleaxe in two hands and wearily dragged it towards her. Seemingly lacking the strength to lift it again, Makennon paused a second, drawing in a deep and contemplative breath, and then turned to face the Pale Lord, her expression devoid of emotion. Then, equally slowly, she began to walk towards Redigor, dragging the battleaxe with her. When she stood in front of him, she stopped and, in a dry croak, demanded he rise.

Showing no fear, no remorse, only the arrogance that had marked the man for all his long and depraved life, Bastian Redigor stood. For a second his eyes seemed to flick beyond her but then he leaned forward, and whispered in her ear.

"Your church will crumble at my hands. I will destroy it."

Makennon's gaze rose until it met his. Her eyes were unblinking, her face blank. Almost imperceptibly at first, the muscles about her mouth began to spasm, her face contorted into a mask of rage and fury, and then she swung the battleaxe up from between her legs with a guttural roar that shook the Chapel.

Bastian Redigor had no time even to cry out. With a sound more at home on a butcher's block than a chapel's altar, the blade sliced into the Pale Lord at the groin and continued up through him until it swung out over Makennon's head. Arcs of blood and entrails spattered the faces of those watching but no one moved. The Anointed Lord held the battleaxe over her head, dripping blood and gore, and then gradually set it down. Before her, the halves of Bastian Redigor parted and crumpled to the floor, landing with wet thuds.

Makennon's words were whispered.

"I'd like to see you try."

Kali looked around her at those assembled, seeing in their eyes the same return to humanity that she had witnessed in Makennon's. Then her eyes moved to the prone, shrivelled form of Gabriella DeZantez and she knelt by her side. The Enlightened One was still alive, just, but the life was already fading from her eyes.

Kali cradled DeZantez's head, wanting desperately to offer

some comfort but not knowing what to say. In the end, it was Gabriella who spoke first, though her voice was not what Kali remembered – a cracked, aged thing, little more than a sibilant whisper.

"Do you see the light? Gabriella DeZantez sees the light."

"The light?"

"Kerberos," Gabriella said slowly, and smiled. Her eyes were focused upward, not on Kali at all. "My time is close."

"You saved my life. Bought the time to save all our lives. Is there anything I can do... to make things easier?"

Gabriella emitted a low chuckle. "Are you offering to pray for me?"

"Yes. Yes, yes, I am, if that's what you want."

Gabriella shook her head, laughed again. "Maybe it would be... more appropriate if... you had a drink for me instead..."

Kali smiled. "I'll do that. More than one. The whole of the *Flagons* will."

A cough. "Such a request from a Sister of the Faith is, of course, prohibited."

"What the hells, eh?"

Gabriella suddenly tensed beneath her. "Looks like we were wrong."

Kali frowned. "About what?"

"My being one of the Four."

"Hey, I don't think so," Kali said. "You did more than your bit to save the world today."

Gabriella shook her head again, but this time didn't laugh. "No. This wasn't the time, I sense that. Not the threat that is meant to bring the Four together..."

Kali turned away, biting her lip. When she looked at Gabriella again, the Enlightened One was staring directly at her.

"There's more you haven't told me, isn't there?" Gabriella asked. "You *know* something, don't you?"

Kali took a second before she spoke. "Not much. Something's coming. Darkness."

Gabriella absorbed the information, swallowed, and her body spasmed once more. But she retained enough control to study

Kali intently. She clutched at Kali's hand, squeezed it. "*Tell someone.* Tell Slowhand. Don't go through this alone."

Kali nodded, while beneath her, Gabriella groaned.

"Do something else for me," she said. Slowly, her skeletal hand slipped into her charred surplice and withdrew the shard of Freedom Mountain, which she pressed into Kali's hand. She swallowed again, dryly, and her next words emerged almost as a wheeze. "Please. Watch me go."

Kali looked at the shard and at Gabriella and nodded. The Enlightened One squeezed her hand in thanks and held her gaze. Only after a few moments had passed did Kali realise that she was never going to look away again.

Kali took a shuddering breath and slowly raised the shard. She gasped, eyes widening, and smiled.

Gabriella's soul rose from her body in much the same way as Brother Marcus's had done, but there was something that distinguished it, not only from the Faith soldier's soul but from every other soul she had now seen.

Gabriella's essence shone brightly, blindingly. As it slowly wove its way upwards, towards Kerberos, it flared with all the colours of the threads, a rainbow burst filled far more with life than it ever could be with death.

Kali thought about everything she'd learned about Kerberos in the past few days. About how it might, despite her previous disbelief, be a part of everything.

And maybe, she thought, Gabriella had been wrong about not being one of the Four. Maybe, just maybe, she might yet still be.

A hand fell heavily on her shoulder.

"Hooper, I'm sorry," Slowhand said. "The Engines – there's something wrong."

Chapter Eighteen

There was something wrong, all right. Great shadows loomed over Kali even as she stood to take in what Slowhand had said. As she looked through the collapsed roof of the Chapel of Screams she saw that the Engines were lower in the sky than on their arrival. Their sirens were blaring in a deafening, urgent tone.

"Oh gods," she said. "They're coming down."

"Down?" Slowhand repeated. "Hooper, I thought you had control of these things?"

"I do... I did! They just weren't meant to come down *so soon*."

"So *soon*?"

"What, you thought I'd leave them up there? Slowhand, there's a reason they're called the Engines of the Apocalypse!"

"Right, right, fine," Slowhand said.

He looked around at the former members of Redigor's High Council, all of whom were shuffling slowly about the Chapel, disorientated "But I suggest we get these people out of here now."

Above them, one Engine tipped suddenly to the left, its siren blaring louder still, and grazed one of its companions. The sound of the immense machines grinding together drowned out even the increasingly distressed wail of the siren, and the explosion that followed drowned out even that. The first Engine shuddered on its axis and sheered off. The second came to a stop, hanging above them like a steel storm cloud.

And then, though strangely slowly for something of its size, it began to drop.

"Move, move, move!" The archer commanded, slapping Kali on the shoulder with his good arm and herding Makennon, Freel and the rest towards the Chapel's exit.

The Anointed Lord glared at him furiously for a moment, snarling over Redigor's remains, but she capitulated, turning to help Freel and Slowhand with steering their groggier counterparts from the Chapel.

As they ushered the nobles, lords and ladies onto the tomb bridge, the first Engine fell, burrowing into the hole left by the exploded chapel roof. As it came, slowly and inexorably, the edges of the hole began to crumble and collapse, bringing a rain of falling masonry. From near the exit, having just manhandled the last of Redigor's victims through, Kali stared back into the Chapel, picking out Gabriella's corpse through the resultant cloud of dust and debris. She started towards it, intending to carry it out with her, but two slabs of the roof collapsed in her path. Coughing and spluttering, Kali staggered back, looking for another way around. The Engine had begun to burrow itself into the base of the Chapel, and great jagged rents were splitting the floor, spidering out in all directions. Kali finally had to concede that there was no way through. Reluctantly, she turned and stepped onto the bridge.

As Kali began to race after the others, making their way slowly across the bridge, the second of the Engines slammed into the chapel roof and through it and the Chapel of Screams was no more. Kali looked back and swallowed as cracks began to pursue them across the bridge. Many of the former soul-stripped still milled by the tombs lining the chamber, free of their possession but lost on the crumbling walkways.

"Get a farking move on!" Kali shouted to those on the bridge, and to those above and below, "Hey, do you *really* want to die?"

Miraculously they all made it, bursting from the entrance of Bel'A'Gon'Shri and racing to safety along the gorge just as the entire necropolis collapsed. Kali and Slowhand ushered them on along the gorge, at last reaching a safe distance where the dust and debris from Bel'A'Gon'Shri choked and coated them but otherwise passed them harmlessly by.

The rest of the party out of harm's way, Kali told them to carry on while she and Slowhand paused for a while. She wanted to make sure that the third and last of the Engines followed its companions, not only to confirm that the peninsula was rid of the things but also because, in a sense, it would be like watching the final nail being hammered into Bastian Redigor's coffin.

Unfortunately, things didn't go quite according to plan. Explosions rocked the third Engine, and it began to spin faster and faster, before it fell.

Kali and Slowhand looked at the crooked remains of its companions beneath it, and did some quick mental calculations.

"Please tell me it's not going to do what I think it's going to do," Slowhand said.

Kali stared. "It's going to do what you think it's going to do."

"Oh. Hells."

"Shall we run?"

"I think we'd better."

Despite their words, they remained where they were for another couple of seconds, staring up.

The third engine was coming down on the other two and still spinning at full tilt. Exactly how the engine would react to that Kali and Slowhand couldn't be sure, but it wasn't likely to be gentle or quiet.

The third engine, its sirens blaring, listed badly to the side as it continued its fall, presenting itself side on to the remains of the engines below. The strangely shaped mass slewed into its companions with a grinding and clashing of metals louder even than the noise of the sirens, jamming itself between them and, with an almighty explosion, hurled itself out from between its grounded companions, tumbling end over end towards the necropolis's entrance. The Engine shattered and scattered statues as it came and, when its nose hit the ground, flipped itself end over end once more, bounced along the gorge for perhaps three or four rotations, and slapped down onto its belly with ground-quaking force, skewing along the gorge towards them.

"Now?" Slowhand asked.

"Now." Kali said.

The two of them turned and began to run like the hells, the engine demolishing trees, boulders, *everything* behind them, and still coming. The pair snatched glances over their shoulders and wished they hadn't, as it was beginning to look as if they had turned to run just a little too late.

The engine, seemingly unstoppable, continued to tear up the ground as it advanced, creating a solid tsunami of soil, rock and shredded vegetation. It would not, both of them reflected, be a very nice way to go.

The first ripples of soil and debris nudged at their ankles.

They looked at each other, and gulped.

Then Katherine Makennon was standing before them and the Anointed Lord was not alone. A group of ten mages, who had presumably teleported in to be by her side when they had witnessed the arrival and demise of the Engines, stood to either side of her. Makennon gestured to them and, as one, they raised their arms, releasing visible pulses of energy over Kali and Slowhand's heads, designed to slow the rampaging Engine down.

The strain was written on their faces. Veins pulsed beneath their flesh. From the noses of one or two blood began to trickle, and then pour.

The Engine began to slow. Gradually, the sounds of destruction from behind Kali and Slowhand quietened. And then it was over, the two of them rather embarrassingly pushed right in front of Makennon on the crest of a final, slow wave of soil.

"Thanks," Kali said, after a moment.

The Anointed Lord regarded her. The cloak she wore to restore her dignity had, it seemed, been 'donated' by the mayor of Gargas, who stood shivering in his britches behind her.

"I think that makes us even," Katherine Makennon said. Her tone made it clear that there would be no discussion as to what had happened. *Ever.*

Kali nodded. As she did, Freel emerged from the undergrowth and stood by Makennon's side. He snapped his fingers at those mages who weren't holding handkerchiefs to their noses, and they began to weave the threads. After a few seconds, the air before Makennon and Freel parted into a rift through which Kali glimpsed a view of Makennon's inner sanctum back at Scholten Cathedral. The rift hovered a couple of feet off the ground but, in an ostentatious touch presumably designed to ease Makennon's passage, a small flight of steps formed so that she could reach it.

As if they were departing after a simple day in the countryside, Makennon's retinue filed through one by one, until only the Anointed Lord and Freel were left. Then it was Freel's turn. At first it seemed that Jenna's husband was going to leave without a goodbye but he paused, one foot on the steps, and turned to Slowhand.

"I'll remember this," he said.

Slowhand nodded and, with a bow to Kali, Freel was gone.

Makennon stepped up to the threshold of the portal. Like Freel it seemed that she, too, was going to depart without another word but then she turned to Kali and beckoned her to her side.

"That girl in the Chapel. Who was she?"

"Her name," Kali said, "was Gabriella DeZantez."

"DeZantez... DeZantez," Makennon repeated as if she were dredging the name up from some dark and forgotten depth. "Ah, yes."

Then Makennon – and the portal – were gone.

"Well, they could have offered us a lift," Slowhand said. But the only response he got from Kali was a crashing of the undergrowth. "Hooper? Hooper?"

Kali was storming away from the necropolis as fast as she could go. Slowhand hurried to catch up.

"Farking woman!" Kali cursed.

"Hooper, I'm not sure you should be storming through the forest like this."

"No? You know any better way to get the hells out of the pitsing place?"

"Hooper, what I mean is *slow down*, or you'll bring every freak and monstrosity within a league's radius down on us!"

"Bring 'em on."

"Don't be stupid."

"I said, fark 'em, Slowhand!"

The archer pulled a face, grabbed her by the shoulders with his good arm, and turned her around. "Hey," he shouted. "Hey!"

Kali wrenched herself out of his grip, turned in a frustrated circle, not knowing what to do with herself, and finally kicked a nearby tree trunk. Something with wings that flapped like wet cloth took to the sky but Kali didn't care, her breathing fast and hard.

"Hooper," Slowhand gasped, "if you don't stop crashing around you're going to get us *both* killed."

Kali bent and ran the back of her hand across her mouth, speaking breathlessly. "Leave it alone, Liam."

"I can't do that. Because this isn't about Makennon, is it?" Slowhand challenged. "It's about Gabriella."

Kali shot him a look, found his firm but concerned blue eyes holding her gaze, and gradually brought her breathing under control. The archer was only partly right, but right enough. It was about Gabriella, yes, but about Makennon, too – the way the woman had swanned off just now. Pits of Kerberos, she didn't want any gratitude herself – gods knew, she hoped she wasn't *that* petty – but she *did* want some kind of acknowledgement for the people who had died to win her the freedom to go home. Not only Gabriella DeZantez but those many who had died at the hands of the juggennath or in their subsequent flight from it. Still, it was Gabriella that stuck in her mind, and what stuck more than anything were Makennon's words about her.

Who was she?

Who was she?

Kali pulled away from Slowhand and continued, with him trailing behind. The pair managed to negotiate a couple of leagues without incident, but found themselves freezing at a sudden thrashing from the bush beside them. Kali drew her gutting knife, ready to wield against whatever warped denizen of the forest had them in its sights. Nothing came at them though, and, after a few seconds, Kali pulled the undergrowth aside.

The source of the thrashing was a warped denizen all right, but not the kind that she or Slowhand had expected.

Querilous Fitch lay in a ditch beneath them, having presumably landed here after he had been struck by the juggennath. The extent of his injuries were plain to see.

Fitch saw Slowhand and the broken body of the psychic manipulator spasmed in the ditch, hands desperately trying to rise and wield some kind of magic, offensive or defensive, but his arms simply flapped by his sides ineffectually.

"That old problem again, Fitch?" Slowhand growled. "You really ought to see a doctor about that."

The archer moved in and took Fitch by the neck, staring him in the eyes as he tightened his grip.

"Liam, don't kill him," Kali said.

"What?"

"I'm asking you not to kill him. He has information that I need."

"What the hells do you mean, he has information that you need?"

Kali hesitated. "Something... well, I don't know if it's important, but it might be."

"Oh, really," Slowhand hissed without loosening his grip. Fitch was struggling, turning blue, his tongue bloating between twisted lips. "Hooper, this guy was responsible for the death of my sister and in case you hadn't noticed has tried to kill me twice, both times without compunction or hesitation, and frankly I don't want him running around anymore. You tell me – what could be more important than that?"

"I –" Kali began, and stopped.

She rocked back and forth on her heels, torn. *Share this with someone*, Gabriella had said. *Don't bear it alone.* But how could she burden her sometime lover with the knowledge that the world he knew – and all of the beds and women in it – might soon be coming to an end? The answer was, she couldn't – at least until Slowhand, with a sigh, suddenly released his grip on Fitch, dropping his choking victim back into the bottom of the ditch, and turned to face her, more concerned than she had ever seen him.

"Dammit, Hooper, this is about that night at the *Flagons*, isn't it? The night you stormed out of the party? Because you learned something in the Crucible, didn't you? Something you haven't told anyone?" He took her by the shoulder again, and this time Kali didn't pull away.

She did just the opposite, in fact.

"Kal, what is it?" Slowhand asked, as she sobbed in his arms.

She told him everything. About what the dwelf had said about the coming darkness and about what she had learned about 'the Four' and how she had come to believe they might have a role in preventing it. When she had finished, Slowhand said nothing, his eyes like those of a drowning man. In the end, it was Fitch who broke the silence.

"Everything your girlfriend says is true," the manipulator admitted, "and I have the information she needs to make sense of it."

"Then spill it," Slowhand said.

Fitch smiled. "Not here. Hidden. I can tell her how to find it, how to retrieve it, but first you have to get me out of here."

"No deal."

Kali looked at Slowhand, hesitant. She knew the decision she was about to make was not going to be popular. "Deal," she said. "Can you help me get him up? We should be near enough to the perimeter now for me to whistle Horse."

"No," Slowhand said.

Kali shook her head and clambered into the ditch. "Fine. I'll do it myself."

Slowhand held her arm. "I mean no, he's not coming, Hooper. The bastard stays here, takes his chances."

"Slowhand, *please*."

"No."

"No?" It was the first time Slowhand had ever openly disagreed with her.

"No, Kal," Slowhand said more softly. "Because it strikes me that if it's your *destiny* to do these things, your destiny to find these things out, then you're going to find them out whichever way things happen. *If* it's Fitch who's destined to tell you what you need to know then he'll find his way out of this and he'll tell you, but I'll be damned if I'm going to help him do so."

"What if that's *your* destiny? To help him?"

Slowhand slapped his forehead in frustration. "No, Kali. No, I'm not having that. I'll not accept that my every move is predestined." The archer felt the need to explain further, sought an analogy. "Look, I believed it was Pontaine's destiny to win the Great War – every one of us did, which is why we fought so hard and for so long – and in the end we *did* win, spilling the blood of thousands on the Killing Ground. *Thousands*, Kal – but you know that. The point is the battle was won as a result of thousands of decisions that I and those fighters made each and every second we fought – split second choices to cut or to thrust, parry or raise shield, shoot or hold that made the difference between our lives and our deaths. And all of those decisions were based on what our *enemies* chose, out of thousands of choices of their own. Just how many choices is that in all, Kal? It was chaos on the Killing Ground, *chaos*, so can you really tell me that every one of those decisions was predestined?"

"Of course not!" Kali said defensively, aware of the strength of Slowhand's argument. "But I'm talking about the bigger picture." She struggled. "The way it needs all the pieces to fit together... like a jigsaw."

"Didn't you once tell me that you were crap at jigsaws?" Slowhand said.

Kali stared up at him, tearful, then down at Fitch, torn.

"Hooper," Slowhand said, "wars are won as they're meant to be won, through dedication to a cause and a determination to see it through. I know you – you might hate every minute of this, but I also know you *will* see it through whether you're one of these fabled 'four' or not. And you know why? Because that's *who you are*, and not because it's your destiny. But if you let Fitch manipulate you like this, you'll be just as much one of his puppets as Jenna was."

"Will you... see it through with me?"

"I don't know, Kal. I just don't know."

Kali bit her lip, then nodded. She whistled for Horse and, a few minutes later, the bamfcat appeared. Kali mounted, slapping the thick of his neck hard in thanks for coming to collect her. "Sorry, Querilous," she said to the protesting, groaning figure in the ditch, and then, to Slowhand, "You coming?"

"Give me a second," Slowhand said, "I'll catch up." He watched as Kali nodded once more then walked Horse forward through the forest, and then he turned back to Querilous Fitch.

"Are you going to kill me now, archer?" The manipulator said. He nodded at Suresight. "I should imagine that would prove difficult, with only one arm."

Slowhand whipped an arrow from his quiver and held its tip shaking above Querilous Fitch's chest. "I only need one arm."

"You really should listen to your girlfriend, you know. It's your *destiny*."

Slowhand almost plunged the arrow down right then, but he held it, his unblinking blue eyes looking into Fitch's, *through* him. *Thousands of choices a second,* he thought, *and through those wars are won.* He stood and began to walk away. Whether it was the low, sick cackling from behind him or the sibilant, murmuring, protesting voices in his own head he didn't know, but a moment later he turned, returned to Fitch and, with a shout, rammed the arrow into the manipulator's chest with such force that it pinned him to the ground. Wide eyed, Fitch was so stunned that he couldn't even wail.

"I make my *own* destiny," Slowhand said, and followed Kali's trail.

Both Kali and Slowhand wanted to take the journey slowly, and, camping at their leisure, took three days to return to the *Flagons*. The last thing they expected when they arrived was an invitation to attend a memorial service in Scholten for those who hadn't made it out of the Sardenne. Kali thought for a second that she had, after all, misjudged Makennon – but on closer inspection it turned out that their invitation had been signed by Jakub Freel. At any rate, the service was scheduled for the next day at Midchime and, after both she and Slowhand had been thoroughly polished and preened by Dolorosa – "you notta go in anything from which your bum sticka out, young lady!" – the two of them set out on Horse, reaching the Vossian seat of power overnight, in four jumps.

They spent the morning in the *Gay Goblin*, the *Kegs O'Kerberos* and the *Bloody Merry*, marking time in the way of those aware that, on a fundamental level, things were moving on. Gradually, eventually, they worked their way towards the cathedral, the front of which, by the time they arrived, was filled with people considerably more sober than they. The two of them were content with a place in the jostling crowd, but one look from a guard at their invitation had them elevated to the front platform where they were positioned instead alongside Freel, the Anointed Lord and a number of dignitaries including Cardinal Kratos and General McIntee.

Freel nodded as they took their places. Makennon, however, did not even acknowledge their presence, remaining aloof. Whether that was because she was maintaining her public face or, as Kali suspected, this whole thing and their part in it had been Freel's idea and Makennon resented it, she didn't know – but it was interesting to note that the Faith's new enforcer seemed far more willing to adopt a prominent public role than Konstantin Munch had ever done.

Quite what he intended to *do* with it was a matter for another day.

Bells rang, silencing the crowd, and Makennon's address began. Kali was hardly surprised that in the Anointed Lord's account of the events in the Sardenne, neither she nor Slowhand got a mention, and in fact she had difficulty recognising any of it. All the crowd seemed to want to hear, however, was that – aided by the Lord of All – the forces of the Final Faith had defeated their First Enemy and that once again its flock could look forward to the glory of the day of ascension. The very mention of the word brought a rousing cheer from the crowd, and both Kali and Slowhand shuffled uneasily as the all too familiar mantra began to sound from the crowd, growing in volume with each repetition.

"The One Faith!"

"The Only Faith!"

"The Final Faith!"

Eventually, the Anointed Lord raised a hand, and the crowd lapsed into silence. Bells rang once more, but this time more slowly, a dirge rather than a call to attention. Makennon nodded to Cardinal Kratos and the robed figure moved solemnly forward. He began, as was way of these things, to intone platitudes about the dead.

The names were read out, the accompanying comments saying nothing at all about the people who had died, or what had led them to make the sacrifices they had made. As banality followed banality, Slowhand saw the growing tension in Kali's face. The thing about Hooper was that she never got drunk unless she wanted to or she was upset. It was almost as if she could open a sluice gate somewhere halfway down her throat, and all the alcohol she consumed simply went somewhere else. Today, however, that sluice gate had remained firmly closed, and while he'd *thought* she was handling herself well, considering the amount of thwack they'd poured down their necks, he now saw that slightly unfocused look in her eyes.

Trouble was brewing, he knew it.

Sure enough, as the roll call of the dead reached Gabriella DeZantez and the platitudes began to spout, Kali suddenly lurched forward and shoved the cardinal out of the way. The noise Kratos made as he tumbled down the platform's wooden steps were amplified by the complex arrangement of shells positioned around the podium to amplify speech, and three quarters of Scholten gasped.

Behind Kali the Swords of Dawn honour guard reached for their weapons, but a subtle shake of the head from Makennon halted them.

"You want to know about Gabriella DeZantez?" Kali began. "I'll tell you about Gabriella DeZantez..."

As Kali began to speak about the woman she had known, her loyalty, her dedication, her embarrassing laugh and even her *eyes*, Slowhand stared at the back of Kali's head and mouthed, *goodbye*. He had decided that morning that it was time to go, that he had to spend time away from Hooper and work out what was to happen in the future on his own, and now was as good a time as any. Maybe he'd be back, maybe not, but whatever happened he knew that at least Kali had another friend she could rely on, one within the Faith itself.

Slowhand nodded to Jakub Freel as he made his way off the platform and down into the crowd. Kali was in full swing now and didn't notice him go.

"...if it wasn't for Gabriella DeZantez," Kali shouted, pointing at the Anointed Lord, "this woman would be spending the rest of her life with tassels on her tits!"

Slowhand smiled, working his way through the crowd. A few days ago he'd have stopped to help with the commotion that comment would cause, but Hooper would be all right.

Look after her, Prince Jakub Tremayne Freel, he thought.

What Slowhand did not know was that as he had left the platform and stared into the eyes of the Faith enforcer, it had been Bastian Redigor staring back.

THE END

Mike Wild is much older than he has a right to be, considering the kebabs, the booze and the fags. Maybe it's because he still thinks he's 15. Apart from dabbling occasionally in publishing and editing, he's been a freelance writer for ever, clawing his way up to his current dizzy heights by way of work as diverse as *Doctor Who*, *Masters of the Universe*, *Starblazer*, *'Allo 'Allo!* and – erm – *My Little Pony*. Counting one *Teen Romance*, one *ABC Warriors* and two *Caballistics Inc*, *Engines of the Apocalypse* is his seventh novel. However, only his beloved wife and tuna-scoffing cat give him the recognition he deserves.

TWILIGHT of KERBEROS

If you enjoyed *Engines of the Apocalypse*, why not try...

The CALL of KERBEROS

JONATHAN OLIVER

ISBN: 978-1-906735-28-9

£6.99/$7.99

WWW.ABADDONBOOKS.COM

Chapter One

Stealing a ship from the harbour at Turnitia would have been an audacious enough task in itself, but stealing a vessel belonging to the Final Faith was another matter entirely. When Dunsany had first suggested it to Kelos he had stared blankly at him for a moment and then said: "Have you seen what they do to heretics? Have you seen the rather fetching collection of heretic skins Makennon keeps as mementos?"

Katherine Makennon was the flame-haired, hot-tempered, Anointed Lord; the leader of the Final Faith. A religious tyrant who kept a firm hand on her church and made sure that its message was heard by all, whether they wanted to listen or not.

"I may have no love for the Faith, Dunsany, but I rather value my fingernails."

"But we're in a perfect position to do this." Kelos said. "We have my contacts on Sarcre and a hiding place that's virtually impossible to find. Besides, who's in a better position to pull this off than the Chief Engineer and the Head Mage on the project?"

The designs for the ship had been found almost a year before in an elvish ruin near Freiport, by an adventurer called Kali Hooper. Hooper had been forced to part with her find once Makennon's people had got wind of the importance of the artefact. Ancient texts had spoken of the elves' mastery of the rough Twilight seas and of how they had ventured far beyond the Storm Wall and the Sarcre Islands but, until now, no reference had been found as to the design of their ships.

And just as Kali Hooper had been forced to part with her find, so Dunsany and Kelos had been forced to work for the Final Faith.

Dunsany had been working as a shipping engineer in Turnitia for the last ten years, before that he had been the Captain of a merchant vessel plying its trade between Sarcre and Allantia. He was a master of the rough seas that surrounded the peninsula and the ships he sailed, and later designed, were considered to be some of the finest in existence. When the Anclas Territories fell to Vos and the Final Faith tightened its grip on the city, Dunsany was the first person corralled into working for the church's naval division.

The second was Kelos.

With the subjugation of Turnitia, Kelos had considered fleeing across the border to Andon, but before he could act on his decision booted feet had kicked down his door and he had been dragged into the night.

Makennon had heard rumours of this powerful mage who worked his magic at the Turnitia docks; of how his wards protected the ships against the ravages of the sea and how his mastery of the elements had guided home many a battered vessel. It was true that his magic was no match for the angry waters beyond the Storm Wall but, even so, it was reckoned that his power was one of the main reasons Turnitia thrived as a harbour town.

When Dunsany had looked up from his diagrams one night to see Kelos standing over him, he had grinned and said: "What took you so long?"

So the two men applied themselves to whatever marine

problem Makennon threw their way; Dunsany maintaining the fleet and mapping routes while Kelos empowered the ships with his charms and wards. The crossed circle of the Final Faith soon became a familiar sight at the docks, as it was painted onto the ships preparing to bring indoctrination to Twilight's coastal towns.

As the Faith's power had grown, so Kelos and Dunsany's resentment had increased. It was true that they were spiritual men, to a certain degree, but they resented being forced along one path of belief. "All paths lead to Kerberos," Kelos's mother had once said. But if either Dunsany or Kelos dared mention the old ways, the penalty would be severe indeed and they'd soon be joining their ancestors.

And so they strengthened their comradeship in the hatred they held for the church and, with the discovery of the designs for the ship, that hatred soon found purpose.

It was called the *Llothriall* and it was a song ship. As Dunsany and Kelos had been presented with the ancient scrolls, detailing the schematics for the vessel, their awe had been palpable. Both men had heard of the song ships but neither had ever imagined they'd see the plans for such a vessel. Dunsany had never thought that a ship could be so beautiful, or so difficult to build. As he and Kelos had worked through the list of materials required they realised that the actual construction of the vessel would be the least part of the project.

The hull was to be composed primarily of a wood found only in the Drakengrat mountains. Even with their enchanted armour and cadre of mages, the detachment of men sent there suffered massive losses when a pride of shnarls smelt the human meat entering their territory. The pitch required to coat the hull had also been somewhat difficult to source, having to come – as it did – from the veins of the many-spiked, semi-sentient and highly poisonous spiritine tree. Twenty-five men were sent into the Sardenne and only five made it out. The fate they suffered, however, was as nothing compared to the torment experienced by the young men and women sent to steal the silk for the sails from the X'lcotl. All forty sent on that mission to the World's Ridge mountains returned, but their minds did not. Their consciousnesses remained with the X'lcotl – now a part of their web – and, as those strange creatures traversed the strands, the vibrations echoed out, inducing visions and delirium in the souls captured there. The shells of humans who sat and muttered in the padded cells of Scholten cathedral would die in time, and their bodies would return to the earth, but their souls would always be caught in that terrible web.

The heart of the *Llothriall* – the great gem whose magic powered the ship – was, thankfully, already in the possession of the Faith. The iridescent mineral had sat in Katherine Makennon's private quarters and had been used, variously, over the years as a footstool, a table and a support for a bookshelf. It was only after the discovery of the designs for the song ship that Makennon realised the worth of the artefact. Originally a general had found it in a field during the last war between Vos and Pontaine, and it had been presented to Makennon as a tribute. When Kelos told her what she had, Makennon's estimation of the general was greatly raised. If he had still been alive she may even have made him an Eminence.

The power within the gem required a key to unlock it, and that was where Emuel had come into the picture.

Elf magic was based on song and no human could achieve the pitch required to sing their spells. No normal human, at least.

Emuel had been the priest of a small parish near Nürn. He was the youngest priest in the Faith, at only twelve years old, and was utterly devoted to the church. Even through the soft, lilting tones of his voice he managed to communicate his passion and devotion to his congregation. His parishioners had often speculated as to whether elf blood ran in Emuel's veins, for he was unnaturally tall, unusually pale and unquestionably feminine. So it was that his was one of the first names put forward for the role of ship's eunuch; a role that he accepted demurely and gratefully. Once the surgeon's knives had ensured that the youthful pitch of Emuel's voice would remain, and the elven runes and songlines had been needled into his flesh, Kelos wondered whether that gratitude endured.

The *Llothriall's* construction was brought through suffering and loss and there was no limit to the number of men and women Katherine Makennon was willing to spend in building the Faith's flagship vessel. Unfortunately, there also seemed to be no limit to the amount of the faithful who were willing to give their lives to the cause. Dunsany and Kelos wouldn't have given their time so freely had it not been for the threat of certain heresies and indiscretions suddenly being 'remembered'. Even through their resentment, however, both men couldn't deny the majesty of what was taking shape at the Turnitia docks.

And it was partly because of that, and partly because of their hatred of the Final Faith and all it stood for, that they planned to steal the *Llothriall*.

"Makennon cannot be allowed to keep it," Dunsany said one evening when they were away from the ears of the Faithful. "It's bad enough that they use the regular ships to enforce their beliefs on the coastal towns, but the *Llothriall* can go further than them. Make no mistake, Makennon isn't planning some altruistic voyage of discovery. She's on a mission of religious conquest."

Kelos stared into the depths of his ale, behind him two sailors were beating a sea shanty into a broken piano. "No one's been beyond the Sarcre Islands and the Storm Wall before. No ship could survive those seas."

"The *Llothriall* can and just imagine what it may find."

"New lands."

"New people."

"New races with new ideologies. What do you think will happen, Dunsany, when those ideologies come up against the Final Faith?"

"What do you think?" Dunsany sighed and ran his fingers through his beard. "Gods, whatever happened to discovery for discovery's sake? Why does every pitsing artefact, every pitsing scroll and spell that's unearthed instantly become a weapon in somebody's war?"

"We could always run away to Allantia. Start up a small fishing concern. I could do cantrips for the locals."

Dunsany shook his head and smiled. "Or we could take Makennon's new toy away from her."

This time, when Kelos looked at him, Dunsany could see something like resolve in his eyes. "Discovery for discovery's sake?"

"Discovery for Discovery's sake," Dunsany confirmed, raising his tankard. "Cheers."

"Get down!"

Dunsany shoved Emuel and Kelos behind a crate as the guard rounded the hull of the vast ship. Beside him the eunuch whimpered, the strange runes and illustrations inked on his body glowing with a blue-black sheen in the Kerberos-lit dusk.

"Was it really necessary to bind him like that?" Kelos whispered, looking over at the shivering, tattooed eunuch.

"If he gets away we're buggered, you know that. No one else can sing to that gem and unlock the magic but him. Unless, that is, you'd like me to perform an impromptu operation on you right here?" Dunsany slowly unsheathed his dagger, a smile playing across his lips.

"No, no that's fine. *Really.*"

It didn't look like Emuel was going to make a break for it though. He'd been close to a state of catatonic shock ever since they had sprung him from his cell in the cathedral. All they had to do now was board the ship, make him sing and they were away.

"Gods Dunsany, are you sure that this is a good idea? I count three men with crossbows on the foremast and I wouldn't put it past Makennon to have a Shadowmage tucked in there somewhere."

"Well then, old friend," Dunsany said, putting an arm around Kelos's shoulder. "You'll just have to weave your own magic won't you? Now, keep Emuel quiet while I take care of this guard."

The guard was coming towards them again, having completed a circuit of the ship. Dunsany knelt down and loaded a quarrel into his crossbow. Slowly, he edged around the crate, carefully drawing a bead on the guard while keeping to the shadows. The weapon was custom made, expertly crafted, and the quarrel made almost no noise as it exited the crossbow and entered the throat of the man in the robes of a Final Faith guard. Dunsany briefly left cover to grab the corpse and pull it out of sight of the ship.

Emuel looked down at the pool of blood edging towards him from the body and, before Kelos had time to clamp his hand over his mouth, emitted a piercing shriek. Instantly there was movement on the foremast. Dunsany glared at Emuel and briefly considered cracking him round the head with the stock of his crossbow, but without the eunuch they weren't going anywhere.

"Kelos, remember that magic I mentioned? Well, now's the time."

Kelos closed his eyes, summoning the threads of elemental power. A coolness coursed through him as the pounding of waves thundered in his head. Beside him Emuel and Dunsany backed away as they tasted the tang of ozone that told them something big was about to happen.

Kelos stepped out of cover and raised his hands.

The ships in this part of the docks were already swaying drunkenly, the fierce power of the sea only slightly dissipated by the massive breakwaters, but the *Llothriall* now began to lurch even more than its neighbours. The guards in the foremast were having great difficulty in keeping their aim on the man who had emerged from the shadows below them. One let loose with his bow just as the boat lurched hard to starboard and the arrow sailed high into the night. A few almost found their target but Kelos didn't even flinch as the arrows thudded into the wood of the crate behind him. Instead, he concentrated on the great wheel of energy that spun through his mind. The sea surrounding the ship began to churn more furiously now and Kelos spat out the syllables that he had memorised five years before from a rare and mildewed book. For each guttural exclamation a thick rope of water erupted from the waves.

One of the guards dropped his weapon as a tentacle of water snaked around his neck. Hearing the snap of vertebrae his comrade started to scramble down the rigging, but before he could reach the deck he was thrown clear of the ship, crashing into the side of a warehouse. The last man was picked from the foremast, where he had been standing frozen in shock. His bow dropped from his numb fingers as an arm of living water encircled his waist. He looked down as the ship receded below him and then he was upside-down and the sea was rushing towards him.

Kelos lowered his hands and edged towards the dock wall but the guard didn't resurface. The tendrils of water fell, lifeless, and Dunsany and a shaken Emuel emerged from hiding.

"I think that you've found a new way to clear the decks. Don't suppose there's anything you can do for laughing boy here is there?" Kelos cast a silence spell on the eunuch. Emuel looked offended and opened his mouth, but his protest failed to emerge. "Thank the Gods for that. I didn't fancy boarding the *Llothriall* while he continued to scream the place down. Now, when we want you to sing, you'll sing okay? Kelos, lead the way."

On board, at the bottom of the steps leading below, they stopped in front of a door. Dunsany cocked his crossbow and put his ear to the wood. He was raising his arm to signal that it was safe for them to proceed when twelve inches of steel erupted from the door just by his nose. The sword was quickly withdrawn and the door burst open. Kelos flung his palms out and a fireball thudded into the chest of the man who emerged, launching him backwards down the corridor behind him.

Dunsany glanced back at his friend as he stepped over the felled guard.

"I'm warning you now that I can't keep this up for much longer," Kelos panted.

"Relax, we're almost there."

Two more short flights of steps and a long corridor led them to the heart of the ship. They stopped in front of a reinforced door, elvish script covering its surface. Kelos traced the design with his fingers, muttering something to himself. Eventually he stepped back and nodded. "That's the advantage of having designed the wards, I know how to counteract them. On three?" He drew a short sword.

"On three." Dunsany agreed, drawing his own blade.

As they charged into the room Kelos was flung against the ceiling. For a moment he thought that the boat had taken a massive hit, but then he saw the man in the corner, smiling as he weaved threads of magic, muttering strange syllables.

Kelos's windpipe started to constrict as the Shadowmage increased his hold. Below him, Dunsany was squaring off against the guards who stood in front of the magical gem that was the engine of the vessel. The stone, sitting in its housing of metal and wood, seemed to whisper to Kelos as he gasped for breath.

He watched as Dunsany swung at one of the guards. The man tumbled to the side to avoid the blow and Dunsany took the opportunity to fire a quarrel at the other guard.

When the quarrel entered his thigh, the man grunted and stepped back. However, the injury hadn't slowed him as he roared and shoulder charged Dunsany into the wall. The guard pushed his blade against Dunsany's throat but Dunsany gritted his teeth, reversed his grip on his sword and rammed the pommel into the base of the guard's neck. The man dropped and Kelos cried out a warning as the remaining guard stepped in to fill the gap.

Dunsany failed to fully evade the blow and the blade sliced into his cheek, flicking blood into his eyes. He staggered and almost tripped over Emuel, who was on the floor behind him, rocking back and forth. The guard took advantage of the stumble and swung again, this time nicking Dunsany's wrist, making him drop his sword. Dunsany raised his crossbow and fired. Kelos saw the mage in the corner blink and the quarrel turned to powder millimetres from the guard's face.

"I knew Makennon should never have trusted scum like you." The guard said, brushing dust from his jerkin. "If you ask me we didn't do enough in converting this shit hole you people call home. Unbelievers should have been put to the sword a long time ago."

Kelos continued to gasp for breath, barely conscious now. The stone was practically screaming into his head and, with a jolt of realisation, he realised what he must do.

He gestured with his right hand and cancelled the silence spell he had placed on Emuel.

"Sing Emuel! Sing or we'll all die!"

Emuel looked up at Kelos and, for a terrible moment, the mage thought that the eunuch was going to defy him. But then, he stood.

"That's it retard, sing a lament for the death of your friends." The guard raised his sword. The sound that emerged from Emuel, however, stayed his hand.

The room shivered as the song reached out to the gem. The magical energy traced veins of midnight-blue fire in the stone and all in the room felt the ship shudder as it responded to the song. The tattoos on Emuel's body flowed as the song possessed him.

The Shadowmage stepped into the centre of the room and Kelos could see a dark warning in his eyes. He could almost taste the magic flowing from the stone now and, concentrating, Kelos called forth a thread of that energy. The mage below him realised what was happening too late. He tried to finish Kelos with a word but, before he could utter the syllable, Kelos concentrated the thread of energy from the stone and blasted it into the Shadowmage. The room filled with a searing light as his body burned.

Kelos dropped to the floor and lashed out with his sword. The stunned guard didn't even feel the blade enter his belly. All he felt was the song and its ethereal cadence as it followed him into darkness.

Kelos put a hand on Emuel's shoulder. "You can stop now. It's over."

As the Turnitia docks fell away, Dunsany nervously scanned the shoreline.

"Don't worry," Kelos said. "I've cloaked the ship."

Dunsany turned to look at his friend. Wisps of arcane energy surrounded the mage in a dark amber corona.

"Shouldn't one of us be piloting this vessel?"

"Actually, I am. And have you noticed something *really* strange?"

"Apart from your new hair-do and ruddy orange glow?" Dunsany looked around him and had to admit that *everything* was really strange. The sails billowed with the wind and were utterly silent, the rainbow sheen of the X'lcotl silk moving like oil on water as it reflected back the soft light of Kerberos. Around them the ship thrummed with magical energy, veins of which ran through every part of the *Llothriall*. The vessel cut through the sea with a sureness and ease that Dunsany had never before witnessed in a ship. "We're so still."

"Indeed, the ship should be furiously pitching beneath our feet and we should be staggering around like two drunks at the end of a wedding party. Instead, we have this unnatural serenity. Deceptive really, as the power of the *Llothriall* is so vast that it should *feel* like something is happening. And it is, look back at Turnitia."

Dunsany turned. The coast was dwindling rapidly behind them, almost imperceptible through the spray and the mist. On any other ship it would have taken them most of a day to leave sight of the peninsula and, even then, they wouldn't have been able to venture too far from land due to the vicious and unpredictable currents that surrounded Twilight. But the *Llothriall* was not at all affected by the pitch of the waves. Instead, it seemed to skim across the surface.

"And this is the least of the ship's abilities," Kelos said. "Do you know, that it is actually capable of sailing under water? We must try that particular feature out some time."

"I'm glad that we took this away from the Faith," said Dunsany. "I just hope that this hiding place you have in mind is as good as you say."

"Oh yes. And, once we reach Sarcre itself I can introduce you to our crew."

"And do they know that they are going to be shipmates on this mighty vessel?"

"Well, not quite. But once they see the *Llothriall* they're not going to take much persuading. Talking of ship mates, where's Emuel?"

"All sung out. Sleeping soundly below. You think that boy's going to be a problem?"

"He's terrified of everything and he's too timid to be a threat. Anyway, there's no way for him to get back to Makennon now."

The sound of Katherine Makennon's rage was so great that the Eternal Choir almost stopped singing. The congregation who sat with bowed heads looked up from their prayers for a moment as they sensed the anger that flowed through the many halls, chambers and chapels of Scholten cathedral from Makennon's quarters. At his pulpit the Eminence's hand was momentarily stayed from making the sign of benediction.

In her private chamber Makennon stood over the priest who had delivered the news of the *Llothriall's* theft and, for the briefest of moments, considered having him excommunicated. But decisions driven by emotion were not becoming of a leader of Twilight's true faith. Seating herself once more Katherine resumed her air of authoritative calm.

"Why is it that Old Race secrets and artefacts have a habit of slipping out of our grasp? Don't these people realise that we are merely trying to use the knowledge of our ancestors to unite the peninsula and spread our message beyond civilisation?"

Around the room, the members of the Faithful looked at one another, wondering if an answer were required. One cleared his throat and seemed about to speak, but Makennon dismissed his words before he could form them with a wave of a hand.

"It was a rhetorical question Rudolph. I do not require your observations. However... do you know whether our guest has regained consciousness?"

"Our guest Anointed Lord?"

"Yes, the marine creature we recently acquired."

"Ah yes, I shall enquire right away."

"Thank you Rudolph."

Rudolph edged slowly from the room, making sure not to present his back to the Anointed Lord. Once beyond the chamber he descended through the many levels of Scholten until he was far below the foundations of the cathedral. In a corridor lined with cells he stopped at a particular door and slid back the viewing hatch. The stench that poured from the room beyond made him take a step back. For a moment he thought that the creature within had died, but then there was a wet sound as it left its water trough and approached the door.

"Prepare yourself to meet the Anointed Lord," Rudolph piously informed the prisoner.

He couldn't be sure but the sound that came in response sounded almost like a laugh.

For information on this and other titles, visit
www.abaddonbooks.com